Heartache? He could write volumes on it.

Conner crossed to the highboy, his gaze snagging on a grouping of three framed photographs. He picked up one, his chest tightening as he studied the picture. It was a snapshot of Abby, one he had taken years ago. She was laughing at him, the wind molding the soft folds of her dress against her protruding belly. When that photograph had been taken, she was pregnant with Cody, and everything that Abby was, was captured in that picture.

Yeah, he could write a book on heartache, all right. And secrets? He had 'em by the truckload. Most of them were stored up in a whole lot of pain. But there was one that gave him comfort. And it was a secret he would take to his grave without ever giving it up.

He touched the face in the snapshot, the hole in his chest getting bigger. No one would ever know that the baby she carried in this picture wasn't his brother's.

It was his.

D1007948

Dear Reader,

Once again, we've rounded up six exciting romances to keep you reading all month, starting with the latest installment in Marilyn Pappano's HEARTBREAK CANYON miniseries. *The Sheriff's Surrender* is a reunion romance with lots of suspense, lots of passion—lots of *emotion*—to keep you turning the pages. Don't miss it.

And for all of you who've gotten hooked on A YEAR OF LOVING DANGEROUSLY, we've got *The Way We Wed*. Pat Warren does a great job telling this tale of a secret marriage between two SPEAR agents who couldn't be more different— or more right for each other. Merline Lovelace is back with *Twice in a Lifetime,* the latest saga in MEN OF THE BAR H. How she keeps coming up with such fabulous books, I'll never know—but I *do* know we're all glad she does. Return to the WIDE OPEN SPACES of Alberta, Canada, with Judith Duncan in *If Wishes Were Horses....* This is the kind of book that will have you tied up in emotional knots, so keep the tissues handy. Cheryl Biggs returns with *Hart's Last Stand,* a suspenseful romance that will keep you turning the pages at a furious clip. Finally, don't miss the debut of a fine new voice, Wendy Rosnau. *A Younger Woman* is one of those irresistible stories, and it's bound to establish her as a reader favorite right out of the starting gate.

Enjoy them all, then come back next month for more of the best and most exciting romance reading around—only in Silhouette Intimate Moments.

Yours,

Leslie J. Wainger
Executive Senior Editor

Please address questions and book requests to:
Silhouette Reader Service
U.S.: 3010 Walden Ave., P.O. Box 1325, Buffalo, NY 14269
Canadian: P.O. Box 609, Fort Erie, Ont. L2A 5X3

If Wishes Were Horses...

JUDITH DUNCAN

INTIMATE MOMENTS™

Published by Silhouette Books

America's Publisher of Contemporary Romance

If you purchased this book without a cover you should be aware
that this book is stolen property. It was reported as "unsold and
destroyed" to the publisher, and neither the author nor the
publisher has received any payment for this "stripped book."

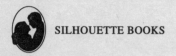

SILHOUETTE BOOKS

ISBN 0-373-27142-5

IF WISHES WERE HORSES…

Copyright © 2001 by Judith Mulholland

All rights reserved. Except for use in any review, the reproduction
or utilization of this work in whole or in part in any form by any
electronic, mechanical or other means, now known or hereafter
invented, including xerography, photocopying and recording, or in
any information storage or retrieval system, is forbidden without
the written permission of the editorial office, Silhouette Books,
300 East 42nd Street, New York, NY 10017 U.S.A.

All characters in this book have no existence outside the imagination of
the author and have no relation whatsoever to anyone bearing the same
name or names. They are not even distantly inspired by any individual
known or unknown to the author, and all incidents are pure invention.

This edition published by arrangement with Harlequin Books S.A.

® and TM are trademarks of Harlequin Books S.A., used under license.
Trademarks indicated with ® are registered in the United States Patent
and Trademark Office, the Canadian Trade Marks Office and in other
countries.

Visit Silhouette at www.eHarlequin.com

Printed in U.S.A.

JUDITH DUNCAN

is married and lives, along with her husband, in Calgary, Alberta, Canada. A staunch supporter of anyone wishing to become a published writer, she has lectured extensively in Canada and the United States. Currently she is involved with the Alberta Romance Writers Association, an organization she helped to found.

Chapter 1

The sun blazed in the bright blue cloudless sky and beat down on the rolling rangeland, the relentless heat shimmering up in waves. The hills and gullies lay like enormous, heaving wrinkles in the earth's surface, the folds held in place by the sharply defined mountains rising up in the west. A vast cloud of dust hung in the air, forming a golden aura that cloaked the landscape and distorted the horizon. Overhead, two red-tailed hawks circled, watching for unwary gophers.

The bawling of calves and the shouts of cowhands carried in the thin mountain air, echoing in the crystal clarity. Hundreds of white-faced cows and their spring calves plodded onward through the rolling terrain, marshalled into a long meandering column by watchful riders. The cloud of yellow dust hung suspended above the undulating herd, the fine grit coating the newly unfurled leaves of the cottonwoods and wolf willow, finally settling on the new shoots of grass struggling through last year's thatch.

It was spring roundup on the Cripple Creek Ranch, and it was a scene that had been played out over a hundred times before. Nothing much had changed, except the faces of the riders. It was a scene that was as much a part of the rolling country as were the great cottonwoods standing tall along the winding creek.

Conner Calhoun pulled up his mount at the crest of the small hill, giving the reins a light jerk as the big buckskin gelding danced and tossed his head. With his gaze fixed on the rim of a far-off ravine, he reached down and flipped open the case strapped on his belt and removed a cell phone. Not taking his eyes off the dark shapes, he hit the redial button, waited, then spoke into the mouthpiece. "Jake, there's four or five strays heading for the south ravine. Send Bud with one of the dogs to bring 'em in."

Conner watched a rider and one dog break from the main herd, then replaced the phone in the case. His horse threw his head again and impatiently tugged at the reins, and Conner gave him a second command, then settled back in the saddle. The slant of the late afternoon sun angled beneath the brim of his Stetson, and he squinted against it, the taste of dust drying in his mouth as he surveyed the state of his grassland.

It was dry—too damned dry—but thick cumulous clouds were racking up behind the jagged ridge of the Rocky Mountains, and Conner could almost taste the rain in that cloud bank. There had been very little snow during the winter, with one Chinook after another drying out the soil. It was the first of June, and they hadn't had one really good rain since the snow-pack had melted. There had been just enough to keep the grass going, but his grazing land needed a good soaking, and soon. Unless he missed his guess, one was on the way—even the animals could sense it.

A series of shrill whistles pierced the din, and Conner's attention shifted as the point man gave the signals to two hardworking Border collies to move up and turn the lead cows into a narrow draw. Three other riders also moved up, hazing the outside stragglers back into the ranks and crowding the herd into the gully, forcing them through the natural funnel. The lead cows, heads swinging, calves crowded against their sides, lumbered through the wide gate, while other riders flanked the herd, trying to prevent any of the range-wary animals from bolting.

The move today was the last stage of the roundup. Over the past couple of weeks, the Cripple Creek cowhands had collected cattle from the winter range. The steers and bulls had been driven onto the summer range and the remaining cows and calves were driven here, onto the home pasture for spring branding. Beyond the gate and hidden from view in a natural holding area, additional Cripple Creek hands were making the final repairs to the vast network of corrals, preparing for the job ahead. Today was the final drive. The cut would take place the following day, when the calves would be separated from their mothers. Then the day after that, the backbreaking work would begin. Tagging, vaccinating and branding each spring calf, and dehorning and castrating those that needed it. A rancher's entire year and the viability of the herd revolved around that operation. And Cripple Creek's future and fortunes depended on it.

And had for over a hundred and twenty years.

A strange feeling unfolded in Conner's chest as he

considered the history behind him. He surveyed the herd, his gaze snagging on the ragged line of old cottonwoods snaking through the valley below.

Sometimes he felt a real kinship with those big old trees. They had stood tall along Cripple Creek for decades—big, indestructible, able to withstand any storm. He respected their tenacity and durability. It was as if they were the silent sentinels, watching over Calhoun land. As if they were a fundamental part of it all.

Just as he was. For forty years, he had breathed this clean mountain air and tasted Cripple Creek dust. Yeah, this land was as much a part of him, as he would, eventually, become a part of it.

He had been born in the huge old Victorian ranch house, and he had spent his entire life in this part of southwestern Alberta, rooted in this ranching country. In fact, the Calhouns had been one of the original settlers in these parts, one of the American families who had been given huge land grants by the British Crown as an inducement to settle the rolling uncharted land. And there were many descendants of the settling families who still ranched in the district—the McCalls, the Ralstons, the Stewards, the Calhouns.

Because of that inducement, his forefathers had come here and put down roots, just like those old cottonwoods. His ancestors had been running huge herds of cattle when that part of western Canada was still a territory. And the Calhouns had been there ever since. Still ranching, still running huge herds of cattle, still part of the never-ending landscape. And although he would never admit it to a living soul, Conner considered it both an honor and a privilege to carry on that heritage—as had his father before him, his grandfather before that, and his great grandfather before that. He felt he had a responsibility to all those who had gone before him, to provide good stewardship of this land.

Impatient with his rider's stillness, the big gelding pranced and yanked on the bit, his hooves striking against a rocky outcropping. A small twist of humor lifted the corner of Conner's mouth, and he reached forward and patted his mount's neck. "Getting antsy, are you, old boy?" Big Mac tossed his head and pranced again, and Conner responded with another half smile. He got the message. Big Mac had been on enough roundups to know his owner had picked one helluvah time to go woolgathering, when a year's crop of calves and their mommas were heading toward the home pasture.

Picking up the reins, Conner cued his mount forward, and Big Mac instantly responded, lunging down the hill, stirring up more dust as he headed toward two stragglers grazing down by a ring of willows. Conner grinned. Right on the money. He'd had cowhands who weren't as smart as this horse.

By the time Conner was ready to pack it in for the day, the sun had settled behind the horizon, setting the gathering clouds on fire. He had been in the saddle since dawn, and he was feeling every second of it. It had been a very long day, and he'd had his fill of range-ornery cows, heat, dust and, most of all, the new saddle he was using. A damned stupid thing to do—to use a brand-new saddle on a cattle drive. But his foreman had a bad hip, and his favorite old roping saddle suited Jake better. The good thing was that Conner's butt had gone numb hours ago.

Turning Big Mac in a pivot, Conner did another

pass of the herd, narrowing his eyes in the fading light as he surveyed the cattle, relying on his years of experience to detect anything amiss. Satisfied that all was as it should be, he turned his mount toward the lone figure of his foreman hanging over the pole gate at the north side of the pasture.

The effects of a fourteen-hour day in the saddle and some hard riding immediately piled in on him, and Conner wearily rolled his shoulders and glanced toward the western horizon. From the fading colors of the sunset, he figured it had to be after 9:30 p.m., maybe even later. Damn. Another day gone.

He shifted against the stiffness and rested his free hand on his thigh, thinking how the time had disappeared. There just weren't enough hours in the day this time of year. It had been the better part of a week since he had made it into Bolton to visit his step-mother, and there was just no excuse for that. Although she tried not to show it, he knew that Mary worried if she hadn't heard from him in awhile. And worrying about him was the last thing she needed.

She was only in her late sixties, but she had been fighting arthritis for many years, and a couple of years ago, she had decided to move into an assisted-care facility in Bolton. He had wanted to get home care for her so she could stay on the ranch, but Mary had been adamant.

And even though it was her decision to move into Bolton, Conner knew that she missed Cripple Creek, especially at this time of year. She had played an active part on the ranch for a lot of years, and had gone on more than her fair share of cattle drives. A skilled and fearless horsewoman, she could ride with the best of them. Though the choice to leave had been hers, he knew her heart was still here, planted in Cripple Creek soil.

Beginning to feel as if he'd gone a few rounds with a bucking bronc, Conner pulled a bandanna from his back pocket and wiped the dust and sweat from his face, then jammed it back in his pocket. He recalled a bright yellow patch of buffalo beans he'd seen at the edge of the driveway, and he made a mental note to pick Mary a bunch of the flowers the next time he went to town. They were particular favorites of hers—''spring sunshine,'' she'd always said.

The fiery sunset reflected off the windshield of the pickup parked alongside the fence, and the sound of country music blared from the radio within. A banty-legged man stood at the gate, one booted foot propped on the lowest rail, his arms hooked over the top one. His battered Stetson was tipped low over his eyes, and he had a piece of straw stuck in his mouth. As horse and rider approached, the Cripple Creek foreman undid the rope hitch and swung the gate open, leaving a space just wide enough for Conner to ride through. A grin split Jake Henderson's weathered face, and he spit out the straw he'd been chewing. ''Took you long enough. What was you doing out there? Picking posies?''

Experiencing a twist of humor at how close his foreman had come to the truth, Conner guided the gelding through the gate, giving Jake a firm reprimand. ''I thought I sent you to the house two hours ago, with specific instructions to get into that hot tub of yours.''

Jake swung the gate closed and fastened it. ''Hell, Conner. The wife would skin me alive if she knowed you was still aworking out here, and I was lazing in the tub. She just might turn up the heat and cook my hide for me.''

Backing the horse away from the fence, Conner watched the older man, another flicker of amusement surfacing. Jake had been telling the same tale about Henny for over thirty years—ever since he'd come to work for Conner's father at the Cripple Creek Ranch. Jake and his stories were an institution.

Hunching over, Conner stacked his forearms on the saddle horn and narrowed his gaze at the older man. His tone was stern when he spoke. ''I don't want you out here again tonight, Jake. You get one of the hands to check the herd.''

The foreman looked a little peeved. ''I ain't an old woman yet, boss.'' He smacked the hood of his truck. ''Me and ol' Bessie here will do that check on our own, thank you very much. I don't trust that bunch to find their butts with a road map, a spotlight and both hands, let alone check this here herd.''

The laugh lines around his eyes creasing, Conner continued to watch as Jake Henderson climbed into his truck. ''You never listen to a damned thing I say, do you?''

Jake grinned and gunned the engine to life. ''Not if I can help it.'' He pointed to the big, muscled, high-spirited buckskin Conner was riding. ''Now you take that puny little horse of yers to the barn and give him his sissy bath. His feelings will get all hurt if he don't get his bath.'' Throwing the vehicle into reverse, the foreman gave Conner a two-finger salute and roared backward toward the buildings, trailing another cloud of dust.

Conner watched his foreman skillfully maneuver up the rutted trail; then he picked up the reins, cueing his mount forward, a wry smile appearing. He wondered if Jake was ever going to let up on Big Mac. Probably not.

True, most working horses preferred a good roll in the dirt after getting rid of their saddles after a hard day. Not Big Mac. Big Mac liked a good, long hosing down, and the longer the better. His shower habits had become the butt of some well-thought out Cripple Creek Ranch pranks. Like bath mitts and shower caps.

Once again aware of the numbness in his rear, he turned his horse toward the trail that led up to the barn. He didn't know about Big Mac, but for him, it was definitely time to call it a day.

By the time they reached the crest of the hill, dusk had settled and a mountain breeze had blown up, carrying the clean smell of rain. The light wind rustled through the leaves, making shadows dance under the high, bright quartz yard lights.

Swinging down from the saddle, Conner pulled the reins from around the horse's neck, then led his mount toward the darkened barn, unbuckling his chaps as he went. He paused briefly outside, straightening the horse's mane as Big Mac took a long noisy drink from the watering trough. Having drunk his fill, the horse tossed his head, flinging water and making his bridle jingle. Noticing the first glimmer of stars overhead, Conner led Big Mac through the wide barn door, reaching for the switch mounted on a panel.

Light sprang from four bare bulbs quartering the long alleyway between the big box stalls, casting the cavernous structure in murky light. The sudden burst of illumination startled a flock of barn sparrows in the rafters, and Big Mac raised his head and paused, pricking his ears as three birds darted through the open door. Responding to a tug on his bit, the horse started moving again, his shod hooves making a hollow clip-clopping sound on the thick plank flooring, the sound echoing in the stillness of the barn.

Conner led his horse past the row of stalls to the far end of the barn, where he looped the reins through an iron ring mounted on the wall. Bone weary, he undid the buckle at his waist and stripped his chaps away, hung them on a hook, then stripped the horse of his tack.

By the time he led Big Mac into the wash area, most of the vibrant color had faded from the sky, and a deepening darkness pressed against the open door. He picked up the hose and turned on the tap, the sound of running water percolating loudly through the silence. For some reason, that sound made Conner very aware of how alone he was, and he didn't like it much. He should be used to that by now; it was a feeling that had become his shadow over the years. And one he did his damnedest to ignore.

Trying to focus on what he was doing, he hosed his horse down. Satisfied that there wasn't a trace of sweat left anywhere, he turned off the water and picked up a lead shank. Then he looped the rope around the horse's neck and led him back to his big box stall, the horse's hooves repeating the hollow clip-clop on the heavy planks. There was a fresh flake of hay and a measure of oats ready and waiting. Removing the lead, he gave the horse a smack on the rump; then he dragged the heavy door shut, shooting the bolt as he hung the lead shank on a hook by the door. He was feeling so damned beat up, he wasn't sure he had the energy to make it to the house.

At the doorway, he paused, resting his hand on the

frame as he stood staring out. Through the row of trees, he could see the darkened shape of the big old Victorian ranch house, the windows black and empty. Not even a glimmer of light to call him in. Knowing his mood was heading into a dark, empty place, Conner pushed away from the door, set his jaw and turned back toward the lighted shed row. He wasn't ready to face that empty house just yet. And there was always tack to fix.

A big old gray tabby cat was already curled up on Big Mac's saddle blanket, and she rose up and arched her back in a mighty stretch when he turned on the light in the tack room. He scratched her neck, then unsnapped his cell phone and set it on the ledge as a reminder to put it on the battery charger.

Selecting three new, unused headstalls from wooden pegs on the bare plank wall, he carried them to the workbench in the corner, then reached for the brown bag containing new snaffle bits and new reins. He always had extra tack on hand during branding— and getting these assembled was a job he should have taken care of days ago.

Turning on the dust-covered radio, he reached for the tray that held his leather tools. Above the soft country music coming from the radio, he could hear the wind change outside, and the fresh smell of rain spilled into the barn. A few moments later, the first raindrops spattered against the small window over the workbench. And Conner could tell by the way it was coming down that it was going to be a steady, all-night rain. Just what his grassland needed.

As he turned his head, his gaze caught on the old faded picture that hung above the workbench, the glass and frame also covered in dust. It was a picture taken of his father and stepmother years ago, shortly after Mary had come to live at Cripple Creek. She was astride a black horse, the wind ruffling through her dark hair. And she was laughing down at his father, who stood with his hand braced on the neck of the horse looking up at her. That dusty, faded picture had hung there for well over three decades—and was identical to the one that Conner's father had always carried in his wallet. It was, in an odd way, a significant marker in Conner's own life. He sometimes wondered how he and his father had gotten so lucky. Because Mary McFie had changed both their lives.

Conner had no recollection of his natural mother. She had died when he was just a baby, and John Calhoun, a taciturn, reserved, unsmiling man had raised his son alone. Then when Conner was four, a pretty district nurse had come to Bolton, and within weeks, Mary McFie and John Calhoun were married, setting the entire district on its ear. And not only had John Calhoun found a woman who changed his life, Conner had gotten the only mother he had ever known. She had fought John over the raising of his son, treating the somber little boy as if he were her own, and she had made a home for both of them. Once Mary came, it was as if a light had been turned on in their lives as she taught John Calhoun how to laugh. And then when Conner was five, Scotty was born, and Conner had learned what being a family was all about. He could understand why his old man had always kept a copy of that picture close by. It marked the beginning of a whole new life.

He was just replacing the screw in the last bridle when his cell phone chirped. Conner glanced at the clock on the radio. Ten-thirty. Strange time to get a call.

He reached for the phone, flipped down the mouthpiece and hit a button with his thumb. Bracing his arm on the top of the workbench, he put the phone to his ear. "Cripple Creek."

There was a brief pause before a tiny voice spoke. "Uncle Conner?"

Going very still, Conner glanced at the clock again, an uneasy feeling unfolding in his gut. It was a Tuesday, a school night. And his eight-year-old nephew was calling from Toronto, which would make it half past midnight there. He straightened and turned to face the door, his hand tightening on the phone. Keeping his voice quiet and easy, he spoke. "Hey, Chucker. This is pretty late for a call. How come you aren't in bed?"

There was another brief pause; then the boy spoke, a funny catch in his voice. "Remember how you told me—remember after Dad died and when I was only six, you said that if I ever was…um…was…um, you know, worried about anything, I was to call. Do you remember saying that?"

The uneasy feeling turned to something sharper, and suddenly Conner's heart felt too big for his chest. His whole body tensed, he licked the sweat off his lips and spoke, forcing himself to use the same quiet tone to answer. "Yes. I remember." He hesitated, looking for the right words, then spoke again. "Maybe you should tell me what's got you worried, all right, sport?"

"Just a minute. I hafta close the door."

There was the sound of a door closing, then a rattle as the boy picked up the receiver. "I'm in the kitchen and I don't want Mom to hear,'' he whispered into the phone.

Conner made himself relax his jaw. ''Where's your sister—is she there with you?''

''No. She's asleep in bed, Uncle Conner. It's only me.''

The anxiety in Conner's gut intensified, and he walked over to the tack room door, then rested his hand on the overhead frame. Bracing himself, he asked the question he dreaded asking. ''Is something wrong with your mom, Cody?''

''Yeah,'' came a soft whisper. Then louder. ''I think so. I think something's wrong. I sometimes hear her crying at night, and she's acting funny and she doesn't go to work anymore. And she forgets things and she yells over dumb stuff.'' He hesitated, then spoke again, a definite wobble in his voice. ''I'm kinda scared.''

A cold sensation spread through Conner's middle and his insides bunched into a hard knot. When he had told the kid to call if he was ever scared or worried, he had done it to offer the boy some reassurance. And he had meant what he'd said. Only this call couldn't have come at a worse time. Cattle rounded up for branding, everything ready to roll—it wasn't as if he could snap his fingers and shut down the entire operation. And with the two new hands he had just hired, he wasn't sure his crew could manage on their own—not with Jake half crippled with that bad hip. His mind racing, Conner considered alternatives. Tanner McCall's spread was just a couple of miles down the road. And it wouldn't be the first time they had stepped in and helped each other out. Maybe if he asked Tanner to help pick up the slack...

Making a snap decision, Conner positioned the phone closer to his mouth and spoke, keeping his tone easy. "Tell you what, Chucker. How about if I come down there and check things out. Do you think that would be okay?"

There was an odd sound, as if the boy was having trouble breathing, but the hope in his voice was unmistakable. "You mean like right now? Like tonight?"

One corner of Conner's mouth lifted, and he hooked his thumb in the front pocket of his jeans. "I don't think I can make it tonight, Tiger. But I could probably get there sometime tomorrow. And I'll find out if your mom's okay."

"For sure tomorrow?"

A touch of real amusement widened Conner's grin. "Unless the planes stop flying—yes, tomorrow."

Another hesitation. "Uncle Conner?"

"What?"

There was an anxious quiver in the boy's voice. "Will you have to tell Mom I called?"

Conner turned and stared down the shed row to the open barn door. "I can't promise not to, Cody. But I won't unless I have to, okay?"

"Okay." Conner could hear him fidgeting with the phone, then his nephew spoke again, another wobble in his voice. "I'm glad you're coming."

Trying to ignore the sudden tightness in his throat, Conner forced a smile into his voice. "I'm glad I'm coming, too. Now you go back to bed and go to sleep. And I'll see you tomorrow."

"Okay. Good night, Uncle Conner."

"Good night, Tiger."

His expression set, Conner pressed the End button,

then stared into space, a hole the size of Texas in his gut. Abby. There couldn't be anything wrong with Abby. Not Abby.

Turning back to the workbench, he stared at the picture of his father and stepmother; then he roughly massaged his eyes. Hell. This was a bad, bad space for him. A very bad space. And one he couldn't get into. Shutting down his emotions, he mentally listed what all he had to do to clear the decks.

Straightening, he lifted the phone and punched in another set of numbers, then walked over to stare out the window. The steady drizzle created misty halos around the yard lights, distorting the illumination.

A voice answered, and Conner moved the phone closer to his mouth. "Hi, Kate. It's Conner. Is Tanner around?"

"He just came in. Just a minute. I'll get him for you."

A man's voice came on and, as briefly as possible, Conner explained the situation to the other rancher.

Tanner McCall's immediate response was, "Let me know what time your flight leaves, and I'll drive you to the airport."

For the first time since he had gotten his nephew's call, the knot in Conner's gut relaxed. "Thanks, but no. I have no idea when I can get a flight, so I'll just leave the truck at Park and Fly." He rubbed his eyes again. "But I'll give you Abby's number and my cell phone number."

It took five minutes to give Tanner the necessary instructions. As soon as he got off the phone with his neighbor, he placed a call to his stepmother. He wished he didn't have to tell her, but above all else, he respected her right to know. Still, it didn't make the call any easier. Not after everything she had been through in the past few years.

But he didn't want to unduly worry her either, and he did his best to minimize it. He told her he was going down to reassure Cody. He could never admit to anyone that he was also going to reassure himself.

After his call to Mary, he called Jake. There were never any embellishments required with Jake. Just the facts and specific instructions. Jake was worth his weight in gold.

Deliberately keeping his thoughts focused on what he had to do, rather than thinking about the phone call, Conner finished up in the barn. He shut off the light and dragged the door shut, then put his head down against the steady drizzle as he headed for the house. He didn't want to acknowledge the sick feeling churning in his belly, or the fear that was fighting to surface. A long time ago, he had learned not to cross bridges, especially those that weren't his to cross.

It wasn't until he'd had a long hot shower, after he'd draped a towel around his neck and pulled on a clean pair of jeans that his mental stockade failed. Knowing from experience that when that happened, there was no easy way out for him, he went over to the casement window and opened it. Then he stood staring out, his own history piling in on him.

He had loved his brother, and right from the time Mary had placed the tiny baby in his arms, he'd had a feeling in his chest that never went away. And he knew it was the same for John Calhoun. Right from the beginning, that baby could do no wrong in his father's eyes. Even when Scotty got into more scrapes than any kid had a right to, John Calhoun would bail out his youngest son. Conner had always been well aware of how the townspeople reacted, shaking their heads, wondering where the boy was going to end up.

When Scott got older and his dad's health started to fail and his mother got fretting, it was Conner who would quietly untangle whatever mess the kid had gotten himself into, then take him home.

But the funny part was that no one ever seemed to hold any grudges against the youngest Calhoun. Everybody liked Scotty. He had been one of those kids born with a special brand of charisma, a personable, good-looking kid full of down-home charm, and probably the best natural athlete within a thousand miles. There hadn't been anything that Scotty didn't excel at, and at the age of eighteen, he had been scouted by one of the big baseball clubs in the States. By the time he had turned twenty-four, he was a star.

The whole district had been proud of Scotty Calhoun, but Conner suspected there were a whole bunch of people who figured that Scotty moving to the U.S., and being accountable to a major league owner and coach, would save his parents a whole passel of headaches. Scotty might have been a talented young man, but even Conner knew he was trouble just waiting to happen.

Some folks openly wondered how Conner could put up with Scotty's shenanigans, but he never made any comment. He had always been the solid, sensible, levelheaded older brother—and it was clear to everyone that Conner was the one person who Scotty wanted to impress, the only one he looked up to. About the only thing the Calhoun brothers had in common was their size, their dark curly hair and the looks they had inherited from their father. Other than that, they had been as different as night and day.

But that was really only part of the history.

Conner knew there was still a certain amount of speculation about him in the small town of Bolton. Pretty well anybody who had roots in the community knew that he'd just turned forty and never married. There had been a time when folks figured he might make it to the altar. Then all of a sudden the pretty little teller at the local bank was seen in the company of other men. And about a year later, she left for the east. And no one ever knew what happened.

Conner wasn't deaf or blind. He knew that in places like the hairdresser's in Bolton, the women still occasionally speculated about the breakup, and what a pity it was that another young thing hadn't come to town to rescue Conner, just like Mary McFie had rescued his father. He knew all of them were convinced the bank teller was the love of his life, and that she had broken his heart.

Yeah, he had been well aware of what had been said over the years, but he had turned a blind eye to the sympathetic looks and the not-so-subtle attempts at matchmaking. The truth was that he preferred to let them think what they did, rather than anyone having an inkling about the truth. And the truth was something he kept to himself.

Rain spattered through the open window, the cool gush of air intruding on Conner's thoughts. He gouged at his eyes, his head congested with old memories. There was a whole lot of stuff that had gone under the bridge, and he wasn't sure he'd ever put it all behind him. Slipping his right hand into the back pocket of his jeans, he leaned against the wall, his expression turning bleak as more old memories surfaced.

The secret he harbored had its roots a long time ago—eleven years to be exact. Scotty had been twenty-four and had made it to the "show," earning more money than was good for him. It had been close to Christmas when he announced out of the blue that he was bringing home the girl he was going to marry.

No one had known what to expect—not Conner, not his mother, not his father. And when Scotty announced he was bringing Abigail Allistair Arlington home to meet the folks, Conner braced himself. With a name like Abigail Allistair Arlington, she could have come from one of the snooty, upper crust areas of Chicago, or she could have been an exotic dancer in a strip bar. With Scotty, either was a possibility.

It had been left to Conner to drive into the city, to pick them up at the Calgary Airport and, as if it were yesterday, he still remembered that night with stunning clarity. His brother coming through the frosted doors of Canada Customs, followed by a tall, natural blonde, with cover-girl good looks, sharply styled hair, wide hazel eyes and an air of sophistication about her. She had looked cool, composed and aloof—until she smiled.

Without even realizing what she had done with that one smile, Abigail Allistair Arlington had altered the course of Conner Calhoun's life. All it had taken was her greeting of a big, warm hug, and within a space of a few seconds, he knew that his life would never be the same.

He had known that Doreen, the bank teller, had marriage on her mind, but there had been no way he could ever consider marrying her. Not then. Not ever. She was a sweet girl who deserved a whole lot more than second best.

It had nearly killed Conner when Scotty and Abby got married, and it was made twice as hard because he had no choice but to stand up for his brother.

It had been one hell of a ride, all right. Heartache? He could write volumes on it. That constant ache had become part of his life. And that was why sometimes, like tonight, he just could not face an empty house. And it was why he'd spent more nights than he could count out in the barn, fixing tack, mending saddles, braiding new reins. A flicker of grim humor lifted one corner of his mouth. Hell, he had the best tended tack in the entire country.

Turning from the window, Conner crossed to the highboy, his gaze snagging on a grouping of three framed photographs arranged on top. His expression softening, he picked up one, his chest tightening as he studied the picture. It was a snapshot of Abby, one he had taken years ago on a South Carolina beach. She was wading in the surf, the wet hem of her full, ankle-length dress plastered against her legs, and she was holding her hair back from her face with both hands. She was laughing at him, the wind molding the soft folds of her dress against her protruding belly. When that photograph had been taken, she was pregnant with Cody, and everything that Abby was was captured in that picture.

Yeah, he could write a book on heartache, all right. And secrets? He had 'em by the truckload. Most of them were stored up in a whole lot of pain. But there was one that gave him comfort. And it was a secret he would take to his grave without ever giving up.

He touched the face in the snapshot, the hole in his

chest getting bigger. No one would ever know that the baby she carried in this picture wasn't his brother's.

It was his.

Chapter 2

A gust of wind rattled the shades, sending more drops of rain spattering through the screen of the open window. The framed photo still in his hand, Conner tipped his head back against the wall and clenched his jaw. It was not a good night for memories. Or for remembering. But that didn't stop the emotions piling up in his chest.

Forcing himself to let go of the air jammed up in his lungs, Conner turned, his gaze going to the remaining two pictures sitting on top of his bureau. He set the third one beside them, then turned back to the window, stuffing his hands in the pockets of his jeans.

It had been one helluvah ride, all right. One that took him places he'd never expected to go. There had been times when his aloneness got so big, he felt buried by it. And he had figured he would go to the grave with that awful hole in his chest. Then something hap-

pened to change all that. Something that gave him a
place to put everything he felt for his brother's wife.

Abby and Scott had been married two years—and
Conner had gone out of his way to keep his distance.
It had been safer and easier that way. Then they had
come home again for Christmas. Which meant that
Conner had been pretty well trapped. Because as far
as Mary was concerned, there was just no good reason
for either of her sons to be away from home at that
time of year. So for Mary's sake, he had stayed.

There had been something different about Scotty—
he was more quiet, always watching Conner, trying
his best to be accommodating. Then on Christmas
Eve, long after everyone else had gone to bed, Scotty
tracked Conner down in the tack room of the barn,
where he was restoring an antique saddle. And he had
told Conner what was on his mind.

They had found out that Scotty was sterile, and
they wanted to have kids—Abby was desperate for
kids. And Scotty made it clear that there was no way
he wanted to adopt—to raise some stranger's kids.
After coming at it from the long way around, Scotty
got to the point, and dropped a bomb that rocked Conner's world. He wanted to know if Conner would consider fathering a baby for them. He figured that they
looked enough alike that no one would ever know
any different, and Conner was the only man alive he
would trust with this—the only man he would ever
consider as a sperm donor.

It had knocked Conner for one hell of a loop. And
he was never sure how long he'd sat there, staring at
his brother, feeling as if solid ground had been blown
out from underneath him. It was as if his mind had
locked on Scotty's words, and it had seemed like for-

ever before he'd been able to get his mind in gear, to ask his brother how Abby felt about this. Scotty had assured Conner that Abby was fine with it.

Feeling as if his whole existence had been turned upside down, Conner had told Scotty he needed some time to think about it. And he had stayed up all that night, thinking what it would be like, knowing she was carrying his child, knowing that a part of him was lodged deep inside of her. It nearly killed him at first.

Then slowly, so slowly, the possibility of his being able to give her his child began to ease that awful hole in his chest—that hole that had become a part of him. And he had realized that part of the burden of loving her was that he could never do anything to validate it. And now he had been handed his chance. He could give her the baby she wanted so much. And slowly everything changed, and the thought of his child growing inside of her gave him the first peace he'd had in a very long time.

It had been as if Abby knew he'd spent the night wrestling with the request. Because long before anyone was up, she had come down to the kitchen, where he was hunched over the table, working his way through yet another cup of coffee. Her hair had been wild around her face, and she'd worn a fuzzy blue housecoat with the belt pulled tight around her. She had sat down across from him, and they had talked. And she had told him, with tears in her eyes, how badly she wanted a baby, and why. If he hadn't already made up his mind, he would have taken one look at the desperate longing in her eyes, and he would have made it up then. With emotion cramping his throat, he told her he'd be honored to do it.

It had been one hell of an experience—when he flew to Chicago to visit their fertility clinic. And no one would ever know what it had been like, shut in that tiny room, doing what he needed to do, everything he felt for her spilling out in that single donation. He had been such a damned mess afterward, he had gone straight to the airport, phoning Scotty from there. John Calhoun had already been diagnosed with bone cancer, and Conner had used that as a cover, making an excuse that some problems had cropped up at the ranch, and he had to get right home. He hadn't been able to face his brother. And he sure in hell hadn't been able to face her.

Ten months later, Cody John Calhoun was born, and sixteen months after that, Sarah Jane Calhoun had arrived. And it had been as if those two kids had given Conner somewhere to place all the emotions he had been carrying around inside of him. He would have gladly laid down his life for either one of them, and somehow their existence made everything right. He had never permitted himself to think of them as his. They were Abby's kids. Always Abby's. They had been his gift to her, and because of that, he'd never allowed himself to think of them as anything but his niece and nephew.

And along with that acceptance came something he had never expected. The hole in his chest had healed over. It didn't mean that he didn't get damned lonely at times, to the point where he would make trips out of town to find a little temporary companionship. And it sure in hell didn't mean he had gotten over her. He would love her until the day he died. But it made a huge difference, knowing that he had given her the two babies she had wanted so much. It meant he could get through one day after another, almost content with his life. Almost.

The midnight chime of the old grandfather clock in the hallway brought Conner out of his somber reverie, and he pulled the towel from around his neck and tossed it on a chair, then raked both his hands through his hair. It was going to be a damned long night.

Leaving his bedroom, he went out into the hallway, to the wood panelled closet under the stairs, and located a very expensive monogrammed leather garment bag. It always gave him a hollow feeling in his chest when he used it. And the only time he used it was when he went to Toronto—because Abby had been so adamant he have it. It had belonged to his brother, and it was the one Scotty had always carried on road trips.

Picking up the bag, Conner turned off the light and closed the door, his expression grim. Sometimes he wondered about the legendary luck of the Calhouns—it had definitely gone astray in this generation, that was for sure.

He took the garment bag back to his bedroom and tossed it on the king-size bed, then unzipped it, that same old feeling of grief unfolding in his chest. *Ah, Scotty,* he thought, *you didn't even know you had it all.* And once again the history piled in, taking him down the path to old, painful memories.

The only good thing that had happened that year was wee Sarah's arrival. The rest had all been bad. Abby's parents had been killed in a car crash, then John Calhoun had died two months after his granddaughter was born. And shortly after that, Mary's health took a turn for the worse, and the arthritis she had been fighting for years had finally taken hold. It was as if John's dying had depleted her resources, and she got considerably worse. They hadn't seen much of Scotty and the kids—Scotty was always on the road, and Abby, with a degree in business management, started working part-time, certainly not for the money. Mostly, Conner had suspected, to compensate for Scotty's absences.

It wasn't until Scotty got traded to the team in Toronto that the cracks in their golden life began to show. Inferences on sportscasts that Scott Calhoun was not performing up to snuff, rumors of trouble with the club. And when Conner had taken his mother to Toronto for a brief visit, there was something frenetic in Scott's behavior. As if he were wired all the time.

Scotty had been a season into a five-year contract when he was abruptly dropped from the roster, and Conner had started to wonder what was going on. But it wasn't until he saw Abby on a trip through Toronto that Conner knew something was seriously wrong. She had started working full-time, and she had been so strung out and tense, it was as if she were fine crystal ready to shatter. Concerned about her, he had taken her aside, telling her that if she ever needed anything, she was to call. Unable to look at him, she had locked her jaw together and nodded. And that had been that.

Until two years ago, when Abby had called him. And he had found out what was really going on. The reason Scotty had been let go was that management found out he was heavily into drugs, and she didn't know what to do. Conner had been in the process of throwing his kit together for an immediate trip to Toronto when he got the second call from Scotty's agent, telling him that Scotty was on his way to the hospital, suffering from a major overdose. It was almost as if Scotty couldn't face Conner knowing the truth about him.

That was one of the hardest things Conner had ever had to do, to tell his mother what was going on and why he was taking the red-eye to Toronto. But she hadn't been in any shape to travel then. So it had been up to him. When he got to Toronto, he'd gone straight to the hospital. The first thing he had discovered was that Abby was barely hanging on. And the second thing he found out was that Scotty was in an irreversible coma. There was nothing they could do.

It had been equally hard, five days later, standing by her during the huge, media-driven funeral, the news of Scotty's overdose plastered all over every sports page in the country.

But the hardest thing of all was leaving her behind when it was time for him to go home. If he'd had his way, he would have bundled her up and taken her and the kids with him. But he couldn't do that. She was his brother's wife.

After Scotty's death, he had made a point of going to Toronto every three or four months, but Abby had totally walled up. That once vibrant smile was like an accessory she pulled out and put on whenever it was required, and she was so brittle, it was hard for him to watch. He had been concerned about her for months—damned concerned. And he had told her countless times that if she ever needed anything, all she had to do was call. But Abby had a whole lot of stiff, chin-in-the-air pride. Rooted, no doubt, in the public humiliation Scotty had put her through.

Conner had known all along things would have to get really bad before she would call. And the feeling of unease never left him. He knew something was wrong. But unless she came to him for help, there wasn't a whole hell of a lot he could do. At least a couple of times a week he would call, and she was always very upbeat on the phone, but he could hear the edge in her voice. She would never talk long— instead she would take the first opportunity to pass the phone off to one of the kids. There were nights when he'd lay awake until dawn, trying to hatch some plan to get through to her. But he knew Abigail, and he understood that stiff-necked pride of hers. And unless she opened up and told him what was going on, he was stymied. It wasn't as if he could play some damned white knight and ride in to rescue her, especially when she didn't want to be rescued. So he had resigned himself to her silence.

Never once had he ever considered that the call for help would come from another source—like his eight-year-old nephew. Which meant it had to be far worse than he'd ever dreamt. It hurt like hell, knowing she was suffering through something all alone—and wouldn't come to him for help. All along he had told himself the only thing he wanted was for her to recover enough to get on with her life.

But as he packed the last of his gear and zipped the garment bag shut, he faced the fact that he would go to his grave wanting a whole lot more.

The sun had not yet reached high noon when the cab passed through a security gate and turned onto a heavily treed cul-de-sac in a very exclusive area of Toronto. His best Stetson settled squarely on his head,

Conner took his billfold out of the breast pocket of his western sports coat, removed two bills and replaced the billfold, then stared down at the toes of his freshly polished boots. He felt as if he had an entire rock pile in his gut. He had been awake all night, trying to figure out the best way to handle this. But he was no closer to an answer than he had been ten hours ago. He'd debated phoning first, but then decided against it.

Disconnecting from that line of thought, he looked out the window as the cab pulled in front of his brother's large and very pricey home. Somehow he was going to have to keep his personal feelings out of this. Somehow.

His face impassive, he handed the driver the two bills, then climbed out of the taxi, hitching the strap of the leather garment bag over his shoulder. He watched the cab disappear down the long curved driveway, then he climbed the steps to the ornate front door. Steeling himself, he pressed his thumb against the doorbell.

His jaw taut, he turned his head, watching a robin harvest worms in the lawn. Finally he heard footsteps from within, and the door opened.

He almost didn't recognize her. Her thick blond hair was pulled back in an untidy ponytail, and she had a tea towel draped over her shoulder. With her skin free of makeup and dressed in jeans and a faded Blue Jays sweatshirt, she didn't even come close to the put-together woman he was familiar with.

Her hand on the door, Abby went dead still; then her face lit up with a spontaneous smile. "Conner! For heaven's sake, what are you doing here? And why didn't you let us know you were coming?" Her hazel eyes bright with genuine pleasure, she stepped closer, reached up and welcomed him with her customary hug. Conner swallowed hard and closed his eyes, permitting himself the brief luxury of hugging her back.

His voice gruff, he relinquished his hold on her and forced himself to smile. "I had some business I had to take care of, and figured now was as good a time as any."

She laughed and grasped his arm, pulling him inside. "Well, this is the best surprise. The kids are going to be wild when they get home."

She closed the door behind them, and he set his bag down in the wide, terrazzo tiled foyer. Keeping his face expressionless, he took off his hat and dropped it on top of his bag, then turned to face her. She was much thinner than when he'd seen her last. There were dark circles under her wide, hazel eyes, and there was a pinched look around her full mouth. But even dressed the way she was, she still had that air of class about her. And the same inner warmth. She grinned up at him, then slipped her arm through his, propelling him down the wide oak-panelled hallway toward the kitchen. "You're one lucky camper, Mr. Calhoun. I just took a batch of blueberry muffins out of the oven, and they look as good as Grandma Mary's if I do say so myself."

Conner looked down at her, humor tugging at his mouth. He clearly remembered Abby and her first attempt at muffins. They had been so hard, Scotty had deemed them his very own cannonballs and made a big production out of pitching them into the creek. "Don't try and kid me, lady. You make lousy muffins. You could use them for ballast."

She grinned again and made a face. "Well, they

aren't as awful as they used to be. You can actually eat 'em now.''

He followed her into the bright spacious kitchen. This room was Abby through and through. There were splashes of bright colors and lush, healthy plants everywhere, and the granite countertops were comfortably cluttered. The stainless steel fridge sported an array of Post-it notes, notices and what looked like Sarah's artwork, and the ceramic pot by the phone was stuffed with a variety of pencils and pens.

The aroma of fresh muffins actually made his mouth water, and Conner allowed himself to be engineered into a chair.

Abby went over and opened one of the cupboards. ''I'll wager you could use a good cup of coffee right about now.'' She glanced over at him. ''Yes? No?''

He stretched out his legs. Even flying business class, he felt as if he'd spent the past four hours in a sardine can. He gave her a wry half smile. ''Coffee sounds great.''

Slouching in the maple captain's chair, he folded his arms across his chest and watched her as she prepared a fresh pot of coffee, his mind absently registering what she was saying, the knot in his gut tightening. She looked like hell. Her hair, now slightly darker than when Scotty first brought her home, had lost its luster, there was a hollowness to her finely sculpted features, and there wasn't a speck of color in her face. Her jeans practically hung on her, and he detected an unhealthy energy in her. There was no doubt about it; something was seriously wrong here. Abby wasn't the type to fade away to nothing without a damned good reason.

Compartmentalizing his observations in another

part of his brain, he responded to her small talk, his gaze fixed on her the entire time.

She set the table, getting coffee mugs for them both, keeping up a steady stream of chatter, which was unusual for her. Abby was not one to chatter. Turning in his seat, Conner rested his elbows on the table and clasped his hands together, trying to figure out what was going on. She wasn't herself, that was for sure.

Setting a basket of still steaming muffins on the table beside him, Abby reached for the drawer at the end of the large kitchen island and took out two linen napkins. She passed him one, then sat down kitty-corner from him and propped her chin in her hand. Sunlight caught in her long lashes and brought out the gold flecks in her hazel eyes as she studied him. "So what kind of urgent business would get you away from Cripple Creek this time of year? Aren't you getting close to spring branding?"

Conner held her gaze for an instant, then took one of the muffins from the basket, broke it open and reached for the butter dish. He had never been good at subterfuge; he always figured the most direct route was the best way to go. Buttering his muffin, he met her gaze.

He stared at her a moment, then spoke, his tone very quiet. "You're the urgent business, Abigail. I'm here to find out what in hell is going on."

Her expression froze and she went so still, it was as if she wasn't even breathing. There was a long, electric silence, her agitation almost palpable. Then she abruptly picked up a muffin and broke it in half. Her face carefully arranged into a non-expression, she spoke, her tone artificially bright. "I don't have a clue what you're talking about, Conner. Everything is fine.''

Conner ate his way through half a muffin, then took a sip of coffee, considering how to play his hand. Finally he brushed the crumbs off his fingers and looked at her. There was a hint of a smile around his mouth when he finally spoke. ''You're a lousy liar, Abby.'' He paused, then spoke again. ''And an even worse actress. So cut the guff, okay?''

Her head came up and her gaze riveted on his face, her eyes as wide as saucers; then she looked down again, her movements jerky. ''I don't have any guff to cut, Conner,'' she said, her tone just a little snippy. ''I think you've fallen off one too many horses.''

She almost made him laugh—Abby had always been able to make him laugh. And he had to admit that he was amused by the way she was maneuvering away from his question, but he wasn't that easy to lose. Hooking his thumb in his belt, he leaned back and considered her a moment, and he could almost feel her squirm. He was also very good at maneuvering. He indicated the muffins. ''These are very good.''

She lifted her chin, and gave him one of her cool looks. ''Thank you. I think.''

He smiled, then leaned forward, braced his elbows on the table and laced his hands together. He studied her, not liking the awful tension he sensed in her. He decided then that their little game was over. Under the circumstances, he figured his nephew would understand. Using that same quiet tone of voice, he spoke. ''Cody called me last night.''

She went very still again, and he caught a glimmer of alarm in her eyes. Satisfied that he had gotten her full attention, he continued. "He was pretty worried. He said that he thinks something is wrong with you—that you don't go to work anymore and he hears you crying late at night, and that you forget things." He shifted his clasped hands, then fixed his gaze on her. "So why don't you just tell me what's going on, Abigail?"

There was an instant, just an instant, where she sat staring at him, almost as if she were paralyzed, then she abruptly covered her face with her hands, a low sound wrenched from her. Experiencing a fierce, painful cramp in his chest, Conner forced himself to keep his hands laced together, the need to touch her almost unmanageable. Sometimes it was damned hard playing big brother around her. Too damned hard.

Unable to watch, Conner looked away, his face feeling like granite as he ran his thumbnail down a pattern carved in the ceramic mug. The sounds coming from across the table were tearing him to shreds inside. But there was nothing he could do. At least not without crossing a line he'd sworn he would never cross.

He had just about reached his limit when Abby finally lifted her head and quickly wiped her face with the napkin, her face swollen and red. She let her breath go in a shuddering sigh, then she began fiddling with the napkin. Finally she lifted her head and looked at him, a depleted expression in her eyes. "I don't even know where to begin," she whispered. "It's all been so awful."

Resting his clasped hands against his jaw, he gave her a small smile. "Then why don't you just start talking and we'll see where it takes us."

She managed a smile, then she pushed her plate

away and began folding and refolding her napkin. "It was more than just a drug problem," she said, her voice barely above a whisper.

Sensing that she was preparing herself for the telling, he waited, his gaze locked on her face. Finally she drew in a deep shaky breath and straightened, folding her arms tightly across her chest. "I didn't find out until months after he died just how bad it was." She turned her head toward the window, her profile stark against the bright light. "I didn't find out until then that he had a serious gambling problem as well—a very serious gambling problem. I knew he gambled, but I really thought it was strictly recreational." She finally looked at Conner, her gaze bleak. "He owed hundreds of thousands of dollars. And when the people started calling his loans, I couldn't believe it at first. He had borrowed from everyone. His teammates, his friends, the kids' educational funds. I found records for all those personal loans in his safety deposit box. I used all our savings and his insurance money to pay off his friends, and I thought I had it under control."

She clutched her arms tighter, then tipped her head back, staring at the ceiling. "Then I started getting calls from a string of his bookies. And there was another huge loan from a loan company in the States— I found out later he'd borrowed that to pay off another huge drug and gambling debt." She closed her eyes, the muscles in her jaw working; then she let out another sigh and looked at him. "To make a long story short," she said, her voice devoid of any emotion, "I had to remortgage the house, and I sold off every piece of art we had, my jewelry, his cars—anything and everything that had any kind of value." She held up her naked left hand. "Even my rings. But I got the bookies all paid off, and I had to cut a deal with the loan company for me to pay them back. Everything was gone—the equity in the house, all our investments...everything. Thank God the kids' school tuition is covered by a trust fund from my parents' estate, or I would have had to pull them out."

As if everything was crowding in on her, she got up and went over to the patio doors and stood staring out, her arms still clutched in front of her. She didn't say anything for a moment, then spoke, her voice barely audible. "I had managed to pay back most of the last loan, except there's still twenty thousand dollars owing. I knew, given time, I'd get it paid off. Then I lost my job. The company I work for was part of a merger, and my position was eliminated. I got a decent severance package, but that was it. Kaput." She lifted one shoulder in a small, defeated shrug. "When the loan company found out, they called their note." She turned and faced him, giving him a wan smile. "Of course I couldn't pay it, so now they've threatened to take me to court." Her face ashen and her hands visibly trembling, she came back over to the table and sat down, not a trace of animation in her. She clasped her hands together on the table, rubbing one thumb against the other. Her attempt at a smile failed. "It's been a bit of a bitch, Conner."

He had forced himself to remain disengaged during her telling—not allowing any kind of feeling to surface. But now, as she sat there, her animation gone, the vibrancy beat right out of her, he experienced a rush of rage. She was out of a job, just about out of money, and her once-perfect life was a total mess. He wanted to kill somebody.

She tipped her head back and closed her eyes, and Conner could see tears gathering in her lashes. Her despair cut him to the quick. And something gave way inside him. He had only ever initiated touching her twice before—once when he'd kissed Scotty's bride after the wedding. And then the night Scotty had died, when he'd pulled her onto his lap like a small wounded child, and held her as she wept for their awful loss. That time had been about offering comfort, and nothing more. This time, though, would be about something entirely different.

Knowing he was stepping across a very dangerous line, and sharply aware of how hard his heart was pounding in his chest, he reached across the table and grasped her cold, thin hands between his. The feel of her was almost enough. Almost.

His heart lumbering, he tightened his hold, rubbing her hands between his, trying to infuse her with his warmth. Then he drew in a deep, uneven breath and spoke, his voice very gruff. "You could have called me, Abby," he said quietly.

She opened her eyes, tears catching in her long lashes. "I couldn't," she whispered. "You had lost him, too. I couldn't dump this in your lap."

Holding her gaze, he managed a lopsided smile. "Well, consider it dumped." He gave her hands a reassuring squeeze. "Between us, we'll straighten this whole mess out. But the first rule is that you're not to worry anymore, okay?"

She stared at him, more tears damming up, and the look in her eyes almost did him in. Disconnecting from the feelings rising up in him, he gave her hands another squeeze, prompting an answer. "Okay?"

She managed a wobbly smile and nodded, and he

rewarded her effort with a smile of his own. "Okay."
He gave her hands another reassuring little shake,
then released her. Leaning back in his chair, he scru-
tinized her. "How much sleep have you had in the
past couple of weeks?"

Some of the old Abby resurfaced. She managed an
almost real smile. "Good grief, Conner. Don't you
know anything? No one sleeps when you're lost in
the swamp and up to your armpits in alligators."

He rewarded her effort with a soft chuckle, then he
stood up. "Well, I'm here to drain the swamp, lady.
So go to bed and get some sleep."

"I can't. The kids are home early from school today, and…"

Conner broke his self-imposed rule for the second
time that day. He grasped her hand, pulled her to her
feet, then pushed her toward the front foyer and the
stairs. "Damn it," he said, trying to sound as if he
meant it, "don't start arguing with me already, Abigail. For the rest of the day, I'm the boss."

She turned at the bottom of the stairs and looked
up at him, a faint glimmer appearing in her eyes. "All
right. I'll give you today, Calhoun. But tomorrow is
mine, and don't you forget it." Catching him totally
by surprise, she gripped his arm, then stretched up
and kissed him on the cheek. "Thank you, Conner,"
she whispered unevenly. Then she turned and went
up the stairs, and Conner watched her go, his lungs
suddenly so tight it was impossible to get air into
them.

A rush of emotion jammed up in his chest, and he
anchored his hand on the heavy oak newel post. God
help him, he had to keep his head on straight. And

he had to do right by her. Because, in the end, that was all he could ever give her.

Beginning to feel the effects of a sleepless night, he returned to the kitchen and poured himself another coffee, then went out and stood on the raised deck, staring out over the expensively designed landscape. Right now a half-hour nap would do wonders, but he knew he'd never sleep with her trapped in his head. Clamping his jaw shut, he forced himself to concentrate on other things, like how he was going to get her out of this pickle without walking all over that damned pride of hers. But he really didn't have a whole lot of options. Yeah, Abigail Allistair had put on a brave face, and she didn't expect anyone to bail her out, but he could tell that she was damned near at the end of her rope. There was no way he could walk off and leave her in this mess. So that gave him only one alternative. He was stepping in whether she liked it or not. And it was too damned bad if he tramped on her pride.

His expression set, he went back into the house. For his own peace of mind, he needed to check on her—she was just too eaten up by stress and strain, and far too thin for his liking.

The master bedroom door was ajar, and Conner pushed it open with one finger. She was curled up on the bed, very soundly asleep, her hands tucked under her face. Resting his shoulder against the door frame, he hooked his thumb in the front pocket of his jeans, his expression fixed as he watched her sleep. She *was* far too thin, but what bothered him more than anything was that her special effervescence was gone— that rare kind of energy that could light up a whole room. It was as if her bright spirit had been extinguished, and she just looked so fragile. He'd give anything if he had the right to hold her, to wrap her up and keep her safe.

Ever since she'd appeared that long-ago Christmas, she had been his still center, and in spite of the emptiness in his life, he wouldn't know what to do without her there. Just knowing she was alive fortified him somehow.

Abby stirred, curling up tighter, and Conner suspected she was cold. Careful not to make a sound, he went into the room, picked up a throw off the wing chair by the bed, then carefully covered her with it. Some of her hair had come loose from the ponytail, and he very gently lifted the strands away from her face and tucked them behind her ear. His throat cramping up, he let his hand linger just a moment— just a brief, perfect moment before he tucked the cover under her chin. Feeling as if he'd just got punched in the gut, he turned and left the room, soundlessly pulling the door shut behind him. Closing his eyes, he took a deep, uneven breath. He had let himself get far too close. But it wasn't nearly close enough.

Chapter 3

It was a little after two in the afternoon when the small yellow school bus pulled up in the Calhoun driveway, a private school logo on the side. Conner, who had been sitting on the wide steps waiting for its arrival, stood up as the bus pulled to a halt. The door opened and a dark-haired boy shot out, throwing his backpack in the air. "Uncle Conner! Hey!"

Cody launched himself at his uncle, and Conner laughed and swept him up, having just enough time to give him a hug before catching the angel-eyed little girl who practically jumped into his arms. "Uncle Conner! Uncle Conner! Thith is a big thurprith!"

Laughing at their antics and Sarah's lisp, Conner managed to wave to the bus driver, the tangle of arms around his neck nearly strangling him. "Hey, buckaroos. How are you doing?"

Sarah gave him a huge hug. "We're doing fine, Uncle Conner. How are *you* doing?"

"Well I'm doing fine, too, angel." He went over
to where Cody had dumped his backpack and bent
over, the two kids still clinging to him. "How about
snagging that bag, Tiger."

Leaning over in his uncle's arm, the boy did as he
was asked, then straightened and looked at his uncle,
his deep blue eyes dark with anxiety. Conner did what
he could to reassure his nephew. He winked and
smiled at him. "We'll talk later, okay, Chucker?"

The boy managed a smile. "Okay."

Grasping Conner's face, Sarah turned him to look
at her. "Where ith my mom?" she demanded.

Amused by his niece's imperious tone, he hitched
her higher. As Jake would say, there were no flies on
this one—nope, Little Miss Calhoun was a handful of
the first order. He gave her a solemn look. "I sold
her to a bunch of trolls."

Sarah narrowed her eyes at him. "What trolls?"

"He's pulling your leg, Sarah," interjected her
brother, sounding disgusted. "Dontcha know anything?"

Sarah lifted her chin and gave her brother a
haughty look. "I know loths of things."

Deciding that with these two it was no wonder
Abby was worn out, Conner tried not to smile as he
climbed the steps. He reached the door. "Let's try to
be quiet, okay. Just in case your mom is still asleep."

They entered quietly, closing the door without
making a sound; then Conner packed them both
through the big foyer to the kitchen. He set them
down on the big work island. Sarah gave him a fierce
hug, then squirmed toward the edge. "I hafta go to
the bathroom, Uncle Conner."

He swung her down and watched her leave the

room, then he turned back to his nephew. His gaze was solemn when he spoke. "You did the right thing calling me, Cody," he said, his tone quiet. "And I'm going to stick around and help your mom get things straightened away."

Cody looked up at his uncle, his gaze still anxious. "Did you tell her I called you?"

Conner smoothed down the boy's tousled curly hair. "Yeah, I did. But she's not upset about it. So don't you worry, okay?" Lifting the boy's chin so he could look him square in the eye, Conner gave his nephew a reassuring smile. "I don't want you worrying about anything from now on—I'm going to do that. And everything will be fine. I promise."

Cody looked up at his uncle, and Conner knew the little boy was doing his best not to cry. "Come here," he said gruffly, gathering the boy up and giving him a big hug. "That was a very grown-up thing you did, Cody. To call me."

The boy wrapped his arms and legs around Conner, then whispered unevenly against his uncle's neck, "I was kinda scared."

"It's okay to be scared, Tiger. But you don't have to be scared anymore, okay?"

"Okay."

"Mom ith up!" announced Miss Sarah as she skipped into the room. Abby followed her in, looking dazed and almost drunk. And she was trembling. His insides bunching up, Conner realized that she was in far worse shape than he'd originally thought. This was a woman who was literally running on empty. Setting his nephew down, he fixed a neutral expression on his face and crossed the room. Breaking his hard-and-fast rule for the third time that day, he took her by

the shoulders, turned her around and aimed her toward the stairs. "You're going back to bed, Abby,"
he said, using a tone that no one in his right mind
would ever mess with.

She looked at him, her eyes dazed. "I can't. The
kids are home. And I'll have to fix dinner."

He shook his head. "You're going back to bed. I'll
look after the kids and I'll fix dinner." She opened
her mouth to respond, and he shook his head again.
"Don't argue with me, Abby."

She closed her eyes and clasped her head, and he
had to fight back the urge to pick her up and carry
her up the stairs. That kind of touching was definitely
out of bounds. Cody seemed to pick up on his uncle's
mood. Taking his mom by the hand, he led her toward
the front hall. "Come on, Mom."

Conner watched them leave the room, then he went
outside on the deck, bracing both hands on the rail
and bending his head, his jaw rigid. For the first time
in his life, he experienced a bitter rage toward his
brother. He should have had his ass kicked for leaving
Abby in such a bloody mess.

"Are you mad at my mom?" came a small voice
at his elbow. Giving himself a minute to get his anger
under control, Conner turned his head and looked at
Abby's daughter. He wasn't going to try any kind of
dodge with this kid. His expression unsmiling, he
shook his head. "No angel. I'm not mad at your
mom. I'm mad at the person who upset your mom."

Her head tipped to one side, Sarah watched him,
considering his answer, and whether it was on the
level.

Conner almost smiled. Both she and her brother
had the Calhoun dark blue eyes and dark curly hair,

but there was a whole lot of Abby in this one, especially in that pointed, determined little chin. As if deciding his answer was on the up-and-up, she announced, "Mom thaid we could have macaroni and cheese for dinner. Do you know *how* to make macaroni and cheese?" His mood lightening, Conner swung his niece into his arms, flipped her over and carried her into the house. He was rewarded with a squeal and a giggle.

"Of course I know how to make macaroni and cheese."

Still giggling, Sarah grasped his pant legs. "You got your boots on, Uncle Conner. Mommy ith going to give you heck for having your boots on in the houth."

He laughed and swung her over his shoulder. "And I suppose you're going to tell her."

She managed to get her arms around his neck. "Nope," she said, squirming around to look him square in the eye, letting him know exactly what side his bread was buttered on. "Becauth you're going to make me macaroni and cheese."

Conner laughed and tipped her upside down again, letting her slide onto the kitchen table. This kid was going to pull out all the stops, that was for sure. He had to admit that his independent, strong-willed niece amused the hell out of him. But he didn't kid himself either. Anyone taking on this kid was going to have to be quick off the mark to keep ahead of her. No doubt about it.

He fixed an early dinner for them and debated about waking Abby up, but decided against it. It was as if having someone there had allowed her to pull the plug on everything she'd been frantically juggling, and her body had simply shut down on her. She was still asleep when he put the kids to bed. And she was still out cold when he decided to turn in. He heard her get up in the middle of the night, and he forced himself to stay right where he was. He reminded himself that he had come here to help her, not make things worse.

In spite of the jumble of thoughts racing around in his head, he actually slept far better than he expected to. He awoke at sunrise, recalling the alarm clock he'd seen on Abby's bedside table. Feeling slightly hungover, he pulled on a pair of jeans, then slipped down the hall and into Abby's room, confiscating the clock. He'd be damned if he was going to let an alarm clock wake her.

He made the kids flapjacks for breakfast, managing to outmaneuver his niece when she tried to exploit his boots-in-the-house misdemeanor. And he didn't even try to play referee when the two of them got into a pitched battle in the front hall over who got to go out the door first. He simply grabbed them both by the back of their school jackets and set them on the doorstep like a pair of boots. Obviously, by the stunned looks on their faces, their mother was more into negotiation and refereeing. Cody looked slightly peeved when the bus pulled away, but Sarah was dramatically blowing kisses from the back window. Conner couldn't help but grin, wondering what nefarious schemes she was cooking up in that little head of hers.

He watched the bus disappear around the curve, then turned and went back into the house, his expression turning grim. It was time to take care of business. And it didn't matter whether Abby liked it or not, he was taking over.

It took him no time to find the information he needed on the New York loan company—all he had to do was go through the efficiently organized desk in Abby's office. With everything spread out before him, he made a list of things he had to deal with today, not the least of which was the branding.

With a fresh cup of coffee at his elbow, he used the phone in Abby's office to handle the loan company, and he used his cell phone to keep up a running dialogue with Jake and Tanner at Cripple Creek. As crazy as it was, he could almost see the humor in it. It was the kind of situation a phone company would have snapped up for a TV commercial—a rancher directing the spring branding operation on one phone, while dealing with a financial institution in a different country on another.

And between specific instructions on the select group of calves he wanted left as bulls, he used Abby's fax machine to fax his bank in Bolton his signature, authorizing his accounts manager to transfer the required funds to the loan company in New York. In less than an hour and a half, he had everything organized and settled. He figured with two phones and a fax, a person could darned near move mountains.

It was just before ten when Abby finally made an appearance. Conner was sitting at the kitchen table, another cup of coffee by his elbow, reading the newspaper when she stumbled in. She looked like hell—and he could tell she was on the verge of panic. He didn't give that panic a chance to gather momentum. Before she could say anything, he held up his hand to halt her. "Kids on the bus, fed, teeth brushed, faces washed, socks matched." He gave her a lopsided smile. "So take a load off, Mother. There's fresh coffee in the pot."

Normally, she would have nailed him with some sharp snippy comment, but she just stood there staring at him, the most awful look in her eyes. Then she covered her face with her hands and simply fell apart. Feeling as if he had inadvertently broadsided her somehow, Conner launched himself out of the chair, forgetting all his rules about keeping his distance.

He was just about to grab her when Abby stuck her arm out, as if blocking him. "Don't," she sobbed. "Don't be nice to me, Conner. I can't handle 'nice' right now."

It was so Abby, that kind of comment, that he stopped dead in his tracks, not sure what in hell he should do. He had never felt so out of his depth in his whole life. She visibly pulled herself together and roughly dried her face on the baggy purple sweatshirt she was wearing. Then squaring her shoulders, she lifted her chin and marched over to the cupboard, yanked a mug off a shelf, slammed it on the counter and slopped coffee into it.

If she hadn't looked so awful, and if she hadn't damned near scared him half to death, he would have laughed. But this was no laughing matter. This woman was running on sheer grit and not a whole lot else, and he wasn't going to stand around, waiting for her to unravel. He was going to start making some critical decisions here, whether she liked it or not.

Acid rolling around in his gut, he went over to the table, sat down and propped his feet up on another chair. Making sure his expression was a whole lot calmer than he felt, he slouched back and laced his hands across his chest. Giving himself a couple of seconds to get a grip, he squared his jaw and spoke. "Sit down, Abby."

He had never used that abrupt tone on her—never—and her head came up and she looked at him as if he'd just said something foul and disgusting.

He fixed her with a steady stare. "You better sit down, Abby. This is going to take a while."

She mustered some attitude and gave him a sour look, but she did sit down, plunking her mug on the table.

Not moving, Conner contemplated what to hit her with first. He figured he might as well start at the top. "I found the statements from the loan company in your desk—"

She started to get up, and he held up his hand, giving her a warning look. "You better get your butt in that chair, Abigail. Like I said, this is going to take a while." She settled into her chair, a stunned look on her face, as if she didn't know this person before her. Which was good. Conner wasn't sure he knew this person either. He kept the same businesslike tone. "As I said, I found the statement from the loan company, and as of an hour and a half ago, the loan has been paid off. They are out of your hair, permanently." He watched her too-thin face, and he caught a glimmer of acute relief in her eyes—as if a huge threat had been removed. He let his expression relax as he continued, his tone softer. "And I looked over your accounts, and the cold hard truth is that you need to unload this house. You can't afford to keep it—it's just going to drag you down deeper. So I have a plan." Straightening, he dropped his feet to the floor, then leaned forward and rested his arms on the table. His expression determined, he fixed his gaze on hers.

"I think we should call a real estate agent and list this place at a price that's going to move it, but where you come out with no debt. Then I think we should get a moving company in here to pack everything up and haul it into storage."

She tried to resurrect some indignation, her chin coming up. "You had no right to go through my finances, Conner. That was damned rude."

Amused at her attempt to cut him down, he looked straight into her eyes. "No I didn't, and yes I am." He leaned back again, continuing with his plan. "After we get all that straightened away, I'm going to call the kids' school, tell them there's a family emergency, then I'm packing you all up and taking you back to Cripple Creek for the summer."

That stark look was back in her eyes and her face was so pale it was scary. Obviously struggling, she clasped her hands between her legs and opened her mouth to speak. Conner knew she was going to set up a big argument. He never even gave her a chance to get started. "Don't even think about arguing with me, Abby," he said, his tone firm. "You're coming home for the summer, and that's that."

She looked like a pathetic waif sitting there, the bones of her shoulders pronounced under the fleece fabric. Her hair was mostly out of the ponytail, and she just looked so damned forlorn. He would have given anything to have the right to go over there, pick her up and just hold her. But that was not his right— or his mission.

She never took her eyes off him, and his gut clenched when he realized she was trembling. He gave her a wry smile, his gaze fixed on her. "It's a good plan, Abby," he said softly. "You'll have the whole summer to get it back together, and the kids will love it.''

Her eyes filled with tears and she bit her lip to keep it from trembling. Then she closed her eyes and swallowed hard, two tears spilling out. ''I would have made it through if you hadn't showed up,'' she whispered brokenly. ''I would have.''

Conner laced his hands tighter together to keep from touching her. She was fighting her little fight, and he respected her for that. And he knew it just wasn't in her to go down without a struggle. ''I know you would have. But it's going to make me feel a whole lot better if you let me help you over this hump.''

She opened her eyes and stared at him, a hollow look back in her eyes; then she took a deep breath, as if fortifying herself. ''This is only a loan,'' she said, trying to call up some of her usual stubbornness. ''I'll pay you back the money.''

Knowing exactly where she was going, Conner decided it was time for him to draw his own line in the sand. His gaze fixed on her, he leaned back and folded his arms. ''I don't think so, darlin'. That money is a gift to your kids, so you don't have a whole hell of a lot to say about it.''

His response caught her unawares. Abby gave a huff of uneven laughter, and clasped her head. ''Ah, God, don't start getting cute, Conner. I can't dance that fast right now.''

A twitch of amusement surfacing, he watched her try to recover, not giving her an inch. ''I don't dance, Abigail. You should know that by now. And I don't want a big argument. All I want from you right now is complete compliance.''

She wasn't so down and out that she couldn't even scrape up a decent dirty look. "And you know where you can stuff your compliance, Calhoun."

He grinned and rocked back in his chair. "It's a good plan, Abigail." His expression turning serious, he spoke again, his tone soft and persuasive. "Like I said, I'd love to have you guys there for the summer, and you know the kids would love every minute of it. And it would give you a chance to regroup."

Clearly struggling with a whole bunch of emotions, she tipped her head back, wrestling with her choices. Conner watched her, his gut in a knot, waiting for her answer. He could almost feel her internal battle—her pride and independence struggling to override her common sense.

Finally she dropped her head and looked at him, a tiny glimmer of humor in her eyes. "Okay. It is a good plan. But you might want to rethink that part about getting stuck with us for the summer."

Liking her spunk, he rocked his chair farther back. "Hey. If I can ride herd on a bunch of range-ornery cows year after year, I can sure as hell manage one skinny woman and two kids for a couple of months."

Clasping her arms around her, she tipped her head to one side, her expression changing as she considered him. Finally she spoke, her voice very soft and very husky. "Did anyone ever tell you that you make one hell of a white knight, Conner Calhoun?"

Discomfited by her comment, he got up and started folding the paper. He didn't want her thinking that. He wasn't a white knight by a long shot. Now that he had gotten what he wanted, part of him felt like a thief in the night.

The next week was absolute chaos, and Conner continued to have concerns about Abby. He could tell she was running on empty, yet she continued to drive herself to the limit. And on top of overseeing all the sorting and packing, she made an appointment with a head-hunting firm to start a job search, even though she was going to be out of the city.

About midway through the week, she managed to dredge up enough spunk to argue with him again over his payment of the loan. He finally got his back up and told her that the money was going to go to the kids anyway, and they just got it a little early, and for her to just drop it. She didn't talk to him for the rest of the day, but she did drop it. Finally. But even in the state she was in, she was amazing. He figured with her organizational skills, she could move a whole city if she had to.

One good thing was that the kids were ecstatic about spending the summer at Uncle Conner's, and they would rattle on to anyone who would listen to them—the real estate agent, Abby's nextdoor neighbor, Abby's friend, Joanne, the guy from the moving company who came out to give them an estimate. Uncle Conner had promised them ponies, and Uncle Conner had a litter of newborn kittens in the barn, and he had dogs that herded cows. And Uncle Conner was going to take them fishing, and was going to let them sleep out on the veranda.

Uncle Conner began to wonder what he had let himself in for.

It took nine days to move the mountain—getting authorization for the kids' early dismissal from school, household effects and Abby's car in storage, mail forwarded, utilities canceled, bank notified. And by the time they boarded the plane for the flight to Calgary, Abby had that glassy-eyed look of a sleepwalker. But in spite of his concerns for her, Conner knew he had done the right thing. Hell, it was the *only* thing he could have done. He tried to convince himself that all she needed was a few weeks with no worries, good food, fresh country air and she would be as right as rain. But once she was settled in the window seat beside him, it was as if she simply let go. She was fast asleep before they'd even left the ground.

The skies in Calgary were bright and cloudless when they landed, and the kids were wound up like tops. Abby had slept the entire flight, and she was still half out of it when he left her with the luggage while he took the kids to pick up his truck from Park and Fly.

He figured she'd be back asleep before he got their suitcases loaded and the kids belted in the back seat of the extended cab, and he was right. Even the kids packed it in before they got out of the city, and he was left with nothing to keep his mind occupied— except his own thoughts. And those were very dangerous. He had been so busy playing big brother and Uncle Conner for the past few days, he had never even considered his own reality. And now here he was, heading home, and for two and a half months his world was going to be complete. And he was going to have to make the most of every second of that time. He had no illusions; that was going to be his allotment—two and a half months to last the rest of his life.

There had been changes since he'd left. The countryside was green from the several good rains and the warm weather. Every depression was full of water, and the ditches were sprinkled with bright patches of dandelions. God, it felt damned good to be back in these wide open spaces.

This was where he belonged—the rolling green hills, the rugged purple Rockies in the distance, skirted with dense coniferous forests and capped with snow. There was nowhere on earth like it. He always felt cramped and crowded in the city, as if everything was crowding in on him. Here a man had room to breathe.

The clock in the dashboard read 3:27 p.m. when Conner turned off the secondary highway onto the long, paved tree-lined lane that led to the ranch. He noticed the mailbox had a fresh coat of paint and someone had planted flowers around the base.

He slowed as he crossed the cattle guard, the tight feeling letting go in his chest. Yeah, this was definitely where he belonged, here in the high country where the air was cleaner, the colors brighter, the smells sweeter. There was a spot, right at the top of the hill, that commanded the most spectacular view in the whole country. That particular spot was his touchstone, the spot that grounded him when he returned home after being away for a spell. If he had his way, he'd be buried on this hill.

He pulled over on the grassy verge and rolled down the window, the scent of silver willow sweet and clear. Conner took a deep breath. A smile surfaced when a mare and her new foal came over to the fence to inspect his presence. Propping his elbow in the open window, he studied the foal. A nice little filly, with the identical markings of her mother.

There was the sound of a seat belt releasing, and he turned as Abby opened her eyes very wide and stretched forward. Her hair wild around her face, she raked it back with one hand, her pricey khaki top so wrinkled it looked as if it had come out of a rag bag. Her voice was thick and groggy. "What?"

He lifted the corner of his mouth. "What do you mean, what?"

She stretched her eyes wide open again, then licked her lips. "Don't start playing dumb games," she said, still trying to wake up. "Why are we stopped?"

He hooked his thumb out the window. "We've got visitors."

Before he could brace himself, she slid across the split-bench seat to check it out. Without thinking, he removed his hand from the steering wheel and rested his right arm across the back of the seat so she could get a clear view.

But that was a big, big mistake. She crowded over, her breast pressing against his chest as she craned her neck to see the foal. There was some of the old effervescence in her voice when she whispered, "Oh, look at him. Isn't he beautiful? And so precious."

Her warmth and scent wrapped around him, and Conner froze, suddenly unable to breathe. She moved her head and her hair brushed against his jaw. Conner closed his eyes, an age-old need roaring through him like a freight train, the sensation completely paralyzing him. It was as if his entire body was retaliating for the mental discipline he had managed to maintain over the past ten days, and he clenched his jaw, his whole body on red alert. He needed her to move away—far away. But his mind rebelled, telling him that was a lie, that he wanted her closer. Much closer.

"Now come on, Conner. I know you're a big tough cowboy and all, but don't you honestly think he's precious?"

Somehow he managed to respond, his voice slightly choked. "It's a she."

She turned her head and looked at him, a glimmer of laughter in her eyes. "You're a pain, do you know that? Couldn't you just have agreed?"

Feeling as if a single touch would put him through the roof, Conner wasn't quite sure how he managed to dredge up a weak smile in return. But he managed. "I agree."

She smacked his shoulder and sat back in her seat, looking better than she had all week. "You need a good woman who'll train you right." She rolled down her window, closing her eyes and taking a long deep breath. "Lord, I love the smell of silver willow. It really does smell like heaven."

His whole body one big pulse point, Conner put the truck in gear and gripped the wheel, his knuckles white. Thank God they only had half a mile to go— he didn't think he could take being closed up in the cab with her for much longer. He felt like a bomb ready to go off.

He wasn't in such bad shape that he didn't notice things. Not only had the mailbox been painted and flowers planted around it, but the row of trees on either side of the drive had been freshly cultivated, and the grass had been recently mowed. Obviously Jake and Henny had gone all out for this homecoming.

When he had called to tell Henny, who also kept house for him, that he was bringing Scotty's family home, he could almost see her perk up and bristle with that take-charge efficiency of hers. The fact that Scotty's wife and kids were coming for the summer was an event that exceeded even *her* expectations.

The Hendersons were an integral part of Cripple Creek—not only was Jake the foreman, but Henny was also the ranch cook. They had been with the Calhouns for over thirty years, and they had raised their three sons there. They were like family, plain and simple.

Conner drove over the stone bridge that spanned the creek and rounded a dense stand of aspen and spruce, the open patch of prairie still yellow with buffalo beans and dandelions. The huge old Victorian house came into view, the front veranda yawning over a lawn that rolled down to the creek, the wide expanse of green anchored by the big old willows scattered along the bank.

The house wasn't the traditional white of most of the old ranch houses in the district. Not even close. When Conner had been about six, Mary had gotten it into her head that the drab, plain white would have to go, and she'd decided to deck it out in the Easter-egg colors of the famed painted ladies in San Francisco. Never one to soft peddle anything, she had chosen robin's egg blue, bright pink, teal green and dark purple. His father had had a fit, but Mary refused to back down. The paint job had taken an entire summer to complete, and Conner could still remember the fights, totally awed by both the yelling matches and the colorful transformation. Mary had altered that big, plain old house the exact same way she had altered their lives.

His three dogs came out to meet them as he

rounded the last curve, the paved road swinging around to the rear of the house. Mindful of the load of luggage in the back of the truck, Conner broke his own rule and parked next to the concrete sidewalk that bisected the high lilac hedge. The hedge, which his grandfather had planted, separated the house yard from the wide paved parking area and the garage. Beyond the garage, a gravel drive continued on, forking just past a stand of towering spruce. One road led to the barn, corrals, massive windmill and other outbuildings; the other led to the house the Hendersons lived in, and the bunkhouse and kitchen. The property was functional and well laid out, considering it had been designed over a century ago.

Not quite sure if he was back to normal or not, he shut off the ignition, then turned and looked at Abby. She gave him a wry grin. ''Aren't you going to say, 'Well, here we are?'''

Her earlier flash of effervescence was fading, and she looked wan and very tired. Her obvious exhaustion extinguished the remaining heat in his body, and it was all he could do not to reach out and touch her. Instead, he gave her an off-center smile. ''Well, here we are.''

He opened his door, then turned around and reached over the back of the seat and gently shook Cody's shoulder. ''Hey, Tiger. Up and at 'em.''

Cody woke up like a normal kid—slow, kind of dozy. But not Miss Sarah. Miss Sarah woke up like a rocket launching. Her eyes flew open and she was trying to scramble out of the truck before she'd even got untangled from the seat belt. ''Come on. Come *on,* Cody. We gotta go find the kittens.''

Jake came hustling from around the corner of the

garage, the hitch in his gait indicating he was still nursing a bad hip. Abby climbed out of the truck, and Jake hobbled around the hood to give her a big hug; then he swept Sarah up. "Well, if it ain't Miss Muffet come to visit."

Sarah acted all sweet and coy. "I'm not Mith Muffet, Jake. I am Tharah Jane."

Jake chuckled and crouched down to shake Cody's hand. "And how are you doing there, young fella. You've grown a foot since I seen you last."

Abby dragged her hands through her hair and stretched, looking suddenly very fragile. In fact, she was so pale, she looked as if she was ready to fall down. Jake shot Conner a quick worried look, and nodded when Conner indicated the two kids with a lift of his chin.

"Tell you what. How about you young 'uns come with me to find them kitties, and Uncle Conner can get your ma settled. How's that?"

Looking sweet and innocent, Sarah batted her eyelashes at Jake. "That thounds fine," she said, taking his hand, looking just a little too cute to trust. Conner restrained a smile. She didn't fool him for a minute. This one was going to take some watching. No question about it.

Slamming the door, Conner scratched each of the dogs, then went to the back of the truck. Hoisting out the two largest suitcases, he gave Abby a warning look when she made a move to get some of the remaining luggage. "Not a chance, Abby," he said, using that same tone he had used a whole lot over the past ten days. "Just leave 'em there. I'll take care of it."

She gave him an uppity look. "I'm not a cripple, Conner. I can carry two little suitcases."

He didn't say anything. He just continued to stare at her, and she gave an exasperated huff and turned up the walk, muttering something under her breath. But she didn't waste any energy arguing with him. It was as if she'd used up the little burst she had, and he followed behind her, watching her every step. It seemed to take what remaining energy she had to make it up the walk. She was so exhausted, he half expected her to trip over a crack in the sidewalk.

Henny met them at the back door, her large frame obscured by a huge butcher's apron, her gray frizzled hair pulled back in a braid. Her weathered faced creased into a huge smile when she stretched out her arms to welcome Abby. "Well, well, well. You made it at last. Jake must have been up that road ten times to see if you were coming." She folded Abby in her substantial arms, giving her a hug, then drew her through the large mudroom into the even bigger kitchen.

If Conner had had any doubts before, it was clear to him as soon as he entered the house that Henny had used the homecoming as an excuse to clean from top to bottom. The fridge and stove gleamed, the pegged oak floor didn't have a smudge of dirt on it, and even the yellow gingham curtains had been freshly washed and starched. A basket of fruit sat in the middle of the round table, so full it could feed half the county, and fresh cinnamon buns were cooling on the counter. Conner gave up a small smile. God only knew what was stuffed in the fridge.

The foreman's wife urged Abby through the spotless kitchen to the dining room, obviously heading for the stairs. "Now you come on along upstairs, and we'll get you all settled."

There was a huge bouquet of lilacs on the dining room table and Abby stopped to touch them. "These are lovely, Henny," she said softly, caressing the thick cluster of blossoms.

Henny puffed up with pleasure. "They're late blooming this year. I expect it's because it was such a late spring. But I remembered that you liked them," she said, looking pleased. "Especially them dark purple ones. They are something, aren't they?" Then she gave Abby a gentle prod. "Now you go on up and get settled, and I'm going to fix some lemonade and cookies for a wee snack."

Feeling as if he'd been consigned to the role of bellboy, Conner continued through the dining room and living room to the front hall. Shifting his grip on the two suitcases, he started up the wide staircase. If he knew Henny, the upstairs would be as shipshape as the downstairs.

When he'd called to say he was bringing them home, he had asked Henny to fix up the original master bedroom for Abby.

After Mary could no longer manage the stairs, Conner had had the huge old formal parlor turned into a bedroom and bath for her. And when she had moved into the extended-care facility in Bolton, he had, to make less work for Henny, moved downstairs into that room. So for the past couple of years, the upstairs had been pretty much closed off.

He turned at the top of the stairs. It was obvious to even him that the entire upper floor had been aired out and cleaned up for Abby and the kids. But the master bedroom was absolutely immaculate—the lace curtains had been freshly laundered, the old hooked rugs beaten and aired, and the antique furniture had been polished within an inch of its life. A tracking dog couldn't have found a speck of dust anywhere. And there was another huge bouquet of lilacs sitting on the two-hundred-year-old blanket chest sitting at the foot of the big, four-poster bed.

He set the suitcases on the floor by the bed, then went and opened the casement windows, the scent of silver willow heavy on the warm spring breeze.

Abby came into the room, and he turned, his expression tightening when he saw how pale she was. Even her lips had lost their color, and he detected a fine tremor in her hands. He suspected that in her physically depleted state, she was probably feeling the effects of the high-country altitude on top of everything else.

Bracing one hand on the wall, he stuck the other in the back pocket of his jeans. His jaw tight, he watched Abby take off the jacket she'd been wearing. His voice was very gruff when he spoke. "I'll look out for the kids if you want to lie down for a while."

She swept her loose hair behind her ear, then looked at him, trying to pull up a smile. "When did you get so bossy?"

He forced a return smile. "It wasn't an order, Abby. It was a suggestion."

She stared at him, her expression unsmiling, then she looked away and laid her jacket on the blanket chest. "Maybe I will," she said, her voice very soft. He watched her for a moment, wondering why she was avoiding looking at him. His expression fixed, he straightened and pulled down the blinds on all the windows. He didn't like her like this. It was as if all the energy and brightness had been sucked right out of her. Reluctant to leave her, he crossed to the bed and pulled back the light quilt spread, then straightened, keeping his expression neutral. "Can I get you anything?"

Her arms folded tightly in front of her, she shook her head, exhaustion etched on her face. He tried to ease his own expression. "I don't want to see you until suppertime, all right?"

She managed a small smile, and he stared at her a moment, then turned toward the door. His hand was on the crystal knob when she spoke, her voice very quiet. "Conner?"

He turned and looked at her, the soft yellow fabric of her blouse clinging to her, making him think of a long, slender rosebud.

She met his gaze, her eyes steady. "I'd like to think I could have pulled out of this tailspin on my own. But the truth is, I don't know what I would have done without you." Her voice got even softer. "Thank you."

The muscles in his face didn't want to work as he tried to erect a smile. "It was my pleasure."

A thick feeling unfolding in his chest, he watched her a moment longer, then left the room, pulling the heavy door shut behind him. His hand still on the doorknob, he locked his jaw and closed his eyes, a thousand feelings lumbering through his chest. Abby. His brother's widow.

It was as if having her there was eroding his old defenses. Because this was the closest to the truth he'd ever come with her—when he said it was his pleasure. Except she would never know just how much.

It was another secret he had to keep.

Chapter 4

The first fingers of sunrise painted the bellies of the fat, cumulous clouds with pink and purple, the angle of early morning light stretching the shadows and making the dew sparkle.

Facing the sunrise, Conner rocked back in the old wicker chair and propped his feet on the spindled veranda rail, a steaming cup of coffee cradled in his hands. It was not quite 5:00 a.m., but in the long days of June, he was always up by then anyway. It was his favorite time of day. He liked witnessing the sunrise, the beginning of a brand-new day. And he liked that particular stillness that came with early morning. But most of all, he liked soaking up that quiet as he watched the sun rise over the closed courtyard on the east side of the house. Even though he didn't have a damned clue about flowers or gardening, he had to admit the courtyard was spectacular.

Filled with flowers and old-fashioned roses and

flowering shrubs, that courtyard was like a little piece of heaven. There was a whole family history in it, and it had turned into a tiny oasis of solitude for him. Coming out here was one ritual he wouldn't want to give up.

When Mary had come to Cripple Creek, she had worked like a madwoman to restore that neglected, overgrown garden to its former glory. And after Henny arrived, she had worked right alongside Mary. Henny still continued to maintain it.

His gaze drifted to the molded lounge chair under the hawthorn tree and his expression altered. Over the past week, at every chance he got, he'd dragged Abby out into the courtyard. He hoped the solitude and quiet would have the same restoring effect on her. More often than not, when he'd come out to check on her, she'd been asleep in that chair. And she seemed to be improving. Conner knew he owed a big vote of thanks to Henny. She had taken the two kids under her wing and they barely saw their mother from dawn to dusk. He took a sip from his mug. He hoped to hell Abby really was getting her feet under her and he wasn't just kidding himself.

There was the click of the release on the high-tech roller screen he had installed for the French doors, and he knew from the scent who it was before he even turned his head.

Abby pulled the screen back across the opening and latched it, a large steaming mug in her hand. She wore a baggy faded gray sweat suit, and her hair, which had escaped from a topknot, was sticking out at weird angles, her cheeks pink from sleep. She truly did look as if she'd just crawled out of bed.

He gave her a reproving look. "What are you doing up at this hour? You should be in bed."

She glared at him, the reflection of the rising sun making the flecks in her hazel eyes look like pure gold. Ignoring him, she sat down on the top step, her shoulder inches away from his thigh, then took a sip from the mug.

Her tousled hair was very close, and Conner tightened his hand on his mug. He spoke again, his tone softer. "You should be in bed, Abby."

"Can it, Uncle Conner. I'm not three years old, you're not my mother and I can manage to get around all by myself." She looked up and gave him a lopsided smile, a tiny glint appearing in her eyes. "I'm not going to expire on your front doorstep, so give it a rest, okay?"

Amusement lifted one corner of his mouth. "Technically, you're not on my front doorstep. The front doorstep is on the other side of the house."

She gave a soft, disbelieving laugh and shook her head. "Lord, you are a contrary animal. You know darned well what I mean." She hunched her shoulders and drew up her legs, locking her arms around them, the mug still clutched in one hand. "It's so beautiful in the country this time of morning," she said, her voice very quiet. "No wonder you come out here every day."

He experienced a funny rush in his belly, and his voice wasn't quite steady when he responded. "How do you know I come out here every day?"

Her profile to him, she took a sip. "I've got ears, Conner," she said, as if speaking to a slow child. "And a nose. Every morning, you get up, go to the kitchen and make coffee—and darned fine coffee, I

might add. Then you come out here.'' She glanced
up at him, a twinkle in her eyes. ''I would have joined
you long before now, but I think you've been slipping
me Mickey Finns. I just couldn't haul my sorry butt
out of bed.''

He wanted to smooth down her hair that was sticking up, but instead he forced a small grin. ''You
should listen to your sorry butt more often.''

She rebuked him with a shoulder nudge against his
thigh, and that one light touch sent a hot-and-cold
sensation shooting through him, making his pulse run.
For an instant, it felt as if his lungs had collapsed.
Closing his eyes and clamping his teeth together, he
forced himself to inhale, a new rush of heat sizzling
through him. Lord, he must be out of his mind, letting
her get that close. But he knew she'd come out because he was there, so he was damned well going to
have to tough it out. Because above all else, he never
wanted to give her one single reason to think her being at the ranch was an imposition. Having her there
was more than he'd ever hoped for.

''Conner?''

It took a huge effort for him to turn his head and
look down at her. ''Hmm?''

There was an odd look in her eyes, just like he'd
seen in Sarah's when she was hopeful of the right
answer. ''You aren't going to baby me the whole time
I'm here, are you?''

The tightness in his chest suddenly let go, and he
was able to respond with a chuckle. ''Ah. Now this
sounds very much like Miss Sarah. Are you trying to
get your own way?''

She narrowed her eyes at him. ''I'm not trying to
get my own way. It was a simple question.''

Wanting to laugh, he held her gaze. "Nothing is ever simple with you, Abigail."

She rolled her eyes, then picked up a dried leaf and rolled it between her fingers. Tossing it away, she looked up at him again, her gaze serious. "I don't want you worrying about me," she said, her voice quiet.

It was so hard to keep from reaching out to touch her face, so hard. Not allowing himself the easy way out, he held her gaze, everything he felt for her crowding up into his chest. He dragged up a small smile. "Let me worry, Abigail," he said, his voice husky. "It gives me something new to get kinked up about other than bad grass, lame horses and a bunch of lazy cowhands."

She grinned, giving him another little jab. "Give me a break, Calhoun. I might be a big city girl, but even I know that big, strong cowboys don't kink up."

Conner managed to grin back at her. "Shows you how little you know."

She made a face at him, then turned her head and took another sip from her mug. "So tell me about the grass, the horses and the lazy cowhands. Especially that pretty mare that Chase McCall delivered yesterday."

Conner told her about the mare he had sent to Chase for training, and from there, conversation drifted to how the spring roundup went and the new crop of calves. From the questions Abby was asking, Conner knew she'd been reading some of the farm magazines that were lying around. And it kind of amazed him, how much she'd assimilated in such a short time. Maybe there was more "country" in her than she thought.

It was just going on six when Conner heard a door slam, then Jake whistling on his way to the barn. As much as Conner hated to break off his time with Abby, he knew he had to get a move on. They had fences to fix, and he wanted to get the cows and calves back to the summer range later in the week. Not to mention he had a dozen other things he should be doing.

Reluctantly lifting his feet off the railing, he let his chair rock forward. He stood up and tossed the dregs of his mug over the rail, then settled his Stetson on his head as he looked down at her. "I hear Jake heading for the corrals, so I'd better get my sorry butt in the saddle."

Her arms clasped around her legs and her chin propped on her upraised knees, she turned her head to look at him, a twinkle in her eyes. "If you're trying to stir up a little sympathy, it's not working. You love every darned minute of it, and you know it."

He tapped the back of her head as he went down the steps. "Feeling a little sassy this morning, aren't you?"

"You bet."

He headed down the flag walk to the ivy-covered trellis and wrought-iron gate, and had his hand on the latch when she called out behind him. "Watch yourself around all those cows, cowboy. There's a lot of estrogen out there."

That made him smile. "And you behave yourself."

"In your dreams," she retorted as he went through the gate. He grinned again. She was slowly getting her feet under her. No doubt about it.

Conner spent the next hour taking care of business. A two-year-old colt had a hot, nasty swelling on his foreleg, and it looked like an abscess. Conner had just let the horse into a box stall when Abby came flying into the barn, more animation in her face than he'd seen for a very long time. And it hit him again, why he had fallen so hard the first time he met her—because of that animation, that zest for life, that unbelievable energy.

She looked like a kid, dressed in blue jeans, what looked like one of his old plaid shirts, her hair twisted up on top of her head. In the dim light, she could pass for eighteen.

"Guess what?" she demanded, practically dancing.

Dragging the door closed on the box stall, he gave her a half smile. "I don't think I want to know."

She tucked a loose tendril of hair behind her ear, excitement practically bubbling out of her. "Yes, you do." Then she narrowed her eyes at him. "Come on, Conner. Play the game, all right?"

Trying not to smile, he rested one hand on the wall and hooked his thumb in the back pocket of his jeans. "Okay. What?"

The effervescence was back. "I just got a call from the real estate agent. And guess what?"

Aware of how much her daughter was like her, he obliged her with the right answer. "I'm guessing."

She grinned and made a rude gesture. "He got not one, but two offers on the house late last night." She did a little dance and raised her arms in victory. "I think I just might unload that money pit. I think I just might."

Before he had time to answer, she turned around and headed back down the alleyway. "He wants me to stick close to the phone, but I just had to tell you."

As if she just couldn't contain herself, she did a perfect pirouette, then danced out the door. "I'm free, I'm free," he could hear her singing out, and Conner looked down at the floor and shook his head, amused by her behavior. He'd never seen her act quite that goofy before. Maybe she had simply lost it.

After her announcement, Conner would have liked to stick around, but he got a call from a cattle buyer. He had to meet up with him, and then he had to go into Bolton to pick up more fencing supplies.

It was midafternoon when he finally returned to the ranch. Needing to check an old invoice, he entered the house. He was just entering the kitchen when Abby appeared in the archway, a look on her face that he couldn't define. A kind of regal, rigidly contained expression, as if she had acquired something she hadn't expected to acquire. It made his chest ache just to look at her.

As though there was an enormous energy built up in her, she met his gaze, her shoulders square, her chin up. And when she spoke, her voice was shaky with emotion. "I sold the house, Conner," she said, as if trying to hold everything in. "There were offers and counteroffers from both parties, and I sold it for more than we listed it for." Her whole body seemed to radiate energy waves as she swallowed and spoke again. "I'm actually going to come out of this with some cold, hard cash. I can't believe it."

His own throat suddenly tight, he abruptly stuck his hands in his back pockets, not trusting himself. Unable to tear his gaze from her face, he spoke, his own voice gruff. "That's great news, Abby."

Her expression transfixed, she stared up at him, then suddenly she covered her face with one hand and started crying. "I can't believe I'm actually out of that whole awful mess."

Feeling totally out of his depth, and not at all sure what was going on, he went to reach for her, then dropped his hands. "Hey, come on," he said, his voice soft. "Tell me what's wrong." But he was certain she never heard a word he said. And in spite of all his rules concerning her, he just couldn't stand to watch her fall apart like that.

His face feeling like cement, he reached for her again, this time pulling her into a tight, secure embrace. As if under enormous pressure, his heart felt suddenly too big for his chest. Closing his eyes, he swallowed hard and tightened his hold, years of rigidly suppressed feelings boiling up inside him. Having her in his arms—with her entire body pressed against his—was almost more than he could handle, and he clutched her closer, grimacing as he pressed his head against hers. Lord, it was as if a dam had broken loose in him, and every single feeling he'd ever had for her came raging out.

He knew that giving in to this impulse was the worst mistake he'd ever made, and he also knew he was going to pay dearly for it. Because there was no way, not after experiencing the feel of her body molded against his, that he would ever be able to beat down all those long-denied feelings. Never in a million years. And knowing that now was the only time he could ever allow himself to get this physically close to her, he eased in a painful breath and pressed his face against her hair, saturating himself in every unbelievable sensation. Dear God, but she was such a miracle. And he loved her. With absolutely everything in him. He knew he had no business feeling that way, but he did. And nothing—nothing—was ever going to change that.

His throat tight and his eyes burning, he held her head against him, his jaw clenched. If he could, he'd take her right inside him and keep her there forever. She was everything to him. Absolutely everything.

As if unloading some terrible stored-up pain, Abby finally cried herself out and she turned her head against his shoulder. She pressed her hand against his shirt and whispered, "I got your shirt all wet."

He couldn't resist the urge to hug her, and he gave her a reassuring squeeze. His own voice was low and rough when he answered. "You could have irrigated a whole alfalfa field with all that water." Loosening his hold, he swallowed hard and braced himself for her to pull away. But Abby never did what he expected. Instead, she nearly knocked the pins right from under him when she slipped her arms around his waist, rested her head on his shoulder and stayed right where she was. She released a long sigh, as if expelling the last of her tears.

With her warm and soft against him, Conner locked his jaw and made himself take a deep, slow breath, the heat from her body making his blood thicken. Ah, but it felt so good to hold her—so damned good.

Imperceptibly he tightened his hold, committing every single sensation to memory. Sensations to call up and remember after she was gone.

The grandfather clock in the front hall chimed the half hour when Abby finally stirred. Releasing a long sigh, she flattened her hand against his back and shifted her head. And just as imperceptibly she tightened her hold. "This is nice," she whispered unevenly. "It feels so good to have someone to hold on to for just a little while."

Her honesty made his heart roll over and his chest clog up. Feeling as if he might turn inside out at any minute, Conner closed his eyes and rubbed her back. His throat was so tight, he couldn't have spoken if he'd wanted to. He had never expected this to happen, this chance to simply hold her like that. And he had never let himself even think about it because it had always been so far out of reach. Until now.

Aware of every curve and hollow of her body, he continued to hold her, wishing this moment could last forever.

After a long silence, Abby sighed and pulled away, then looked up at him, her face still puffy from crying. With so much gratitude in her eyes that it nearly broke his heart, she met his gaze. "Thank you for making that decision for me, Conner," she said softly. "And for taking such good care of us. I don't know what I would have done without you."

She reached up and kissed his cheek, then turned and walked away. Conner stood there and watched her leave, unable to move, feeling as if someone had just dropped a boulder on his chest. He tipped his head back and swallowed hard. He knew he would relive that interlude thousands of times in his mind. If he lived to be a hundred, he would never forget it.

His jaw locked, he turned and went outside, wondering how in hell he was going to make it through the next couple of hours, let alone the rest of the summer.

He got maybe a whole minute and a half to worry about it, because as soon as he turned up the path to the barn, he saw Jake marching young Sarah to the house, stomping so hard that little puffs of dust were rising up with every step.

Expelling a weary sigh, Conner hooked his thumbs in the front pockets of his jeans and waited for them, knowing from the look on Jake's face that he did not want to hear this.

With steam practically pouring out his ears, Jake came to a halt, still holding Sarah by the back strap of her overalls. The foreman was fuming. ''The wife had to go into town for an appointment, so I told her I'd watch the tads. But I jest caught little Miss Sarah here out in the west pasture, trying to lasso one of them there horses.'' His eyes snapping, the foreman lifted himself to his full height. ''Then this little missy informs me that there's no way she's going to ride them ponies you got from Tanner no more—that they're for babies and she ain't no durned baby. I tell you, boss, if she was my own, I'd hogtie her to the front porch for a day or two.'' And as an afterthought, he added, ''And she lost that good crop of Miz Mary's—said she lost it in the pasture.''

Suddenly wishing he were somewhere else, Conner looked at little Miss Sarah, who was staring up at him, her arms folded, her chin stuck out a mile, her hair full of straw and grass. She had stubbornness written all over her.

Conner considered his options. Jake had every right to be fuming. The very first day they were there, Conner had taken both of Abby's kids aside and set down some rules. And he had specifically warned his small defiant niece and his try-anything nephew to stay out of that pasture. He had made it crystal clear to them that Cripple Creek stock horses were not docile little ponies—not by a long shot. Hell, most of those horses were barely broke, and some of them were downright wild. But he knew by the ornery look on Sarah's face that she was going to march to her own tune, come hell or high water.

His jaw bunching, he narrowed his gaze. It was time to give Miss Sarah a new set of marching orders.

Folding his arms, he spoke, his tone ominous. "Thanks for bringing her down here, Jake. I'll take it from here." Still clearly upset, the foreman whacked his battered Stetson against his leg, raising another cloud of dust, then turned and stomped off, muttering under his breath.

With the hot sun beating down on them, Conner glared down at his niece. And with that pointed little chin stuck out, she glared right back at him. There wasn't a hint of remorse in her. It was like having a miniature, dark-haired version of Abby staring at him, and suddenly it was all he could do not to laugh. He had to remind himself that the stunt she'd pulled was no laughing matter.

His tone was stern when he spoke. "You were told not to go into that pasture, Sarah. And if you refuse to obey the rules, then you won't be allowed out of the house yard. Do you understand?"

She lifted her arms higher and stuck her chin out at him. "I don't like those dumb ponies. They're fat and stupid, and they just stand there. I want to ride a real horse."

Conner knew that he had to win this round—to instill some fear of repercussions. Somehow he was going to have to make her understand that a ranch was a dangerous place. Somehow he had to get this little firecracker's attention—because he knew if he didn't, they would all be basket cases by the end of the summer.

Shifting his stance, he rested his hands on his hips. Miss Sarah did the same.

He fixed her with a level gaze. "So. If you were back in Toronto, would you simply run out in the middle of Yonge Street without looking?"

She rolled her eyes. "Course not. That would be dangrous."

He narrowed his gaze, realizing her lisp was gone. Now what was she up to? He decided on a frontal attack. "So what happened to your lisp? Did you lose it in the pasture along with Grandma Mary's crop?"

She gave him an imperious look. "I didn't lose it," she said, acting very regal. "Cody kept saying I sounded like a baby, so I got Henny to teach me to say 'sss'."

He wanted to laugh all over again, but he got that no-nonsense tone back in his voice. "Well, you'd better get Henny to teach you the meaning of no, because if you don't, you're going to spend the whole summer confined to the veranda."

She frowned and made a face. "But I don't like those dumb ponies. They won't even move. You said I would learn to ride. We just *sit* on them, Uncle Conner. They're no fun."

Realizing that she was trying to manipulate him and that he was getting nowhere, he took a different tack. Crouching down in front of her so they were eye to eye, he did a little manipulating of his own. He kept his voice quiet but stern when he spoke. "I know what you want, Sarah. But maybe it's time you started thinking about something other than getting your own way. How do you think your mother would feel if you got kicked out there? Have you ever thought about that?''

If he wanted results, he certainly got them. It was definitely the right button to push, because she immediately burst into tears and clambered into his arms.

''She would feel really bad,'' she sobbed.

Feeling like a louse for going that far and making her cry, Conner snuggled her up in a secure embrace, a sudden rush of feelings for this little tiger making his chest hurt.

Full of remorse, Sarah wrapped her arms around his neck and hugged him back, her voice muffled when she whispered, ''I'm sorry I made you mad, Uncle Conner.''

Sharply aware that she hadn't said one word about being sorry for not obeying the rules, Conner had to work really hard not to laugh again. He hadn't fallen off a turnip truck—he knew darned well that little Miss Calhoun was still trying to outmaneuver him.

It was pretty obvious even to him—and he also suspected the only way he was going to get anywhere was to negotiate. So he picked her up and carried her over to the battered picnic table that sat under the gnarled old willow tree.

He pulled a tissue out of her pocket and had her blow her nose, then he sat down on the seat so they were eye to eye again. ''Tell you what. How about we make a deal? You can go into the pasture if there's an adult with you. And when I have time, I'll take you for rides on Big Mac.''

Clearly considering her options, she rolled the corner of the bandanna around her finger, then looked at him with a mutinous set to her chin.

"I want to ride by my own self." Then, as if realizing that kind of attitude wasn't going to get her anywhere, she brightened and made a counteroffer. "I promise I won't go in the pasture unless there's an adult with me if I can ride a real horse every day by my own self."

Amused by her tenacity, Conner considered her. He countered. "All right, but you'll have to ride in the round pen, and you'll have to be supervised. And I get to pick the horse. And," he added when he realized he'd left some gray areas, "you have to understand that you can't just go riding whenever you want, Sarah. We've got a ranch to run, so you can't expect us to drop whatever we're doing so you can have your own way. That has to be part of the bargain."

His niece pondered his renegotiation as she picked at a mosquito bite, then she met his gaze. She gave him her best smile. "It's a deal, Uncle Conner. I won't go in the pasture, and I get to ride in the round pen by myself when you say."

Watching her, Conner held his amusement in check. He reached out his hand. "Deal."

She solemnly shook on it, then clambered onto his lap and latched her arms around his neck. "Whatcha going to do now, Uncle Conner?"

He got up and set her on the ground. "I'm going to go check on that colt in the barn."

"Can I come?"

"Yes, you can come."

It was as if their negotiated deal cemented a good-buddy relationship, because she took hold of his hand and skipped along beside him. They'd only covered a short distance when she decided it was a good time to squeal on her brother. "I betcha don't know what

Cody's been doing. He's been taking an old inner tube he found in the big metal thing. What's it called again?''

Suspecting that she was about to spill the beans on her brother as long as she didn't get distracted, Conner kept his answer brief and to the point. ''It's called a Quonset.''

''Yeah. The Quonset. He found an old tube in the Quonset, and he's been floating down the creek on it. And,'' she continued, skipping along, ''he tried to ride the calves when nobody was watching. I told him not to, that they were only babies. But he told me I was a baby, and to go suck my thumb.''

Conner stopped in his tracks and massaged his eyes, not sure if he wanted to laugh or bang his head. One thing was for sure, the summer was not going to be dull. Compressing his mouth into a hard line, he released Sarah's hand. ''Where is your brother?''

Sarah bent over to pick dandelions. ''He's at the creek.''

Turning on his heel, Conner headed off to give his nephew the same lecture he'd just given his niece. He was beginning to understand why there was gray in Abby's hair.

Sunday dawned, one of those perfect summer mornings. Clear sky, the countryside lush and green from the recent rains, and the wild roses along the fence line filling the clean mountain air with their heady scent. It was the kind of day that made Conner glad to be alive.

As soon as the morning chores were finished, Conner loaded up the kids and drove into Bolton to get their grandmother for the day. They had been to visit her several times, but this was the first time Mary had been out to the ranch since Abby and the kids arrived.

Conner took his SUV to get his stepmother. He actually bought it so he would have something comfortable to transport her in. And it was what Abby drove whenever she went anywhere.

The kids, who kept talking over each other, filled their grandmother in on all their legitimate escapades during the drive back, and they were still going a mile a minute when he parked by the lilac hedge. Conner got out of the vehicle, amusement altering his expression. He noticed that neither one of the kids had apprised their grandmother of their unapproved escapades, like the trips to the pasture to catch wild horses, or the trips down the fast-running creek on an inner tube. He went to the back of the vehicle, lifted the hatch to retrieve Mary's wheelchair, unfolded it, then set her carryall in it.

Then he went around to the front passenger door and opened it. His stepmother looked at him, her slender body twisted with arthritis, her snow-white hair cropped short for easy care, but there was a bright twinkle in her clear brown eyes. She met his gaze, a wise look on her face. "I expect the little darlings aren't telling me everything, are they?"

He grinned at her. "I think you could safely assume that." She laboriously undid her seat belt with her crippled hands, then Conner carefully picked her up, mindful of the joints that were the most painful.

Mary awkwardly slipped her arm around his shoulder. "My, I'm so glad we can spend the day outside. It's just so glorious."

He carried the older woman through the break in

the hedge. "I thought maybe you'd like a picnic down by the creek."

His stepmother patted his back. "Exactly what I would like to do, Conner. It's a wonderful idea." She inhaled deeply. "Ah. Wild roses. You can smell them from here."

Abby had been in the shower when he'd left with the kids and now was down by the creek, stretched on her stomach in the grass, reading a book. Earlier that morning, Conner had moved some of the lawn furniture down, including a well-padded chaise longue he had set up for Mary.

With the kids following behind, scrapping over who got to push the wheelchair, Conner carried his mother across the broad expanse of lawn that rolled down to the rocky creek. It was going to be very hot, but the huge old willows provided a broad expanse of dappled shade, and a slight breeze fluttered their leaves and made the patches of shade dance.

Abby got up as they approached, a grin on her face. She gave her mother-in-law a wide smile of welcome, then aimed her you'd-better-behave finger at her two kids, giving them a silent warning to cut it out.

"Hi, Grandma," she said, coming toward them, brushing grass off her legs. "I suppose they talked your ear off all the way here."

Mary chuckled. "It was a bit of a competition all right." She awkwardly slipped her arm from around Conner's neck as he eased her gently and carefully onto the longue. Once settled, she reached up and patted his cheek and smiled. "Thank you, son. This is wonderful."

Pulling the light shawl out of her carryall, Conner covered her legs with it. He had nothing but unlimited admiration for this woman. People could say all they wanted about heroics or courage, but as far as he was concerned, this woman's day-to-day battle told him more about heroics and courage than anyone could.

Abby sent the kids off to get into their swimsuits, then came over and kissed her mother-in-law on the cheek, her affection for the woman clearly obvious. And as far as Mary was concerned, Abby was her daughter. Plain and simple.

After Conner got Mary settled, he went up to the barn to check on the colt. The vet had lanced the abscess on his foreleg, and he wanted to get some ointment on the sutures.

By the time he got back, the kids were in the creek, making enough racket to raise the dead. Some former Calhoun had dredged out the shallow creek, creating a wide pool deep enough to swim in. Conner wasn't sure if they were actually swimming or simply trying to drown each other, but their mother didn't seem too worried.

Abby had dragged a chair over to Mary's longue, and the two women were deep in conversation, periodically checking on the children. There was a large rock under one tree, and Conner stretched out on the grass and propped his shoulders against it, his straw Stetson pulled low over his eyes. Chewing on a stem of grass, he folded his arms and watched the kids splashing around in the water.

It was funny, how their being there put a quarter turn on everything. Having Abby and the kids around on a regular basis was like acquiring a whole new perspective on life—as if he had a whole new focus. Humor creasing his mouth, he decided it was like living in a constant state of alert, as if waiting for the other shoe to drop, knowing that one, or both, were going to try something that they knew damned well they weren't supposed to. Or like knowing, without a doubt, that one of them was going to come out with something that would amuse the hell out of him. But there was more to it than that. It was also knowing, when he went to bed at night, that there was someone else in the house—two little souls who, for at least the next couple of months, were his responsibility.

Two little souls who were really his.

Jarred by that renegade thought, Conner hardened his expression and looked away. He could not allow that kind of mental slip. Those two little souls belonged to Abby, and he couldn't forget that. They were hers. His gift to her. And she had done a damned fine job of raising them.

A wet beach ball whacked him on the side of his head, snapping him back to reality. Cody was standing waist deep in the water, a huge grin on his face. "Gotcha, Uncle Conner!"

Aware of the smug look in the boy's eyes, Conner got up, hooked off his boots, peeled off his socks and waded into the stream, clothes and all. Squealing at their uncle's approach, they tried to get away. But Conner got to them first. Grabbing Abby's son around the middle, he pitched him into the deep part of the pool. "Gotcha, Chucker."

Other than that one mental lapse, the rest of the day was great. And he knew that Mary enjoyed every second of it. She loved her daughter-in-law, her grandchildren delighted her, and she thrived on spending time on the ranch.

But by early evening, Conner could also tell that she was ready to go back to the nursing home. She was exhausted, and more than ready for her evening medication when he and the kids took her home.

Even the kids had burnt off most of their energy, and the ride home was quiet, both of them content to look out their respective windows, with Sarah very nearly falling asleep.

The shadows were starting to lengthen by the time they got back to the ranch. Both the kids perked right up when Henny came out to meet them, telling them she had found two robins' nests in one of the fir trees. As they traipsed off to check it out, Conner entered the house, aware of how still it was. Suppressing a twist of amusement, he went into the living room. The stillness was the clue. And if Abby was running true to form, he'd be willing to bet his next crop of calves that he'd find her out cold on the living room sofa.

He was wrong. She wasn't asleep. But she was curled up on the sofa, her hands tucked under her face, watching a muted TV. She had on the same baggy sweats she'd worn that morning, and she looked like a larger version of a very sleepy Sarah.

He grinned. "Ah. You're awake. I thought you'd be dead to the world."

She didn't even have the energy to move, but she managed to offer up a sleepy smile. "Don't you ever get tired of being so big, smug and virile?"

He chuckled. "I was just making a comment. After all, you did make it through the whole day without a nap."

"Get lost."

Grinning at her sass, he turned. "I'll round up the kids and get them ready for bed. You just continue vegetating." He got as far as the archway to the dining room when she spoke, her voice very soft. "Conner?"

He turned, resting his hand on the archway. "What?"

She looked at him a moment, her gaze unwavering; then she finally continued, her tone very quiet. "I saw you watching the kids in the pool today. And I wondered what you were thinking."

Conner gripped the wall. He didn't know what he had expected her to ask him, but it sure in hell wasn't that. Feeling as if he were standing on a high, narrow ledge, he stared down at the floor, trying to come up with a safe response. Finally he lifted his head and met her gaze, his expression unsmiling. "I was thinking what a damned fine job you did of raising them," he answered, his voice gruff. "With Scott gone so much, I know that most of that fell on your shoulders." He forced a small smile. "You did a good job, Abigail Allistair."

Her expression remained very sober, and she continued to stare at him. She had that same quiet tone in her voice when she spoke. "Do you ever think of them as yours?"

His gut knotted, and he found it suddenly hard to breathe. It was as if she had just reached inside his chest and grabbed his heart, and he had a hard time keeping it together. He forced another half smile. His voice was so gruff it didn't even sound like his own when he answered. "No. I think of them as yours."

"I never, ever thanked you for that," she said, her tone very husky.

He thought of all the reasons why he'd fallen in love with her, but that directness of hers, that honesty, which was a fundamental part of her, was one of the things he admired most.

And it made his chest tighten even more.

He ran his thumbnail over an imperfection in the varnish, then he worked his throat and met her gaze. And he came as close to being honest as he dared. "I didn't expect any thanks. I was happy I could do it for you."

Feeling suddenly very exposed and needing something to do, he picked up a throw off the back of a chair, then went over to the sofa and carefully covered her up. There was a funny ringing in his ears, and his voice seemed to come from a long way off. "Go to sleep, Abby," he said, his tone strained. "I'll take care of the kids."

Then he turned and walked out of the room, his heart thundering like a freight train in his chest.

He hadn't been prepared for that, for her to address the fact that they had created two children together. Never.

And the asking had stripped away a defense system that had been in place ever since that long-ago Christmas.

Chapter 5

A loud crack of thunder brought Abby sharply awake, her heart pounding, adrenaline racing through her system. For an instant, she didn't know where she was. She remained perfectly still, the disoriented feeling fading when familiar things began to take shape in the darkened room. Finally she realized she was curled up on the sofa in the living room.

Another crack of thunder reverberated through the house, and she launched herself off the sofa, heading for the stairs. All the windows were open in the bedrooms—every darned one. And by the way the sky was rumbling, she suspected rain wasn't very far behind.

The wind had picked up and was rattling the shades and whipping the curtains when she went into Sarah's room. She closed the window, then covered up her daughter, smiling faintly when she saw that Sarah wore one of Conner's old shirts. No doubt about it;

the Calhoun women definitely had a propensity for those shirts. Maybe it was because they made a girl feel warm and safe.

Rain started to spatter through the screen by the time she entered Cody's room, and she pulled both casement windows closed, then rested her shoulder against the wall of the alcove, watching the lightning roll across the sky. There was a sound from the bed, and she turned her head. Her son was flat on his back, both arms extended, absolutely dead to the world. Her shoulder still against the wall, she folded her arms, her expression altering as she watched him sleep. It still caught her unawares at times—how much of his biological father she saw in her son. The angle of his chin, the shape of his hands, his build—even his mannerisms—reminded her of Conner. In a thousand little ways, he truly was his father's child. But that recognition was something she had always kept to herself. She had never shared her observations with Scott.

Feeling oddly unsettled, she turned back to the window, watching the wild display as lightning rolled across the blackened sky, flashes zigzagging up the towering thunderheads, arcing from one cloud to another.

Her expression sober, she hugged herself against a sudden chill. She had no idea why she'd asked Conner if he ever thought of the kids as his. It had come from nowhere. But, she mentally rebutted, that wasn't exactly true. It had come from somewhere. Or she wouldn't have asked it.

Nor could she fathom the underlying nuance of his answer—about his thinking of them as her children. It had been oddly ambiguous. Oddly disturbing. But there was one thing that wasn't ambiguous. The fact that he had given them the most extraordinary gifts. He was a good man, the best. And she had never understood why some smart woman hadn't snapped him up.

A strange, heavy feeling unfolded in her chest, making her suddenly restless. She pushed open one window so she could smell the rain, the heavy feeling climbing higher. Folding her arms tightly around herself, she tried to will away the heaviness inside her. She didn't know why she felt suddenly so exposed. Especially when Conner always made her feel so safe.

She had loved Scotty, really loved him—but then he had started down his tormented road to self-destruction and everything had begun to unravel. When his addictions became his mistresses, everything they'd shared as man and wife was eventually destroyed. In the end he had become so dependent, it was almost as if he had turned into her handicapped child—someone she had to protect and shelter, someone she had to take care of.

Then there was Conner—rock solid, steady, dependable. She didn't know what she would have done without him when things got so bad after her parents were killed. And she really didn't know what she would have done without him when Scotty died. It had been so awful, so emotionally devastating—to watch a bright, talented, full-of-life man brought down by all his demons. And it had been even worse when Conner left after the funeral. Then she had been truly left on her own. There had been at least a thousand times when she'd wanted to call him, after she'd started finding out what a mess Scotty had left behind. But even as shell-shocked as she'd been, she'd known that her problems could not be turned into his problems—that she simply had to pull her socks up and get on with it.

But Conner always seemed to know. And he was doing it again, quietly picking up the pieces and putting everything back together again. Only this time, it was different. This time it wasn't his brother he was rescuing. This time it was her.

And for the first time since Conner had ridden in and rescued her, Abby spent a sleepless night. She berated herself over and over. She never should have asked that question. When she had done that, she had breached some unspoken pact of silence.

The storm spent itself by dawn, and with all the broken clouds drifting toward the eastern horizon, the sunrise was spectacular. But Abby couldn't really enjoy it. She was too busy worrying about facing Conner. Her gut told her she had crossed a sacrosanct line, when she'd asked him about the kids. They had only spoken of it once—that Christmas years ago, when she had screwed up her courage to talk to him, to plead their case with him. And as if by some tacit agreement, they'd never spoken of it since.

Only now it was out in the open. It had been a reckless question, a question that moved them from a friendly comfort zone to a not-so-comfortable zone of intimacy.

And it had become intimate. Because finally, after years of avoiding the truth, they had openly acknowledged that they had made two children together.

She didn't know how it had affected Conner, but it had left her feeling oddly exposed inside. She didn't have a clue how she was going to handle it—not a clue. But she knew she had to face him.

Abby waited for the smell of coffee and the sound of him on the veranda, but by seven o'clock she realized that he was not there. And it was obvious that he had slipped out—deliberately, no doubt. He probably didn't know how to handle the breach any more than she did. But she had to admit that she was relieved. Lord, but she was a coward.

She caught herself as she started to rummage through her thoughts again, and she shoved the windows wide open, then took a deep, cleansing breath. It was time to get a grip. She had done nothing but wallow for the past several months, and she was wallowing again. And even she could see that she'd spent far too much time picking at emotional lint. Knowing the best thing for her to do right now was to get busy and stay busy, she squared her shoulders and straightened her spine. It was darned well time to get with a program. She could at least do something to earn her keep.

She went a little crazy, really. Once she got the kids fed, dressed and outside, she turned into an insane cleaning person. It was just too bad that Henny was such a fastidious housekeeper, because there wasn't a whole lot to do. But there was laundry. With kids and Conner, there was always laundry. And when she found the oven actually had some spatters in it, she really went into hyper-drive. Now here was something to do; so she ripped the stove apart. After taking steaks out of the freezer to defrost, she attacked the pantry and the rows of cupboards in the big back porch, which obviously had been overlooked for some time. She was thrilled—something else to keep her occupied.

But once that was finished, she had nothing, nothing, nothing. At least not anything that wouldn't be an insult to Henny. Briefly she considered attacking the attic, but it was full of trunks and old furniture, and boxes upon boxes—truly a treasure trove of all the family history, and using that as a distraction seemed dishonest somehow. So she decided to go out and weed the perennial garden along the garage. It was clearly not on Henny's work roster, and it was one huge mess. Abby felt as if she had discovered gold.

She planned her assault. Hoes, spades, trowels, hedge clippers—she had every weapon in Henny's arsenal in the garden shed. With a pair of Henny's garden gloves on, her hair yanked through the back of a ball cap advertising the Bolton feed store, and dressed in a pair of old shorts and a halter top, Abby attacked the overgrown garden.

The sun beat down upon her, sweat trickled down her face, and her knees felt as if someone had pounded rocks into them, but she was determined to conquer the garden. Darn it, she had to win at something.

"Jeeze, Mom. Whatcha doing?"

She looked up from under the brim of her hat, wiping a trickle of sweat away with her wrist. Cody was staring at her as if she were nuts. "I'm weeding."

"Why?"

Because I asked a question I never should have asked. She jabbed a trowel under the root of a thriving, giant-size dandelion. She could have made a very substantial grass skirt out of that one dandelion plant.

"Mom?"

Experiencing that quaky feeling all over again, Abby stared at the freshly turned dirt, facing up to what was behind this frenzy. By asking that question, she had stripped away Conner's right to privacy. And that upset her. The last thing she ever wanted to do was to make him uncomfortable. Not Conner. Not her knight in shining armor.

Plastering what she hoped was a reasonably normal expression on her face, she sat back on her haunches and looked at her son. Her stomach did a barrel roll when she realized Conner was standing across the paved parking area, his hand resting on the open door of his truck, watching her with an intent gaze. Feeling exposed all over again, she slapped a smile on and came up with what she hoped was a reasonable response. "It just feels good, honey. I haven't done anything like this for a long time."

"You mean because we used to have gardeners?"

No, that wasn't what she meant at all. She smiled at her son. "Yeah. Something like that."

"Oh." He fidgeted with his T-shirt. "Uncle Conner is going over to check the calves, and he wants to know if it's okay if we go along."

Taking off her glove, Abby reached up and tucked in the label of his not-so-clean T-shirt. "Yes, you can go." Then she fixed him with a warning look. "But you do as Uncle Conner says, Cody. Or you won't be able to go again."

He rolled his eyes. "I will."

Abby knew she should get up, go over to the truck, look her small daughter square in the eye and issue the same directive. But she just couldn't get that close to Conner. At least not yet. Instead, she sent the message with her son. "And you tell your sister. I'll ground her for life if she doesn't behave."

Cody perked right up. "I'll tell her." He ran back

to the truck and climbed into the back with his sister, obviously wasting no time in passing on the message. Abby braced herself to meet Conner's gaze. He stared at her for a split second, then turned and climbed into the vehicle, slamming the door shut behind him.

Abby's heart was beating a mile a minute as she turned back to her ruthless reclamation. Lord, what was going on with her anyway? She felt as if she'd just overdosed on chocolate.

It took her another hour to fight the garden into submission. But she won, darn it. She won.

Hot, dirty and feeling the effects of too much sun, she went upstairs, had a cool shower, put some cream on her mild sunburn, then pulled on a clean pair of shorts and a tank top. Picking up her dirty clothes and wet towels, she ran down the stairs, the stillness in the big old house wrapping around her.

She loved that house—the high ceilings, the leaded windows, the elaborate Victorian moldings, the gleaming woodwork, the pegged floors. And she especially loved all the nooks and crannies—and the spaciousness. And the history. She loved the history most of all.

Humming to herself, she went through the kitchen into the laundry room. It was a small room behind the kitchen and was the Victorian equivalent of the hired girl's room. But when Mary had come to Cripple Creek, she'd changed it into a much-needed laundry and sewing room.

Abby tossed the tan towels and her shorts and top into the washer, adjusted the setting and turned it on. The last load of blue jeans and denim shirts was still in the dryer, and she took the still-warm clothes out and folded them. As she hung one of Conner's shirts on a hanger, she noticed a tear in the sleeve, and a weird, protective sensation rolled over her, clutching her heart. He had no one to look after him. No one at all. He was walking around with holes in his shirts.

Closing her eyes and flattening her hands on top of the dryer, Abby struggled to squash the reaction, a thick ache stuffing up her chest. Her eyes still tightly closed, she gave herself a stern lecture on growing up and getting a grip. This was becoming ridiculous.

Lifting her chin and setting her resolve, Abby avoided the rip and resolutely laid the shirts on top of the laundry basket containing his other clothes. Honestly, she was acting like some silly adolescent.

Giving the room one last check, she squared her shoulders and picked up the laundry basket, bracing it on her hip. She'd put these things away, then she would find something else to do. Like start dinner.

Conner's room was at the front of the house, directly across the wide front hall from the archway to the living room. It had once been the formal parlor, with a wide oriel window that housed an elegant Victorian window seat. It also had a fieldstone fireplace, and on either side of the fireplace, glassed-in bookshelves, with the glass beautifully etched, as was the glass in the French door that opened onto the front veranda. When John Calhoun was still alive, it had been his den, and it was Abby's favorite room in the whole house. She had only been in it a couple of times since the renovation, when it was Mary's room.

Now it was Conner's private domain. Feeling as if she were about to trespass, Abby paused at the heavy, panelled pocket door, her pulse suddenly skipping. *Don't go in there,* a tiny voice spoke in her head. "Don't be ridiculous," she muttered out loud. Now she really was acting like an adolescent. Bracing herself, she grasped the brass latch and slid the heavy pocket door open, her heart giving a funny little skip as she entered.

And stopped. It was not the same at all. It was not John's. And it was not Mary's. This room was unquestionably Conner's. Right from the somber colors to the solid heavy furniture. Uncluttered, unadorned—masculine. Very masculine.

The sight of the unmade king-size bed set off a funny fizzle in her middle, and Abby tried to ignore it. Setting her spine, she reminded herself that she was on a keep-busy schedule. Bolstered with determination, she set the loaded laundry basket on the bed, then considered the old highboy dresser. Okay. Now what?

Hooking her still damp hair behind her ear, she also considered the fact that Scott had the mate to that highboy, and she wondered what the chances were that both brothers had the same preference for dresser drawers. She grinned to herself. Now she was being downright nosy.

Curiosity getting the better of her, she opened the top drawer, expecting to find socks but instead discovered a catchall. She opened the next one, expecting to find underwear, but discovered socks. Getting into the game, she opened the next one, which should, according to reverse order, be underwear.

But there was more than underwear in the drawer. Feeling as if her heart had stopped working altogether, Abby stared at the items lying on top of the folded clothing, her mind screeching to a halt. Transfixed, she stared at the contents, getting a funny rush from her head to her toes. Lying there, carefully placed, were three beautifully framed photographs. Each one of her.

The shock of her discovery left her lightheaded, and Abby stared at them, unbelieving of what was lying there before her very eyes. Oh, Lord, it didn't make any sense.

Completely stunned, she finally picked up one, her hands becoming unsteady as she recognized when and where it was taken. It had been taken years ago. The second picture was taken just before Scotty died, but it was the third one that nearly brought her to her knees. It was the only full shot, and it had been taken at the beach, when she was very pregnant with Cody. She was laughing at the camera, standing ankle deep in water, holding her disheveled hair back, the wind flattening her sundress against her ripe, gravid body.

It was that picture that brought everything sharply into focus. And comprehension dawned in a sickening rush. Hugging the picture against her chest, she closed her eyes, her knees suddenly weak. With a sharp stab of realization, she knew exactly what they meant. Oh, God. Oh, God. She had never once suspected. Never guessed.

In another dizzying rush, it hit her why they were in the drawer—put away so she wouldn't see them. Hidden from view as he had hidden everything else. All those years.

Her mind numb with stark comprehension and her whole body suddenly filled with a churning feeling, Abby carefully replaced the picture with unsteady hands, her heart laboring heavily in her chest. Making sure that all three pictures were exactly as they had been when she'd discovered them, she pushed the drawer shut, then closed her eyes again. Lord, she didn't know how to handle this. She didn't have a clue.

Her body feeling stiff and unnatural, she straightened, then turned and picked up the laundry basket, the numb feeling spreading. Looking straight ahead, she left the room and carefully closed the door behind her. Standing in the dim hallway, she stared straight ahead, trying to think, to sort it all out.

There was only one thing she could do. She had to cover her tracks, but above all else, she had to keep his secret safe. Swallowing hard against the sudden contraction in her throat, she placed the laundry basket in front of the closed door with inordinate care, fixing the shirts on top. Then feeling as if she were walking down a long, thin tunnel, she passed through the living room, heading toward the dining room and the French doors that opened onto the veranda and the courtyard garden.

But for the very first time, the fenced-in garden gave her no solace. No comfort. It felt like a cage, and she stood blindly staring out, her insides cold. All those years, and she'd had no idea. Hadn't a clue. But the little voice in her head came up with a "Yes, but—"

And she had to think about that. Up until now, not once had she ever stopped to consciously assess why Conner had done what he had—why he had agreed to father Scotty's children. She had just been so grateful, she hadn't considered anything else. But if she had stopped to take it apart back then, she would have eventually realized, as young as she was, that Conner never would have agreed to father their children for Scotty alone. She was a part of the equation all along.

But until she discovered those pictures, she had never realized just how significant a part.

Her vision blurring, Abby hugged herself, guilt welling up inside her. Conner had given her so much. And his gift wasn't just the babies. He had always given himself. Every time she'd been up against it, Conner had been there for her—every single time. And as messed up as her and Scotty's life had been toward the end, she had unconsciously known that Conner would come through for her. And he had. Just as before.

And she had given him nothing. Except a life of loneliness and lost dreams.

That recognition made her chest ache even worse, the pain blinding her, and she paced down the flag walk, trying to put things back in perspective. The one thing she couldn't do was start picking at emotional lint again. That got her nowhere. And it wasn't as if she could do anything to make it right. It wasn't as if she could confront Conner with her findings. Because if she did… If she did…

As if that thought opened a forbidden door in her mind, a recollection swarmed up, blocking out everything else. And in living detail, she suddenly recalled that day he'd come into the kitchen and she had just gotten the call from her real estate agent. She remembered as if it was happening all over again, how wonderful it had felt to be held by him. How hard his body was, how the scent of outdoors, horses and sweat was so much a part of him. How their bodies fused together, and how his strength and warmth wrapped around her, making her feel more protected than she had ever felt in her entire life. And she remembered how she wanted to hang on and never let go. She recalled the warmth of his breath against her temple, the weight of his arm across her back, the pinch of his belt buckle against...

Letting her breath go in a rush, Abby grasped her hair back with both hands, her heart pounding in her chest. Realizing she was going places in her mind that she had no business going, she took a deep, uneven breath and held it, forcibly pulling herself together. Lord, what was she doing? She exhaled and turned toward the house. If there was ever a time to get with a program, it was now.

Feeling as if she had an overdose of adrenaline racing around inside her, she poured herself into a renewed attack on dirt and grime with a nearly frenetic zeal. As long as she was doing something she loathed, like vacuuming, she was able to stay focused. She had to stay focused. Because if she didn't keep her mind from wandering—well, she simply *had* to keep her mind from wandering.

Otherwise, she was going to work herself into an awful state, worrying about how hard it was going to be to face Conner. Just the thought panicked her. She felt as if she was going to fly apart like an overwound watch.

It was midafternoon when she realized she'd been so intent on vacuuming every nook and cranny that, except for taking the steaks out, she hadn't even so much as thought about supper. Almost giddy with relief, she threw herself into another frenzy of preparation, knowing deep down that she was acting like a crazy person. Conner couldn't care less if she presented him with a culinary work of art or something she'd tossed together. All he'd want was food on the table, and lots of it.

With the steaks marinating and the vegetables all prepared, she decided to head down to the garden to see if there was enough fresh mint to make a salad dressing.

Thin whiffs of clouds hung in the bright blue sky, and a million scents accosted her. Not the most subtle, she thought, smiling to herself, was eau de ranch. Thank heaven her big-city sensibilities didn't take offense—actually she kind of liked it. A light breeze rustled through the trees, making the leaves flutter. As she made her way along the narrow path, long grass along the trail brushed against her bare legs, ejecting clusters of mosquitoes. One of the Border collies joined her halfway down the trail, his tail wagging. She stopped and scratched his neck, then patted her thigh for him to heel.

There was an old wire gate hung between two fence posts in a break in the lilac hedge, and as she opened it the dog trotted in ahead of her. She took a deep breath, savoring it all. The high hedge was still heavy with blossoms, and the fragrance washed out every other scent.

Henny was in the garden, busily hoeing the long rows, a battered yellow straw sun hat on her head, her old transistor radio sitting on the wheelbarrow, tuned to a county music station. Abby grinned. She wondered if Henny ever got more than two steps away from her country music.

It was a picture, this setting. The yellow sun. The bright blue sky. The purple hedge of lilacs. Henny's bright red shirt and faded yellow hat. And the perfect, straight rows of green tender shoots. It was like stepping into a painting, and an odd, calming effect washed over her.

And as that strange peacefulness settled on her, she had a huge revelation. It was right and good that she'd asked that question. It was time that it was out in the open—that she acknowledged that her children were also Conner's. And as for the pictures—well... Her throat closed up and a funny ache settled around her heart. It wasn't as if Conner would ever know she'd found them. His secret was safe. Still tucked away in the drawer. And no one would ever know—except her.

Feeling as if she'd been abruptly relieved of a horrible weight, Abby tipped her face into the breeze, the frenzy of tension letting go. That was one thing she could do for him. Keep his secret safe.

"So are you just going to stand there spitting into the wind, or are you going to get over here and slop some of that iced tea into a cup for me?"

Abby grinned and started down the path toward Conner's housekeeper. "I'll slop some of that tea." She skirted a tiny patch of stinging nettles and picked up the thermos sitting in the grass. Then she took the cup-shaped top off the thermos, poured some iced tea into it and handed it to Henny.

"The garden looks great, Henny."

Pushing her hat back, the older woman considered the straight rows. "It should be a good one. Lots of rain." She drained her cup and handed it to Abby, a twinkle in her eyes. "And that good organic fertilizer we produce here."

Abby brushed a mosquito off her cheek, then turned back to the rows. She glanced at her watch; she figured she had at least an hour to kill before Conner got back with the kids. Kicking off her shoes in the grass, she picked up a hoe and started working on the row next to Henny's.

They fell into an easy conversation, punctuated by long, comfortable silences, the smell of freshly mowed grass and newly turned soil mingling with the smell of lilacs.

And Abby found her thoughts drifting back over old history. Maybe it was the absolute peacefulness of the garden, or maybe it was the feel of the sun on her back, or maybe it was her long-standing ease with the older woman, but Abby found herself revisitng the past. After finding the pictures, there were things she needed to know.

Her expression thoughtful, she bent down and pulled out a tenacious thistle that had taken root in the rich loam, then spoke, her voice quiet. "What do you know about that girl Conner was seeing years ago?"

Straightening, Henny waved her hand at a small cloud of gnats hovering about her head. Her hand resting on the handle of the hoe, she stared off at the horizon. "Doreen Lantry. Nice girl, Doreen." She began hoeing again. "Nobody ever really knew what happened. Just all of a sudden they weren't seeing each other anymore. And about a year later, Doreen quit her job at the bank and moved to Ontario." Henny bent over and firmly reset a corn plant she had loosened. "Nothing was ever said. Of course, Conner was always tight-lipped about stuff like that." She straightened again, fixing the cuff on one of her gloves. "But I'll tell you this. I'd be willing to bet my new stove that it wasn't Doreen's idea. That girl was plumb nuts about Conner. But as to what happened, it's anybody's guess." She shook her head.

"Sad, really. He shouldn't be rattling around in that big house by himself." Henny went back to her hoeing. "He should have a passel of kids by now."

The mention of kids made Abby's stomach twist. Feeling strangely chastened and very responsible, Abby picked up a rock and tossed it out of the garden, her expression stricken. She wondered what Conner's life would be like if he hadn't walked away from someone who apparently cared for him. But as emotionally tangled up as she was about her conclusions, her common sense told her that she was assuming a whole lot, based on three pictures.

Silently she continued to work her way down the row, a strange hollowness settling in her chest. It was a feeling she really couldn't define. As if she had missed out on something—or lost something very rare and special. Something that was really not hers to lose.

But she left it at that. She was not going to start digging around to try and analyze the feeling. There were some things that were just better off left alone.

That somber, reflective mood held. And she was almost back to where she'd started by the time she went into the house to make supper. She didn't have a clue how she was going to face Conner across the table. But if the tightness in her temples got any worse, she wouldn't have to worry about it, because she'd be able to legitimately excuse herself with a blinding headache.

However, her worries got abruptly shelved when the back door slammed open, and Cody came tearing into the kitchen. He was grubby from head to toe, his hair was plastered to his head with sweat, there was mud smeared across the front of his logo-crested T-shirt. And he had a triumphant look on his face.

Abby expelled her breath and rolled her eyes. She knew that look. She had a whole lot of experience with that look. And she knew as sure as she was standing there that his sister had gotten into trouble, and from the expression of malevolent delight on her son's face, it was no little trouble. No. That delighted look on Cody's face meant Sarah had found *big* trouble.

Fixing him with a baleful gaze, she folded her arms. "This had better be good, Cody. I'm in no mood for games."

Practically dancing, he opened his mouth. But he shut it abruptly when Conner entered, marching a wet, bedraggled, muddy Sarah into the kitchen. And Conner was just as muddy and as wet as her daughter. It looked as if they had both just crawled out of a swamp.

Expelling a resigned breath, Abby stared at her daughter, waiting for an explanation, knowing she really didn't want to hear this.

Clearly agitated and with the muscle in his jaw twitching, Conner opened his mouth, but Abby held up one finger in a gesture of silence, then fixed her gaze on Sarah. Her own jaw just a little tight, she leveled the finger at her daughter, a silent indicator that she was to speak. And speak fast. Both Cody and Sarah knew that look, and Cody had the good sense to wipe the grin off his face and start squirming.

Not so Miss Sarah. Miss Sarah folded her arms and stared right back at her mother, lifting her chin.

Out of the corner of her eye, Abby saw Conner also fold his arms and lean back against the counter, the tension gone from his face, amusement settling around his mouth. Wanting to level her you're-in-big-trouble finger at him as well, she fixed her gaze on her daughter. Her tone meant business. "Sarah?"

Clearly offended that she was on the hot seat, Sarah lifted her chin a notch higher. "We went to a whole bunch of places to check cows, but the last one had a big pond in it."

"It wasn't a *pond,* stupid," Cody interjected, now fluent in ranch lingo. "It was a *slough.*"

Sarah sent her brother a scathing look, then defiantly faced her mother. "There were flowers floating on the water—pretty yellow ones. And I wanted to pick some to bring home. And I got wet." She narrowed her eyes. "And that was all."

That was all. The total explanation. End of story.

And pigs could fly.

Knowing there was more—much, much more—Abby fixed her gaze on her son. "Cody?"

No longer grinning, Cody fidgeted and didn't quite know what to do with his hands. "Well..."

"Well, what?"

Looking as if he were somehow culpable, he blurted out the rest. "Uncle Conner had to fix the gate—there were some wires broken. And he told Sarah not to go near the slough because it was deep, but when Uncle Conner was at the truck, she said she could walk out on the log to get the flowers and I said she better not but she did anyway. And the log sank and flipped her in the water and Uncle Conner was right—the water was deep, and Sarah tried to swim but she got tangled up in the weeds and Uncle Conner had to jump in and fish her out."

Dropping her arms in outright indignation, Sarah

glared at her brother. "He did not hafta. I could have got out my own self."

Well acquainted with the urge to throttle, Abby watched her daughter with a stern, reprimanding stare. "What have you been told about listening?"

"But I coulda—"

Abby quelled her with a look, using the tone that no one in his right mind would ever argue with. "I asked you what you were told."

Rolling her eyes, Sarah listed it all off. "I'm not to go in the pasture by myself, and I can't play around any of the trucks or cars. And I hafta be careful not to walk behind a horse, and I can't go near Henny's beehives. And I gotta remember that a ranch is a dangrous place to be, and I'm supposed to listen. But—"

Her arms still folded, Abby stared at her daughter. "I'm not accepting any 'buts,' Sarah. Uncle Conner had a good reason for telling you not to go near the slough. What you did was very wrong, and very thoughtless. Did you stop to think how Uncle Conner would have felt if you had drowned? Your careless actions can be hurtful to other people, Sarah Jane, and you'd do well to remember that."

Finally chastened, Sarah looked up at Conner. "I'm sorry, Uncle Conner. I didn't mean to scare you."

Abby tapped her toe. "Well, sorry doesn't cut it this time, kid. So you'd better decide what your punishment is going to be, or I'll do it."

"I will make my bed every day without being told."

"Not good enough."

"I will brush the dogs every day."

"I'm not buying that either. You have to accept some responsibility here, Sarah."

It took some doing, but a self-imposed punishment was finally agreed upon. Sarah would faithfully help Henny pull weeds in the garden for a whole week. And she would give up four whole days of riding lessons.

Abby knew her daughter got the message when she offered up four days of riding lessons. Relaxing her stance, Abby issued one last warning. "But you'd better live up to your end of the bargain, Sarah Jane, or I will impose my own punishment. And you'll lose a lot more than four days of riding."

Heaving a big, martyred sigh, Sarah let her shoulders sag in a disgruntled posture. "I will."

"Fine. Then both of you go get changed and bring me down your dirty clothes. And don't leave a big mess in the bathroom."

There was some whispering and jostling as they left the room, and Abby blew out her breath. Those kids were enough to test a saint sometimes.

She shook her head and turned to face Conner, about to apologize. But he was standing there, his arms still folded, and he was clearly laughing at her. Okay, maybe not out loud, but his laugh lines were all crinkled, and there was a wicked, wicked sparkle in his eyes.

She cast him an annoyed look. "It's not funny, Conner."

The glint intensified. "Oh, but it is."

There was a patch of mud drying on his cheek, his hair looked like there was glue in it, and his clothes were plastered with slime. And no doubt his boots were ruined—and he thought it was funny.

She made an exasperated sound. "And I was going to apologize for her scaring the wits out of you."

His amusement still clearly evident, he tipped his head in acknowledgment. "She did that right enough."

"And you think it's funny."

Still watching her, he gave his head a small shake. "No, I don't think that's funny. It's the pair of you. You put on quite a show."

Abby lifted her chin. "I don't have a clue what you're talking about."

The laugh lines deepened. "I know where she gets that stubborn streak, and it ain't from the Calhouns, darlin'. The source is standing about eight feet in front of me."

Her insides responding to his comments about the Calhouns, Abby acted out her response and jammed her hands on her hips. "I was never that—that willful."

His eyes glinting, he shook his head, watching her with those piercing blue eyes. "Ah, Abby," he chastised softly. "The lies you tell. And you sure in hell can't ride home on that one. It's just too damned lame."

The way he said it made her laugh—really laugh. As she passed by him, she gave him a hard shove, knocking him off balance. The surprised look on his face made her laugh again, and she started toward the door, knowing she had better check on the kids, or the bathroom would be a disaster. Her hand on the doorjamb, she narrowed her eyes at him. "Go away, Conner Calhoun. You're cluttering up the work space."

He grinned at her, meeting her gaze directly, and

they exchanged a long, silent look—a shared joke, a companionable closeness, a kind of unspoken honesty. And she could see it in his eyes. He understood why she'd breached a nine-year-old silence, and everything was okay. No damage done. Their long, solid friendship was intact. She wanted to hug him, but she flipped her nose at him instead, then turned into the dining room. Hugs were just a little too dangerous right now.

Later that night, she lay in bed, staring into the darkness, a lightness inside her that she hadn't experienced for a very long time. It was as if that exchange in the kitchen set the tone for the rest of the evening, and she couldn't remember the last time she'd laughed like that—laughter that had come straight from her belly. She had never realized it until now, the wealth of easy camaraderie she and Conner had always shared. He was the kind of person she valued highly as a friend. And in many ways, he had become her most significant friend. It hit her just how much she'd always *liked* her brother-in-law. The man who was the father of her two children.

That wayward thought made her stomach do a wild flip-flop, and suddenly her insides were churning up heat. That was one place she could definitely not go. She rolled over on her stomach and dragged the pillow over her head. Definitely a place she couldn't go.

There was a subtle change in things after that night. It was as if the episode with Sarah established a wider, deeper, broader comfort zone between Conner and her. And a comfortable, day-to-day routine developed between them, a kind of warm and easy companionship that Abby had never, ever experienced before with anyone. She tried really hard not to think about the pictures in the drawer, or Conner's solitary life. She didn't dare. It left her feeling far too vulnerable and shaky inside when she did. Instead, she tried to focus on the here and now. And making every moment count.

Suddenly making moments count became a priority. One thing she started doing was joining him every morning on the east veranda. It got to be a ritual, and she loved that time together. Just the two of them, with no interruptions from the kids, no one to call him away. She wouldn't have missed that time together for the world. After a week, he expected her, and he would have a mug of fresh coffee waiting.

She could hardly wait to get downstairs those mornings, and sometimes she was even awake before he was, her stomach full of crazy little butterflies, and she would lie in bed, waiting for the sound of his movements.

This morning was no different. As soon as she heard the roller screen open, she bounded out of bed, yanked on a pair of sweats and flew down the stairs.

He'd given up sitting in the big wicker chair, and was sitting on the second step, his forearms resting on his thighs, his coffee clasped between his hands. And there was the second mug sitting on the step beside him.

Buoyed by the perfect morning and this private moment of companionship, Abby picked up the mug, then sat down next to him, her shoulder rubbing against his. The physical contact filled her with a fuzzy heat, and she didn't pull away, soaking up the feel of his warmth.

He gave her a small, knowing grin. "I see your batteries are all charged up this morning."

She grinned at him and gave him a little jab with her elbow. "And there's even gas in the tank, Calhoun. There's just no stopping me."

He chuckled, then took a sip from his mug. Grasping the cup between both hands, he looked at her. "So what does this big bundle of energy have planned for today?"

"Well," she said, looking pious, "I'm going to work in the garden this morning, then I think I'll take the kids to town this afternoon to see Grandma—maybe she'll want to go for a drive." That was one thing Abby was absolutely faithful about, making a daily trip to town to see Mary. She rolled the coffee around the inside of her mug, then met Conner's gaze and spoke, her voice quiet. "I was hoping she'd feel up to coming out for the day, but she said she'd rather leave it until later in the week. So I expect she's not feeling that well."

His gaze was level and somehow reassuring. "But she's been having more good days than bad lately, so maybe the change in therapy and medication is helping."

Abby sighed. "We can only hope." She drew up her knees and looped her arm around them, then took a sip. She looked at him again. "So what's on your agenda today?"

A glint appeared in his eyes, and the lines around his eyes creased as a smile worked one corner of his mouth. "I expect keeping your daughter out of trouble. The farrier is coming to shoe the roan stud—he's got a quarter crack that needs tending. So we'll probably find her out in the round corral, trying to shoe one of the ponies.''

Abby gave him a wry look. "Well, I can fix that. I'll take her to town with me.''

His gaze glinting with humor, he shook his head. "Naw. It's okay. Having her around keeps everybody on their toes.''

Abby gave him a narrow, chastising look. "And you still think that's funny.''

He didn't respond. Instead he gave her a slow, lazy grin, then drained his cup. His coffee finished, he reached behind Abby to set his empty mug on the low wicker table behind her. And Abby's heart nearly stopped. The warmth and weight of that touch set off such a commotion in her middle, it was hard to catch her breath, and she shivered.

"You're cold,'' he said, his tone suddenly gruff.

Unable to get anything else out, Abby forced herself to respond. "A little.''

He reached behind him and got his jean jacket, then tucked it around her shoulders and across her back, and Abby had to grit her teeth and close her eyes, his careful ministrations setting off another rush inside her. She felt as if she just might expire if he stopped touching her, and she leaned closer to his warmth, needing him to keep her steady.

Lord, he was so warm and safe and solid. Easing in a deep, uneven breath, she steeled herself, expecting him to withdraw his arm. But he didn't. Instead, he braced it on the step behind her, and it was almost as if he had physically enveloped her. Abby focused on breathing in and out, a new rush of heat surging through her. More than anything, she wanted to turn

into his arms. More than anything, anything, anything.

She sat there, not moving a muscle, afraid she'd
scare him off if she moved. It mesmerized her—that
thick, fuzzy feeling that sizzled through her. And it
was a sensation she had never experienced before—
and one she did not want to end. Ever.

Once she got used to it, she was even able to hold
a halfway coherent conversation, and Conner seemed
as reluctant as she to break the contact. But the sound
of Jake whistling echoed in the early-morning stillness, and Conner heaved a sigh and pulled his arm
away. Her pulse frantic in her throat, Abby had to
lock her arms around her legs to keep from grabbing
onto him as he stood up. And it was all she could do
to look at him. He stood staring down at her, his eyes
dark and unreadable; then he ran the back of one finger along her jaw. "See you later," he said, his voice
husky.

That single soft touch nearly took her down, and
her whole body went berserk. It took every ounce of
will she had to smile up at him. "Later," she whispered.

With her lungs seizing up and her heart pounding,
she watched him walk away, things happening inside
her that made her heart pound even harder. As soon
as he disappeared, she got up, clutching his forgotten
jacket around her as she stumbled up the last step.
Like a robot, she went into the house and blindly
ascended the stairs, the clamor inside her getting
worse. Once in her room she shut the door, then
flopped face down on the bed, burying her face in the
pillow as she clutched the jacket around her. This was
crazy. Crazy, crazy, crazy. She wanted him to touch

her all over. She wanted to step into his arms like she had that day in the kitchen, and she wanted to hang on to him and never, ever let go.

Chastising herself for thinking that way, she dragged the garment off, trying to disconnect from the unsatisfied ache lying thick and heavy in her. But she couldn't disconnect. No matter how hard she tried. Feeling shaky and out of control, she sat up and put his jacket on, hugging it around her, her insides crawling with emptiness. God, it would be hours before she'd see him again. She didn't think she could stand it.

She really was losing her mind.

Chapter 6

A breeze swept in through the open window of the pitch-black room, stirring the blinds and making them flutter, the sound intruding on Abby's dream. She came awake, her heart pounding and her breathing so labored she felt as if she'd been running, with the dream still fresh in her mind. Clutching her robe, she stumbled into the bathroom, her heart galloping like a wild horse as she pressed her hot face against the cool tiles. Again. It had happened again. That startlingly real, erotic dream, the one that made her whole body throb with a heavy, pulsating ache—the one that left her with a fierce emptiness when she woke up.

It was bad enough that Conner infiltrated her waking thoughts, but now he had also infiltrated her dreams. Sweet, sensual dreams, hot, erotic dreams—dreams that left her so shaken, so aching, she was a mess inside. And now she'd had that same hot, erotic dream three nights in a row, only it was getting worse.

More intense. More explicit. More real. It was as if Conner were right there in bed beside her—and it was such an awful wrench when she woke up, she could barely stand it. Her nerves were absolutely raw.

Lord, she had to make them stop. But she didn't know how. *Yes, you do. Yes, you do,* answered that little voice in her head. Groaning out loud, she tossed the robe on the floor, yanked open the shower door and wrenched on the faucet. Maybe if she simply stayed away from him, it would help. But would she give up morning coffee with Conner? Not a chance. She lived for that time. But one thing was for sure, she was going to come apart at the seams and become a total wreck if this kept up. One very hygienically clean total wreck.

For the first time ever, Abby beat Conner into the kitchen and, still feeling strung out, she started the coffee. She didn't even want to know what she looked like. There were some things not worth knowing. But she knew she had to pull it together. It was Sunday, and they'd been invited to Tanner and Kate McCall's for a picnic. And she couldn't back out even if she thought it was any kind of solution. The kids would go into full revolt if she did. The truth was, they'd probably eat and sleep with the six McCall kids, given a chance. Which was a thought she just couldn't handle that early in the morning. As a unit, they'd terrorize the entire neighborhood. Especially Casey and Sarah. Trouble squared, Conner called them. Little terrors on their own, together, they were downright scary.

As if conjured up by Abby's thoughts, Sarah came bouncing into the kitchen, her eyes bright. "We're going to the McCalls' today, right, Mom. Right?"

Forcing herself to take a deep, calming breath, Abby answered, "What are you doing up, Sarah Jane? It's not even five o'clock yet."

Sarah gave her mother her best smile. "I didn't want to sleep in and miss it."

"Miss what?" Conner entered the kitchen, smiling at his small niece.

Sarah batted her eyelashes. "The picnic."

"Ah," he said knowingly. "The *McCall* picnic."

She swirled her long nightgown, and slipped into her long-ago lisp. "Yeth."

Amusement still hovering around his mouth, he glanced at Abby, his expression going still. Without saying anything, he studied her a moment longer, his gaze narrowing, but if he read something in her face, he left it alone. His tone was noncommittal. "You're up early."

She gave him a lame smile. "I couldn't sleep." A flicker of genuine humor surfaced. "I just can't wait to see what crisis befalls us today."

One corner of his mouth lifted in a semblance of a smile, but Abby knew he wasn't entirely satisfied with the answer. However, he said nothing as he poured himself some coffee, then leaned back against the counter to drink it.

Still feeling strung out and needing something to do, Abby fixed Sarah half a grapefruit, a million butterflies breaking loose in her stomach. More than anything, she wanted to stand by Conner and lean into his warmth. She should run screaming from the house. Because if she couldn't get a grip, she'd never make it through the day.

Engaging Conner in conversation, Sarah shoveled

her way through the grapefruit, telling him in endless detail what all they were going to do that day.

Not hearing a single word, Abby went to the counter to pour herself a cup of coffee, her insides still in turmoil. She heard Conner tell Sarah to go wash her hands, then she heard him set his empty cup in the sink. He spoke, that same neutral tone in his voice. "I'm going to ride out and see if I can find that one mare that's due to foal. But I'll be back in plenty of time."

Abby knew about the mare—she was unbroken and mostly wild, but she threw the best foals on the place. Sensing him watching her, she turned, dragging up a smile. "Believe me, we won't leave without you."

There was no returning smile, not even in his eyes. Instead he was watching her with an intent, steady look, as if assessing the situation. His voice was quiet and low when he spoke. "You look tired. Go back to bed."

Abby could handle that kind of concern. Barely. But she could handle it. But then Conner blew it. As if not even realizing he was doing it, he reached out and ever so carefully tucked her hair behind her ear.

It was too much. Abby's knees went immediately weak, and her breath jammed up in her chest. It was all she could do to keep from folding into his arms. And all those feelings she'd tried to hold at bay came rushing through her, sending a fountain of need surging up inside her. As if trapped by his gaze, she stared back at him, unable to break away—not really wanting to. She was so lost in his eyes, in the pulse-racing weakness….

The sound of feet on the stairs shattered the spell, and Abby struggled to keep from closing her eyes.

His gaze dark and steady, Conner lightly ran his knuckle along her jaw, his voice very gruff when he spoke. "See you later."

She couldn't speak. She nodded instead. He gave her one last long, steady stare, then left the room, picking his Stetson off the hook by the door.

Dazed and devoid of coherent thought in her head, she reached for the chair, her knees so wobbly they wanted to buckle. She barely made it to the table. Her heart pounding and her pulse thundering in her ears, she weakly rested her head on her folded arms. She felt as if she suddenly had too much blood in her body. Too much heat. Too heavy a response. Closing her eyes, she tightened her hands into fists, trying to bring her body under control. This was not supposed to happen—not all these primitive feelings, not this fever of need. She had always considered herself fairly low-keyed sexually, never given to excesses. But she had excesses now—hot, pumping excesses that made her whole body throb. God, everything had gotten short-circuited. This had all started out as a simple rescue mission—Conner rescuing her—but all of a sudden, it had gone way beyond that. Never had she wanted anything the way she wanted to rescue him.

The rest of the morning was a total loss. Abby couldn't keep her mind on anything. She bounced from one thing to another like a ricocheting tennis ball. Finally she shut herself in the laundry room, determined to get at least one job finished. There was a mountain of laundry to be folded. There was *always* laundry to fold.

Matching the corners of a sheet, she turned and just happened to glance out the window. And her heart stopped dead in its tracks. She could see the barn from that window, and the loft door, and her son trying to attach a rope to the heavy wooden door handle on the front of the door, his sister on her knees beside him. It didn't take a genius to figure out what they were trying to do—these two little angels were trying to kill themselves. They were going to tie that rope to the handle, and they were going to slide down that rope.

Dropping the sheet, she sprinted for the door, her heart racing frantically in her chest. If Cody didn't kill himself, she was going to do it for him. Couldn't there be just one day when one of them didn't try to break their necks?

She rounded the pump house, trying to get enough air into her lungs to give her son royal hell, but she didn't get the chance. Conner was already there, and he had obviously witnessed the whole thing. Cody and Sarah were on the ground, standing in front of him, huddled together like scared sheep. She had never seen them so still or their eyes so big and wide. Bending over at the waist, she braced her arms on her thighs, trying to haul air into her lungs. She couldn't get one word out. She didn't have to. Conner was doing it for her. And for a man who said he never thought of them as his kids, he was looking and acting like one very irate dad. With her breathing so labored and the blood pounding in her ears, she couldn't hear what he was saying. But she got the message.

And the kids were getting it, too. Where she would have gotten a bunch of sulky looks, a whole lot of pouting and a dozen excuses, Conner was getting a whole lot of "yes, sirs" and "no, sirs." If they hadn't scared her half to death, and if she could have gotten enough wind to do it, she would have laughed. He had gotten their attention, all right. And he was definitely acting like their father. No doubt about it.

Before anyone spotted her, she slipped back around the pump house, then leaned against the red clapboard siding, waiting for her pulse to settle. She closed her eyes, a huge, wonderful feeling unfolding in her chest. He *was* acting like their father. And that was as it should be.

She stood there for a long time, then she went back to the house, feeling impossibly light. It was going to be a good day. A very good day.

When Conner and the two kids came in, she was putting the finishing touches on a huge potato salad. The kids were hot and sweaty, and very subdued. The veins in Conner's neck were still visibly distended. But she pretended not to notice anything was amiss. His tone was not one to mess with when he spoke. "Now you two get upstairs and get cleaned up, then straighten up your rooms and make your beds. And you better do it right, or you won't be going anywhere."

Her expression wide-eyed and bland, Abby folded her arms and leaned back against the counter. She didn't say one word. Her only response was to raise her eyebrows in a silent, you-heard-him expression when her two kids looked to her for support. And that was all that she did. But it was enough. Once they left the room, she looked at Conner, nearly choking on the need to laugh.

Obviously still shaken, he held up both his hands, his tone clipped when he spoke. "You don't want to know."

She gave him a serene smile. "You're right. I don't."

His expression going still, Conner narrowed his eyes at her.

She mimicked his gesture, holding up both hands. He stared at her a moment longer, then turned to go. But he turned back, intently assessing her. His tone was blunt. "You're laughing at me, aren't you?"

Knowing darned well her eyes were giving her away, Abby held on to her bland expression, her tone pacifying. "I wouldn't laugh at you, Conner."

He held her gaze for a long moment, then the corner of his mouth lifted just a little. "The hell you wouldn't."

Using Sarah's techniques she batted her eyelashes at him. He was about to say something when Cody came tearing into the room. "Mom! Mom! Sarah stuck her finger up the tap and got it stuck."

Conner's face got a strained, martyred expression on it. He held up his hand again. "I'll get it," he said, waylaying her. "This will nicely round out my morning."

Abby watched him leave, then covered her face with her hand and gave way to silent laughter. God, he was just too precious for words.

The kids were on their best behavior the rest of the morning. Abby had never seen such compliant, eager-to-please children. And they were clearly trying to mend their fences with Conner. But he never brought up their swinging-from-the-barn escapade, and Abby never asked. It was pretty obvious that he'd had his say and it was over and done with, so she left it alone. But it was darned interesting to watch her kids bending over backward to get back in his good graces. It was also obvious that Uncle Conner swung a whole lot of weight. Abby couldn't help it; she kept grinning for no apparent reason.

And she was still smiling to herself as she loaded up the big cooler. The kids were on the floor, stuffing swimsuits and beach towels into their backpacks, fighting over who got the blue towel.

Abby glanced over as Conner appeared in the kitchen after having a shower. He paused in the archway as he rolled back the sleeves of his new plaid shirt. All he did was glance at the kids, and Sarah turned all sweet and accommodating. "You can have the blue towel, Cody. And I'll take the orange one. I like orange."

Wanting to laugh all over again, Abby met Conner's gaze, and he raised one eyebrow, unmistakable amusement glinting in his eyes. It was such a commonplace exchange, but it hit Abby just how much like a real family they were—Mom, Dad, two kids bickering over beach towels. Her heart rolled over, a strange fluttery feeling unfolding in her middle. And another startling realization hit. They weren't like a real family. They *were* a real family. The realization made her heart roll over.

The picnic was exactly what a picnic should be. Lots of food, lots of fun and even the required ants. Which Sarah kept bringing to the picnic table on bits of food to show her mother, fascinated by their industry.

The picnic site was a familiar one to Abby. The best swimming hole in the country was on the McCall ranch. It was at a sharp bend in the river, and the water was so clear, it was like looking through glass.

Someone had hung a rope from one ancient, stalwart tree leaning over the high cut bank, and the kids took turns swinging from it, giving Tarzan yells just before they hit the water. And with the three eldest McCalls and Cody trying to outdo one another in high-flying acrobatics, Abby found it was easier on her nerves if she sat with her back to their daredevil stunts. Having had enough of the other kids hogging the rope, the two little girls, being little angels for once, dragged their beach towels into the clearing, and were busy weaving field daisies into wreaths for their hair. Abby knew better than to turn her back on them.

With the two men seated on the bank, supervising the four-year-old twin boys, Kate McCall and Abby stayed at the picnic table, drinking icy lemonade. Their friendship had developed years before, right after Kate had married Tanner, and it had continued to develop over the years.

Kate flipped back the tea towel covering a container and pulled out a cookie, then flipped the towel back. She took a bite and looked at Abby. "I gotta tell you," she said, a sparkle in her eyes, "this Alberta climate suits you, Abigail. You've lost that awful Toronto pallor."

Abby grinned at her. "Give it up. I'm not going to get into an east-versus-west battle with you today. I haven't got the energy."

Kate chuckled and took another bite of cookie. "You're no fun." Turning her head, she watched her eldest daughter do a perfect somersault fifteen feet in the air as she let go of the rope. "This is really good for Conner," she said, her voice turning quiet, "having you and the kids here."

Experiencing a funny lifting feeling in her stomach,

Abby schooled her expression. Needing a second for the sensation to settle, she took a drink of lemonade, then answered. "I know, and it's good for the kids, too."

"It's nice that he can play such a big part in their lives. He needs that."

Abby stared at her friend, the fluttery feeling climbing higher. It was as if Kate knew a whole lot more than she let on. But Abby dismissed that sensation as overactive nerves. She couldn't help but wonder, though, if Kate had any idea just how big a part Conner had played in her children's lives. Or in hers. Any idea at all.

Kate glanced at Abby, her expression placid; then she began brushing cookie crumbs off her T-shirt. "I can't get over how much Cody is like Conner. It's funny how genetics play out in some families."

Feeling as if she'd just been zapped with a live wire, Abby got up and started picking up empty plastic glasses. She wasn't going to touch that with a ten-foot barge pole.

They stayed at the swimming hole until the sun started to go down, then they went to the McCalls' for coffee. It was dark by the time they called it a day. The entire McCall family had followed them out to the truck, and Kate tucked a bag of cookies in the back seat as Abby helped Sarah with her seat belt. With both kids loaded and belted in, Abby closed the back door and stood by Conner. She smiled at their hosts. "Thanks, guys. We had a great time."

Kate leaned back against Tanner's chest as he slipped his arms around her waist. She teased. "Well, I expect at least a seven-course meal the next time we come to Cripple Creek."

Conner chuckled. "As long as you'll be satisfied with seven courses of good Alberta beef." He opened the passenger door and placed his hand on Abby's back. "We'd better get this show on the road, or we're going to have two sleeping beauties by the time we get home."

It was nothing—just his hand against the small of her back, but it had such a dizzying effect, it nearly paralyzed her. It was the kind of touch a man gave a woman—a familiar, intimate, protective touch—and it was all she could do not to close her eyes and lean into that light pressure. At one far-off level, she was grateful it was dark. Because she knew Kate would have seen the reaction on her face.

She wasn't sure how she made it into the truck, and the only thing she was aware of was Conner's strong, masculine hand clamped around the open window as he closed the door. Swallowing hard, she fixed her gaze straight ahead, her heart skipping frantic beats in her chest. She felt as if she was suffocating.

The trip home was a silent one. The kids fell asleep before they were off McCall land and neither she nor Conner spoke. But it wasn't a strained silence—just a heavy one, and Abby concentrated on breathing in, breathing out. And it took every ounce of concentration she had to do that.

By the time they reached the ranch, the last traces of the sunset had faded from the western sky and stars had started to appear. A full moon hovered just above the horizon, and Abby heard a chorus of coyotes as Conner parked beside the garage. Cody spoke from the back seat. "Are we home?"

Conner's voice was quiet. "Yes, we are."

Abby reached back to wake Sarah but Conner spoke again. "Just leave her, and I'll bring her in."

Still fighting the effects of his hand on her back, Abby picked up towels and sandals and handed Cody his backpack, then gathered up Sarah's belongings and some other odds and ends. All that was left was the empty cooler, and it could wait until tomorrow.

She followed her son into the house and dropped her load on the mudroom floor. She couldn't cope with it tonight. It would also have to wait until tomorrow.

Making sure the screen door was closed against the flurry of moths, she picked up Sarah's sandals and headed for the stairs. For once, she issued no reminders about teeth brushing. She figured their teeth wouldn't rot away to nothing if they missed one night's brushing. Cody was face down on his bed when she entered his room and she heard Sarah whining from the other room. "I wanna sleep in the window box in my brother's room. Mom said I could sleep in the window box."

Conner appeared at the door carrying Sarah, and even in the faint light from the hall, she could detect the glint in his eyes. "I think we'd better switch kids. This one thinks she's a pansy or something," he whispered. "She wants to sleep in a window box."

Abby took her daughter from him, then set her on the chair. "She means window seat." Grabbing a folded quilt from the end of Cody's bed, she made a makeshift bed on the low, wide window seat, then stripped her daughter down to her panties and T-shirt and helped her crawl into the space.

Abby was so aware of Conner's presence, it was as if her body had a million little sensors in it. And to make matters worse, it was oddly intimate, the two of them putting the children to bed—the thud as Cody's jeans hit the floor, the rustle of bedclothes being drawn back, Conner's quiet tone as he spoke to Cody. It was as if her skin was electrified, and her heart was pounding so hard it made her lungs seize up. Struggling to hang on to her equilibrium, to maintain some balance, she swallowed hard, then bent down to tuck her daughter in. She almost smiled when she realized Sarah was dead to the world.

There was another rustle, then Conner spoke. "Good night," he said, his voice very low and gruff.

Abby wanted to grab his arm, to keep him there. Clasping her hands into fists, she eased in an unsteady breath. "Good night, Conner." Feeling unexpectedly close to tears, she bent over and kissed her daughter good-night, her chest unbearably tight. She had never felt so alone or bereft in her entire life.

Nearly overcome by that feeling, she kissed Cody good-night then closed the door. Knowing she was not going to be able to sleep a wink, she went into her darkened room and opened all the windows wide, letting the cool mountain breeze in. Her expression taut, she kicked off her shoes, then stripped off her clothes and climbed blindly into bed. Draping her arm across her eyes, she tried to will away the ache, tried to collect a modicum of common sense. *Proximity,* her rational inner voice whispered. *The pictures in the drawer,* countered that other little voice. *Just two lonely people,* she mentally argued. *You're kidding yourself,* responded her conscience.

Feeling totally shredded inside, Abby wrestled with all the voices, part of her arguing that it wasn't right, having those kinds of feelings for your husband's brother. *But,* countered that sly little voice that refused to be silenced, *your husband was not your husband for a very long time before he died.*

Turning on her stomach, Abby pulled the pillow over her head and groaned. She didn't think she could stand that awful unsatisfied ache throbbing through her whole body. Even the weight of the bedding sensitized her.

Feeling as if she was going slowly crazy, Abby got up and went to stand by the window, hoping the crisp mountain breeze would have some calming effect on the fever inside her. Trying to reclaim some control, she closed her eyes, willing some semblance of calm into her body.

But the squeak of the door directly below her—that door that led from Conner's room to the south veranda—snapped her eyes open, and her pulse began hammering all over again. And she knew, as sure as she was standing there, that he was on the veranda, also unable to sleep. Just like her. And she wondered if he was restless or if he, too, was wrestling with something.

As if that one thought connected her with him, Abby got nailed with another immobilizing rush. Her mind spinning, she rested her face against the cool glass.

God, he was so alone. She couldn't stand the thought of him down there, struggling with that aloneness. She remembered that day in the kitchen, how he had held her, and a terrible ache settled around her heart. And she remembered how it felt to be held safe in his arms.

Experiencing another heavy rush, Abby clenched her jaw, her whole body responding to that memory.

She was losing it, really losing it. It was almost as if he'd reached out and touched her, caressing her in the most intimate way. She flattened both her hands against the glass, her breathing coming in ragged intakes. She could not bear his aloneness. She just could not stand it anymore.

Never in her life had Abby acted on impulse, but she acted on impulse now. Her eyes burning with tears, she snatched up her robe and roughly tied the belt around her waist, a weird kind of anger setting her resolve. She just could not—could not—leave him out there alone. Not Conner. Not her rock. Her anchor. Her knight in shining armor.

Fortified with a crazy kind of determination, she slipped down the stairs, her heart growing larger and more cumbersome with every step, her nerves vibrating so badly that she was shaking. She didn't have a clue what she was doing. But she didn't care. One thing she did know for sure—going to Conner could never be a mistake.

She accessed the veranda through the dining room, carefully latching the roller screen so it didn't make a sound. Clasping the front of her robe, she turned, the flooring cold against her bare feet.

The full moon cast long milky shadows in the yard, and far in the distance the hoot of an owl broke the silence. Her pulse sounding like a heavy surf in her ears, she rounded the corner of the house, her insides doing a crazy barrel roll when she spotted Conner.

The south veranda was heavily shrouded in vines, closing it in, but the moonlight draped him like liquid silver. He was standing with his head bowed, both hands clamped on the railing. Dressed only in jeans, his bare back gleamed in the moonlight, and even in the faint light she could see the awful tension in him.

Her vision blurring with the enormity of her feelings, Abby spoke his name and started toward him.

Conner abruptly straightened, his body going still. Abby could swear she could feel the tension leaping between them. She didn't have a plan, she hadn't thought it out, but just when her nerve nearly faltered, Conner shifted and she got a good look at his face. Seeing the agony in his eyes, she simply reacted.

Her voice catching on a sob, she spoke his name again, then stepped into his arms, his agony becoming hers.

Another sound was wrenched from her as Conner crushed her in a hard, fierce embrace, his hand roughly tangling in her loose hair as he jammed her head against him.

Immobilized by the onslaught of need, Abby clung to him, certain she would collapse if he let her go. She had never experienced anything like it—the heavy, surging feeling of two halves coming together, the awesome power of two universes colliding, the stunning rush of wanting. It had been too long for her, this man-woman thing. And now it was all too much—too much need, too much unsatisfied hunger, too much raw emotion. Yet not nearly enough. Lord, not nearly enough.

Her breathing out of control, she locked her arms around him, pulling herself flush against him, needing him, needing more.

Hoarsely whispering her name, Conner backed her into the shadows, then spread his hand wide in her hair and turned her head. His heart pounding in tandem with hers, he brushed his mouth across hers, and the surge of raw sexual energy was like being struck by a lightning bolt.

Her breathing paralyzed, she lifted herself higher and opened her mouth, needing the heat of him. Conner shuddered, grinding his mouth against hers as he crushed her even tighter. Body to body, heat to heat, he took her mouth, and Abby yielded everything to him, her need fired higher by his.

Everything she had ever believed about herself—about the kind of woman she was, about her moderate level of sexuality—was simply incinerated by that hot, wet plundering kiss. Making a low sound of restraint, he tried to tear his mouth away, but she grasped his face, holding him to her, unable to bear a separation. She knew if they didn't finish this, if they didn't take this to the final completion, she would simply disintegrate into a million frantic pieces.

His breathing raw and labored, Conner ripped his mouth away and clamped her head against his, then fumbled to untie the belt of her robe. Another tremor shuddered through him when he touched her nakedness beneath the garment.

Terrified that he might stop, that he might do the honorable thing, Abby locked her arms around his neck, her breath catching. But he had no thought of stopping. Yanking back the robe, he hooked one arm under one leg and lifted her up. Pelvis against pelvis, he held her fast as he claimed her mouth again, his thick hardness fused against her.

Abby had never known this fever of need, this raw, urgent hunger, and she gave herself up to the frenzied sensations, knowing Conner would not let her fall.

Roughly changing the angle of his mouth, Conner

thrust against her, and the pulsating heaviness in her groin intensified. Desperate for more, Abby sobbed and locked her legs around him, transfixed by the unbelievable sensations he'd set off inside her. He moved again and she clutched him, her senses disintegrating, desperate for more, much more.

Tearing her mouth away, she lifted herself higher, her voice barely coherent. "Please, Conner. Please," she begged hoarsely, rubbing against him again. The unsatisfied pulse thickened and she found his mouth, desperate for the taste of him, wanting to center her pulsating need.

On a jagged intake of air, Conner caught her jaw and dragged his mouth away, then jammed her head under his jaw. His breathing still raw and labored, he tried to gentle his hold. Fighting in a lungful of air, he stroked her head, his voice so rough, it was as if he was speaking through some unmanageable pain. "Abby," he whispered brokenly, his breath hot against her ear. "Ah, Lord, I can't take that kind of risk with you."

But Abby was too far gone to stop. The hunger was centered in her and getting stronger. She rocked her pelvis, her breathing just as labored as his. "It's okay," she pleaded with him, her voice breaking. "It's okay. Please, Conner."

Desperate to persuade him, she moved against the hard ridge under the placate of his jeans, and he clutched her and stiffened, his body rigid with tension. She moved again, and he clutched her tighter, then abruptly he turned, backing her against the side of the house. Bracing her weight, he fumbled with his jeans, and Abby cried out when she felt him free and hard. Blinded by sensation, she arched, expecting him to thrust into her, but instead he pressed his hard heat against her moistness. Thrusting his hand under her head, he started to move, sensitizing her even more. The sensations began to gather and Abby stiffened, right on the brink. On the very brink. As if aware of what was happening to her, he choked out her name and thrust his hardness into her, his body grinding into hers. And in that instant, Abby lost contact with reality.

Every thrust sent her higher and higher, until her whole body focused into one white hot light; then everything exploded, and pulses of relief ripped through her, a million lights going off in her head. And on a tortured groan, Conner twisted his hips, his own release pumping into her.

Incoherent and shattered, she hung on to him for dear life—on to her lifeline, her rock, her still center.

It seemed like an eternity passed before bits of consciousness sifted down, like the remnants of fireworks. Trembling and weak, and feeling as if every bone in her body had been liquefied, she folded around him, aware of how tightly he was holding her, aware of how badly he was trembling.

Her face wet with tears, she wrapped both arms around his head and tightened her legs, an unbearable tenderness welling up in her as she cradled him against her.

She was so shattered, she was incapable of speech. But she was filled to the brim with feelings for him, and she gently combed her fingers through his hair, wishing she could wrap up every inch of him. He was so infinitely special. So infinitely precious.

Conner turned his face against her neck, his hand wedged under her head. Then as if too spent to move, he tightened his hold. His voice muffled, he spoke, his tone very gruff. "Are you okay?"

Moved beyond words by his concern for her, and overcome with the need to comfort him, she pressed her mouth against his temple. Her own voice was very uneven as she whispered, "I'm better than okay." She stroked his head, then hugged him. "I think I've died and gone to heaven."

His chest rose on a deep intake of air, then he tightened his grip on her head. He didn't say anything but she felt him smile. And she hugged him again.

As if gathering together what remaining strength he had, Conner slid his other hand up her back. "Hold on."

She nodded, wrapping herself around him even tighter.

The muscles in his back bunched as he carried her across the veranda. With a minimum of fuss, he carried her through the door, down the hall and into his room.

Abby knew she should let go and stand on her own, but the thought of separating from him was just too much to bear. Instead, she hung on even tighter, her throat cramping. She could not bear to let him go. She just could not. It would be like ripping her own body in half to disconnect from him.

At the edge of his bed, and with Abby still wrapped around him, he paused and pushed his jeans down and stepped out of them, then slid his hand under her robe. His touch was gentle, caressing. "Let's get rid of this," his said, his tone very husky.

Trusting him to hold her, Abby straightened and let the garment slip off her arms, then she wrapped herself back around him. She felt him take a deep breath as she kissed him just beneath his ear. Another faint tremor coursed through him, and he tightened his hold on her, the movement driving him deeper inside her.

His breath caught and he clutched her. Abby closed her eyes and hung on, his movement bringing on another contraction.

Finally, after what seemed like eons, Conner locked his arm around her hips, turning his face against her neck. He spoke, a tinge of amusement in his voice. "I think we're just going to have to trust the laws of gravity here."

Smiling in response, Abby flattened her hand between his shoulders. "Tell you what—I'll leave the logistics in your capable hands."

She was rewarded with a husky chuckle. "Well then, you'd better hang on." He shifted his hold, then with sheer strength and physical finesse, he got them into his bed, with her flat on her back and him cradled between her upraised knees. The feel of his body on top of hers made her go breathless and fizzy all over again.

Bracing his weight on his elbows, he lifted his head and gazed down at her, the moonlight washing his face. Taking her face in his hands, he studied her, a slow smile appearing. His voice was like rough velvet when he spoke. "Ah, Abigail, Abigail. You are full of surprises."

Holding back a grin, she reached up and caressed his mouth. "You have a few surprises yourself, Calhoun."

His smile deepened. "You're a little piece of dynamite, you know that?"

She did grin. "Did I blow you to smithereens?"

He laughed, a low throaty laugh that sent delicious shivers up her spine. "Something like that."

Aware that they were both avoiding what had brought them together, Abby raised her head and kissed him along his jaw. It was almost as if they'd silently struck another pact not to open too many doors, and that was okay. This was too special to risk.

Wanting to keep that comfortable easiness between them, she looped her arms around his neck and gave him another grin. She didn't know why, but she wanted to see if she could make him blush. Keeping her voice deliberately provocative, she murmured, "You're very, very good, Mr. Calhoun."

He saw through her immediately. Chuckling, he gave her head a little shake. "Very funny, Abigail. If you want to make me squirm, you'll have to do a hell of a lot better than that."

Smiling at his astuteness, she ran her thumb down his spine. "I bet I can make you squirm."

His expression altered, and even in the faint moonlight filtering in, she could see his eyes darken, his gaze becoming hot and intimate. Gazing at her, he stroked her cheeks with his thumbs, then he lowered his head, brushing his mouth lightly against hers. "Oh, yeah," he breathed, caressing her bottom lip. "You can definitely make me squirm."

With that one light touch, Abby's heart started stammering, and suddenly it was impossible to breathe. Pulling his head down, she brought his mouth into full contact with hers.

The kiss was slow, soft and so unbelievably gentle that it left her absolutely breathless, and her whole body turned to jelly. A sudden urgency sizzled through her and she locked her arms around him, lifting her hips to urge him on.

Dragging both her arms from around his neck, he laced his fingers through hers, holding her hands against the bed. ''Easy, darlin','' he whispered, moistening her bottom lip. ''We're going to take our time—slow and easy.'' He stroked her palms with his thumbs and shifted ever so gently against her. ''This time we're going to make it last.''

Abby's heart nearly climbed right out of her chest. She didn't think she could stand it. She really didn't. He'd only started and it was too much already.

And Conner did take his time—goodness, did he take his time. It was just like the kiss, slow, soft, gentle. And painstakingly thorough—inch by inch. Abby had no idea a man could be that dedicated to detail, and he set off reactions she'd never, ever experienced before. And she couldn't think of anything, except what he was doing to her. He took it so slow and easy, he nearly drove her crazy, and she was practically clawing at the bedding before he gave in to her. She was sure she was on the verge of losing her mind when he finally thrust into her, driving her up and over into a soul-shredding release. It was so unbelievable, so explosive, it was as if she came right out of her body. And he was the only thing that held her together. But then, he had always been there to hold her together. Always. Always. Always.

Chapter 7

The first faint hint of dawn had already crept into the room when Abby awakened, a heavy lethargy swimming through her, the weight of Conner's arm around her middle anchoring her. She felt as if she didn't have a muscle left in her entire body.

But the pleasant feeling was suddenly dominated by a feeling of enormous responsibility. This was all her doing. All hers. Closing her eyes, she tried to will away the feeling. She was not going to go there. She was not going to let anything detract from what had happened the previous night. She just wasn't. For once in her life, she was not going to assess her actions—or his. And for once in her life, she was not going to be logical and rational. Her much-vaunted sensibleness could just get stuffed. For once, she was going to follow her heart.

It was an easy road to take, snuggled securely in the curve of Conner's body. Tucking her hands under her face, she watched the curtains float in the cool mountain breeze, her heart stumbling as she recalled everything that had happened in that bed. He was amazing, and she had lost count of how many times they'd made love.

Her thoughts stirred up a sexual restlessness in her. She closed her eyes, wanting it to happen all over again. Wanting to turn into his arms, wanting to feel him come awake, wanting him to slip inside her.

Her breathing suddenly uneven, Abby swallowed hard and opened her eyes. Knowing she couldn't stay there beside him and remain still, she eased out of his hold, her skin turning to gooseflesh the instant she separated from his warmth. She carefully covered him up, then located her robe on the floor and slipped it on. Trying not to make a sound, she crept out of his bedroom, soundlessly pulling the heavy door closed behind her.

Knowing that there was no way she was going to be able to go back to sleep, not with all that restlessness, all that need pumping through her, she wandered through the dusky house as first light bled in through the east windows. She ended up in the huge dining room, standing in front of the French doors, staring out over the courtyard. Her arms tightly folded, she realized that the summer perennials were beginning to bloom, and a terrible starkness welled up inside her. And it hit her that she'd never once thought about the passage of time. But as she stood there, watching the clouds lighten in the east, she faced the fact that time was flying by. Here it was, the second week in July—almost six weeks to the day since Conner had appeared on her doorstep. And somehow or another, time had simply evaporated. In less than two months, they would have to head back to Toronto.

Maybe, she thought, a lick of panic twisting through her, she hadn't been aware of the days disappearing because, for the first time in years, she had nothing to worry about. Thanks to Conner. She closed her eyes and hugged herself tighter. She felt stripped naked inside.

Taking a steadying breath, she opened her eyes, an ache snaking around her heart. She had to be realistic. This was only temporary. It was not forever. Even if Conner asked her to—even if she were to consider staying, it could never be.

She was his brother's widow, with all the implications that went with it—and Conner would never forget that. There was more than them to consider— there was Mary. There was the whole damned community. Privacy had always been Conner's psychological armor. Since she'd first met him, she had known that about him. And to step out in the public— Lord, she couldn't even imagine how that would affect him.

But most important of all were the kids. They'd give up Toronto in a minute, and they adored their uncle. But how would they handle a relationship between her and Conner? She didn't have a clue. Couldn't even hazard a guess. It was all just too damned complicated.

Her practical side told her she was simply going to have to get on with life. And it wasn't as if she were destitute. Thanks to Conner, she had enough money in the bank to get them all resettled, enough to carry them, if she was careful, for three or four months.

And she had the capacity to make a darned good living.

Except the thought of leaving here—of going back to Toronto—made her insides hollow out. She tried to reason with herself. What she had this summer was more than she'd ever hoped for, and all she could ever expect.

Determined not to start analyzing everything, she straightened her spine and tightened the belt on her robe. She was not going to wallow. And she refused to spoil the time she had left with him by feeling sorry for herself.

Fortified with resolve, she marched through the kitchen to the laundry room. Thank God for laundry. She could always count on it being there when she needed it.

She began stuffing clothes into the machine, but she got ambushed by one of Conner's work shirts. It was the smell—the lingering male scent of him that did her in. She got such a rush of heat, it made her insides turn over. Clutching it against her, she closed her eyes and leaned her head against the cupboards above the washer, her heart flip-flopping crazily in her chest, her lungs jammed up and unable to function. It was as if last night was happening all over again. Phantom touches—at every pulse point she experienced phantom touches, and she clutched the shirt tighter. It had been so unbelievable. So intense. So…

A sound intruded, then a strong male hand cupped the back of her neck as Conner murmured something. He took the shirt out of her hand, then ran his hand down her back. Her heart struggling to keep on beating, Abby turned into his arms, certain she was simply

going to fly apart. He was dressed only in jeans, and
the feel of his warm skin nearly took her down.

"Hey," he whispered softly. "Hey." Holding on
to her with one arm, he closed the door and set the
lock; then he wrapped her up in a tight, enveloping
embrace. His fingers tangling in her hair, he clasped
her head against him as he brushed her forehead with
a soft kiss. There was a trace of humor in his voice.
"Wow," he murmured, massaging her scalp. "If I'd
known this was the kind of reception I was going to
get, I would have gotten up sooner."

Abby tried—she really tried to speak, but there was
just no way she could. It was as if his touch had
uncorked an even more desperate need in her, and she
hauled in a lungful of air and flattened her hands
against his back. Closing her eyes, she turned her face
against him and held on for dear life, a litany of need
running through her.

Tightening his hold, he turned with her, folding her
even tighter in his strength and warmth, and Abby
clung to him, her whole body vibrating with need.

His breath was warm against her neck as he pressed
his face against hers. "Hey, it's okay," he whispered,
his voice husky. Then ever so gently he angled her
away from him, and his hand cupped the juncture of
her thighs. The touch was so electric that Abby jerked
and tried to yank his hand away. But he cupped her
even tighter. His voice very gruff, he spoke, "There
is no way I'm going to take any more chances with
you." He tightened his arm around her shoulders.
"Not without anything."

Beginning to tremble, Abby nodded, acknowledg-
ing what he'd said. Then Conner moved his hand, and
she made a low sound and tried to disengage his

arousing touch. Pulling her against him so his mouth was next to her ear, he whispered, "Let me, Abby. I want to do this. You don't know how badly I want to do this."

Her mind filling with red haze, she tried to respond. "I can't—"

"Yeah, you can," he answered, his voice rough. Hooking his thumb under her jaw, he tipped her head and brushed his mouth against hers, telling her exactly what he wanted to do and how he was going to do it. His explicitness knocked the wind right out of her as her strength crumbled, and Abby hung on to him, feeling as if she was about to disintegrate. Then he covered her mouth in a hot, wet kiss, and she relinquished conscious thought. All she could do was hang on to the one solid thing in her spiraling universe.

His touch dragged her down deeper, and she gripped his arm, her senses spinning out of control. He tightened his hold on her, his voice rough and ragged against her ear as he urged her on. Then all that burgeoning need started to pull together and narrow, and with one last stroke, he took her over the top. She stiffened and sobbed out his name as the paralyzing release ripped through her, turning her into raw, exploding energy.

His hand still hard against her, he whispered his approval to her. Then he turned so she was flush against him, wrapping her up in a fierce hold. Decimated by his generosity, by his thoroughness, Abby clutched him, raw emotion reducing her to tears.

Smoothing down her hair, he turned his face against hers. "It's okay," he said softly. "It's okay." Shifting his hand in her hair, he expelled a shaky sigh and slid his other arm around her hips, his strength welding them together. He said nothing; he simply held her, as if knowing she could not stand to be separated from him just yet.

Feeling all torn apart inside, she twisted her face in the curve of his neck, trembling from head to toe. She hadn't known it could be like this—so shattering, so powerful, so unbelievable.

Long minutes passed, and bit by bit the discombobulated sensation passed and her ability to think was restored. But she felt as if she didn't have a whole bone anywhere in her body. She was sure that if he let go of her, she would simply turn into a puddle at his feet.

Taking a deep, shaky breath, Abby ran her hand up the back of his neck. What did one say after something like that? A simple thank you hardly seemed appropriate. And stating that he had absolutely rocked her universe seemed woefully inadequate.

Conner rubbed her back, and she could feel him smile. "I've gotta do this more often—check out the laundry room. I think maybe I could even get into doing laundry."

Abby loved him for that, and she smiled back. "Well, you certainly turned my pockets inside out."

Conner grinned and gave her a hard hug. "Is that what you were doing when I came in, checking my pockets?"

She felt herself blush and pinched his back, reprimanding him. "You weren't supposed to notice what I was doing, Conner. So don't be rude."

She felt him grin again, and she closed her eyes and hugged him, her throat suddenly tight. Lord, he was such a miracle—this man who had been part of her life for so long.

Several more moments passed, then Conner let go a heavy sigh and eased his hold. The grandfather clock chimed out the hour, six deep bongs, and Abby also sighed. At any second now, two kids could be banging on the door, and that was one reality she just wasn't ready to deal with quite yet.

She looked up at Conner, her heart skipping a beat when she saw the dark, unsmiling expression in his eyes. He held her gaze a split second; then he lowered his head. Cupping her jaw to protect her from his heavy stubble, he brushed her mouth with the softest, slowest kiss, and Abby's breath caught and her pulse stumbled. His lips moving against hers, he spoke, his voice very low, very raspy. "I think you'd better get while the getting is good, Abigail. The top of that washer is looking pretty damned good."

What he implied made her knees start to buckle, and Conner caught her and gave her a hard quick kiss, then turned her toward the door. He reached past her to unlock and open it, then gave her a push through. "Now go put some clothes on before I say to hell with good intentions."

The last thing she wanted to do was leave. Knowing it was unfair to him if she stayed, she took a deep breath and gathered her resources. But she simply had to get in the last word. "You could make a fortune selling that line, Calhoun." Then tightening the belt on her robe, she took aim at the doorway leading from the kitchen.

She had the quickest shower ever and threw on some clothes, anxious to get back downstairs. She

didn't want him to leave for the day without her
having a chance to say goodbye.

She re-entered the kitchen to find her son seated at
the table, his head propped on his hand, watching his
Uncle Conner. The last thing she needed right now
was a spectator—especially one of her kids. She felt
just a little too sensitized for that.

Conner appeared oblivious. Shaved and showered
and dressed in blue jeans and a denim work shirt, he
was standing in front of the stove, scrambling eggs
for breakfast. When he heard Abby enter, he turned
and gave her a thorough scrutiny from head to toe,
his gaze so potent, so heady, that Abby had to reach
out and grab the doorjamb to steady herself. As if
attuned to her reaction, he gave her a small half smile
that spoke absolute volumes. He spoke, his voice
husky. "Good morning."

Abby wet her lips. "Good morning."

The devil glinted in his eyes, and his laugh lines
deepened. "I think you must have had trouble dressing yourself this morning," he said, indicating her
sweatshirt with a lift of the egg turner. The glint intensified. "You look like you just crawled out of a
laundry basket."

Cody chortled and smacked the table. "That's a
good one, Uncle Conner."

A hot flush climbing up her face, Abby could have
strangled the pair of them. That was a very low ball,
the crack about laundry. Very low.

A huge grin on his face, Cody waggled his finger
at her. "Hey, Mom. Wake up. Your T-shirt's on back-
wards."

Abby looked down. Sure enough, her shirt was on
backward. She blushed again, recalling her earlier

comment about his turning her pockets inside out. She also wanted to laugh. Trying not to let that bubble of amusement get away on her, she shot Conner a warning look and aimed her finger at him. He grinned and winked. Then he turned back to the stove.

Pushing up her sleeves, Abby wasn't quite sure what to do. Under any other circumstances, she would have gone over and finished making breakfast. But after what had happened this morning, she knew she didn't dare get within ten feet of him, or she might come unglued.

So she opted for a cup of coffee and a chair at the safe end of the table. If she tried to do anything else, she was sure she'd look like a moth, trying to beat itself to death around an open flame.

Breakfast proceeded nicely on course without her, and she was beginning to feel as if she was regaining some control over herself. About halfway through the meal, Sarah appeared, looking just a little cranky, a bedraggled bunny clasped under her arm. Sarah was like her mother. You didn't expect Miss Sunshine unless you fed her first.

Abby got up to fix Sarah her half a grapefruit, and Sarah plopped down on her mother's chair. Conner looked at his niece, a twinkle in his eye. "Good morning, Sarah."

"It's a stupid morning."

The twinkle in his eyes intensified. "So it is."

Abby placed the bowl holding the grapefruit in front of her daughter, then put the spoon beside that. Playing along, she gave Conner a solemn look. "We don't talk to Sarah in the morning, Uncle Conner. Not until she gets her happy face on."

Conner nodded his head wisely, and Cody rolled

his eyes. Without thinking about what she was doing, or the problem of proximity, Abby pulled out the chair next to Conner. Which would have been okay, if she hadn't brushed against him when she sat down. She felt that contact right down to her toes. Conner stiffened, and she heard him suck in his breath.

She knew exactly what he was experiencing, because she was experiencing it, too—that hot rush, the debilitating weakness. Just the thought of what had happened in the laundry room made her senses swim.

Feeling as if she had somehow betrayed him, she looked straight ahead and swallowed hard. Then she moved her hand under the table. With her pulse running heavy and her respiration rate accelerating, she touched his thigh, trying to communicate by touch alone, trying to tell him that she had not meant to ignite the need in him again. Without looking at her, he grasped her hand, his grip almost crushing. She heard him take another uneven breath; then he pressed her hand flat against his thigh, the muscles in his jaw rigid.

His gaze fixed straight ahead, he rubbed his thumb against the palm of her hand, and that hidden caress sent such a fizzle of sensation through her, it was all Abby could do to keep from sliding under the table.

The tension was so unbearable that Abby could barely breathe. So she sat there like a statue, the heat from his thigh radiating through her and making her heart pound, making her whole body hum.

His chest rose and Conner squeezed her hand, then met her gaze, his eyes so dark and dilated, they appeared almost black. He stared at her a moment, then spoke, his voice gruff. ''I've got to hit the road.'' He gave her hand a squeeze. ''I'll see you later, okay?''

She had to moisten her lips before she could speak. "Okay."

Without looking at her again, he pushed his chair back and got up, ruffling both the kids' hair on his way out the door. Abby clasped her hands between her knees, a terrible hole forming in her chest. Lord, she hated him leaving like that.

Pushing her chair back, she hurried to the mudroom, pulling the door closed behind her. Conner had just finished putting on his boots when she entered, and he straightened, his expression tight.

Afraid she was going to cry, she went to him and touched his face. Conner closed his eyes, his jaw flexing. "Please stay safe," she whispered.

He muttered something, then grasped her by the jaw and yanked her face up, covering her mouth with a kiss that nearly blew her socks off. She tried to move closer, but he held her back, his mouth hungry against hers. Then he abruptly stepped away and dragged his hand down his face. "Damn it all to hell, Abigail. What am I doing to myself?" He grabbed his hat and jammed it on his head, and Abby stood staring at him, not sure if he was angry or what. He looked at her, then heaved another sigh and kissed her again. Only this was soft—heartbreakingly soft. Breaking off the kiss, he raised his head and looked at her, finally managing a warped smile. "You're trying to kill me, aren't you?"

Feeling oddly flustered, she stuck her hands in her pockets. "I just wanted to say goodbye."

There was a glint of real amusement in his eyes. "Goodbye, Abigail." He squeezed the back of her neck, then left.

Her arms folded, Abby stood at the open door and

watched him disappear around the hedge, her insides feeling suddenly empty. He was barely out of sight, and she was missing him already.

It was going to be a *very* long day.

It *was* a long day. And it got worse. The kids had declared open warfare on each other by midmorning. And they got on her nerves. The ceaseless wind got on her nerves. The mosquitoes in the courtyard got on her nerves. Everything got on her nerves.

And by noon, she swore the clock hands had stopped moving altogether. All she wanted was for Conner to come home.

She finally left the two hellions in Henny's care and drove into town to see Mary, but she felt like an overextended rubber band the entire time. Her only solution was to start vacuuming the minute she got home, and she actually found some minute dust balls under Cody's bed. She felt as if she had discovered gold.

Abby thought she'd actually gotten a grip until Henny showed up with the kids, passing on a message from Conner that he wouldn't be home until after supper. She was devastated. Though she managed the must-do stuff, like feed the kids, supervise baths and nag them into bed, that was about all she could muster.

However, putting them to bed was a mistake. Because once she was alone, that restless feeling got even worse, and all she could do was pace. Unable to stand the feel of her clothes against her skin, she finally went upstairs and had a shower, then put on a huge, old T-shirt that almost skimmed her knees. But it was only a temporary fix. By ten o'clock, she truly felt like a cat on a hot tin roof, and she was ready to climb right out of her skin.

She finally went out on the south veranda, trying to appreciate how the color was fading from the sky. Through the open door, she heard Conner enter the kitchen. Closing her eyes, she forced herself to stay calm and to stay put, her heart pounding, her chest full of butterflies. That resolve lasted maybe two whole seconds, and she simply could not stand it any longer. The butterflies getting wilder, she went inside, her stomach tied up in knots. He was just entering the living room as she rounded the corner.

He looked like hell. His face was haggard, and she had never seen such a haunted look in someone's eyes. He stopped, his expression rigid with tension. His gaze fixed on her, he spoke, his voice gruff. "I had to pick up some things."

Abby's gaze dropped to the white paper bag in his hand, her own tension climbing a notch, and she swallowed hard. She knew what was in that bag.

His face looked as if it were chiseled out of granite when he drew a deep, uneven breath. "I'm sorry, Abby," he said, his voice strained. "I didn't dare come home until I was sure the kids were in bed."

Abby's vision suddenly blurred. With her chest filling up with feelings for him, she crossed the room and stepped into his arms. Emitting a choked sound, Conner swept her up in a crushing embrace, and Abby molded herself against him, holding the back of his head as he buried his face against her neck. She could feel it—the need vibrating in him, the energy that just kept building and building. He was literally trembling with it.

Unable to do anything else, Abby hung on to him,

a thousand sensations raging through her. It was as if they were welded together—locked together by need. It helped, having his arms around her, to take the edge off, to ease the desperateness that held them both.

He turned his head and shifted his hold, a shudder coursing through him. It was as if they were both paralyzed, unable to move, unable to separate.

Abby could feel him gather his control, his whole body tensing; then he gripped her arm and pulled it from around his neck, clasping her by the wrist. His face hardening into stone, he turned and headed for his bedroom, and Abby followed, so disoriented she could barely walk. Once in the dimly lit room, he tossed the bag on the bed, then set the heavy brass lock. The look on his face was one of rigidly controlled discipline as he ripped his belt loose, then tore open the snaps on his shirt. With the unbearable tension radiating like a force field around them, he reached for her and hauled her into his arms. And their common desperation took over.

This time it was like a storm breaking over them. There was no restraint. There was no gentleness. It was desperation all the way. And his only concession was to caution. It was as if they were trapped in this frenzy, and there was only one way out.

It was a night Abby would never forget. It went from hot, wild and urgent, to sweet, tender and slow, with absolutely everything in between. She had never realized a man could have so many sensual layers— so many facets—so much stamina. It was as if he was trying to make up for an entire lifetime in a single night. And Abby reveled in it. She had never felt so cherished. She wanted that night to last forever.

Morning, however, was a different bag of beans.

She could have sworn she had just fallen asleep when Conner was nudging her awake, muttering something about the kids and how they would be getting up soon. The last thing on earth she wanted to do was move from his bed, but Conner had other ideas. "Come on, darlin'," he coaxed, trying to get her to roll over. "I don't think it would be a good idea if they found you here."

Refusing to move, Abby hung on to the pillow that smelled of him. "Leave me alone, Conner."

She felt the bed shift under his weight, then she heard the sound of clothing being pulled on. Fine. He could deal with the kids.

Conner had other plans; he ripped off the comforter, then simply picked her up and set her on her feet. She wavered, squinting at him through bleary eyes. Grinning and looking like a desperado with his dark stubble, he dropped her T-shirt over her head. "Atta girl," he encouraged, the glint in his eyes intensifying. She felt like a rag doll as he stuffed her limp arms through the sleeves, then pulled the garment down. The glint intensified. "As much as I prefer you without this, I think you better have it on."

Abby was still half-asleep and very cranky. "Leave me alone, Conner."

Grinning even more broadly, he gave her a quick kiss. "I can see this is going to take some drastic action." And before she had a clue what he had in mind, he tossed her over one shoulder and headed for the door. Amusement was ripe in his voice. "You'll thank me for this later."

With so much blood suddenly rushing to her head, Abby got dizzy, and all she could do was grasp the waistband of his jeans. As if she were a bag of feed grain, he dumped her on the sofa in the living room, compressing an "oomph" out of her.

Laughter in his eyes, he braced one arm on the back of the sofa and leaned over her, gazing directly into her eyes. "Are you conscious yet?"

She was cold and exhausted, but she wasn't dead. She slid her arms around his neck, trying to pull him down next to her. "I'm cold, Conner."

The laugh lines around his eyes deepened, and he dipped down and gave her a quick hard kiss. "Nice try, Abigail. But I'm not taking the bait this time." He dragged her arms from around his neck and straightened, then pulled the afghan off the back of the sofa. He covered her up, carefully tucking the blanket around her shoulders. His gaze softening, he bent down and gave her another soft, sweet kiss. "Go to sleep."

And that was the last thing Abby remembered. The next thing she was aware of was the sound of children's voices in the kitchen. Feeling as if she had been anesthetized, she forced her eyes open wide, then lifted her wrist to check her watch. Both hands pointed to the twelve. It couldn't be. But then the grandfather clock chimed off the hour and Abby let her arm fall. Lord, she felt like a bag of mush. It took her a moment to scrape up enough energy to stumble to her feet. She hoped a cold shower would bring her around—if she could even make it that far.

It wasn't until she got upstairs that she realized it was raining—not a nice soft drizzle, but one of those steady downpours, as if the whole sky had opened up. She was just coming out of the bathroom, hair pins in her mouth, when Conner's head appeared in the stairwell. He looked good enough to eat.

His expression softened into an intimate half smile when he saw her. "How are you doing?"

Wishing she could touch him but knowing she didn't dare, she reached back and twisted her hair into a knot, then jammed the pins in to anchor it. With that excuse gone, she clamped one hand on the rail and smiled down at him. "Well, I've got my pockets tucked in."

He stared at her a moment; then he shook his head and chuckled, turning to go back down the stairs. "You're a menace." He turned partway down and looked back up at her. "We've been to town to get movies, and the kids are making popcorn. So hustle your butt, woman. Walt is waiting."

Abby rolled her eyes. Just what she needed. An afternoon with Walt Disney.

Actually, it was a nice way to spend a cold, rainy afternoon. A fire in the fireplace, the kids rolled up on the floor in the quilts off their beds. And Conner. But that part was hard. Because more than anything, Abby wanted to curl up beside him, her head on his chest, snuggled up in his warmth. Instead, she had to settle for the other end of the sofa. But he did pull her feet onto his lap, and she nearly dissolved on the spot when he started rubbing them. She had no idea the nerve endings in her feet were connected to so many other parts of her body.

It was midafternoon when Abby woke up for the second time, the afghan once again drawn over her. The kids were still there, watching yet another movie, but Conner was gone.

Pushing back the blanket, Abby sat up, feeling only slightly hungover. It was then that she realized Sarah had also fallen asleep, burrowed under her quilt like a snail.

Abby fixed her hair, then hunched over, stretching the muscles in her back. "Where's your uncle?" she whispered, her voice still thick from sleep.

Cody never took his eyes off the TV. "In his office."

Experiencing a strange quivery feeling, Abby drew her legs up and hooked her arms around them, resting her chin on her knees as she stared into the fire. And for the first time in forty-eight hours, reality checked in, and she thought about what had happened between her and Conner. She had never done anything quite this reckless before, or so out of character. It wasn't like her to jump into something without considering the consequences. It wasn't as if she had any regrets about it—she didn't, not one—but she wasn't really sure where it left her. Or what she was supposed to do about it.

Closing her eyes, she tightened her grip on her wrists and pressed her forehead against her knees. She felt as if she'd been dumped off a bridge, into fast-moving water that was twenty leagues deep. Part of her was so damned uncertain. And the other part of her didn't even want to think about it—it was just too important to start dissecting. But after the past two nights, she couldn't exactly ignore it either. Only the thought of talking to him scared her to death. What could she say without diminishing it? Because she knew it wasn't just casual sex for either one of them. It was real, and it was honest. And it had so many complications tied to it, she couldn't even think about them. But the straightforward, direct person in her could not leave their involvement unacknowledged.

As much as she dreaded it, she was going to have to say something. Screwing up her courage, she got up and headed to Conner's office, her heart in her throat.

His office was down the hall from his bedroom, and had once been an elegant little study. With cherry wood wainscotting and built-in bookshelves, it was a gem of a room, with the alcove windows overlooking the backyard. But with all of Conner's office equipment jammed in, elegance was lost to function.

Conner was standing by the four-drawer filing cabinet when she entered, leafing through some papers he had obviously taken from the top drawer.

He looked up, amusement relaxing his expression and glinting in his eyes. "Ah. The Sleep Queen. You seem to be taking an unusual number of naps lately."

Abby tried to smile, but the nerves beating around in her belly made it almost impossible. Consciously resisting the urge to fold her arms, she stuck her hands in her pockets. Her voice was not quite steady when she spoke. "I think we need to talk about what's happening with us, Conner."

He gave her an inscrutable look, then shoved the file cabinet drawer shut, his expression tightening. He turned so she couldn't see his face, and her stomach dropped. Forgetting her earlier restraint, she tightly folded her arms, a chill running through her. Her voice was very soft and uncertain. "Conner?"

Tossing the papers down on his desk, he turned to face her, resting his hands on his hips. He stared at her a moment, then his expression eased just a little. "I don't want to talk about it, Abby," he said flatly. "I don't want to pick it apart, and I don't want to rehash it." His expression changing again, he reached out and cupped her jaw, running his thumb along her bottom lip. His eyes were dark and shadowed, but she could see the hunger in them. "I'm a realist," he said, his voice gruff. He caressed her mouth again. "And I know that life is going to jump up and bite us in the ass pretty damned soon. So all I want to do is hang on to whatever we have for as long as we've got it."

Abby comprehended probably more than he knew, but once again she sensed that terrible aloneness in him, a kind of self-imposed isolation. And without responding, she closed her eyes and went into his arms. She slid her arms around his waist, and her eyes burned as he caught her up in a fierce hold, his face turned against hers. "That's what I want, too," she whispered. And it was true—she didn't want to jeopardize what time they had together, but she wasn't sure why she was so relieved by his answer. Because she didn't want to dig around in it either. And she wasn't sure why. *Maybe,* whispered a little voice in her head, *you're afraid.* And maybe it was because she might discover something she did not want to know. Or have to face.

Chapter 8

It was as though that conversation in the study set the tone for the rest of July and the first part of August. As if by some unspoken pact, they'd agreed to put time on hold. And Abby refused to think about where she was going to be or what she was going to be doing come September. It made her insides go cold whenever she did. Her time with Conner was simply too precious to waste.

And every day was like a whole new beginning. Stolen kisses. Secret touches. And the nights—ah, God, the nights were unbelievable. It didn't matter if they made love or not—it was how he held her that was so incredible. There wasn't a night that went by that she didn't go to sleep in his arms, or a morning when she didn't wake up snuggled in the curve of his body. She loved it. And she especially loved the way he touched her. Quiet, unobtrusive touches, like placing his hand in the small of her back. Bold touches when no one was looking. Or subtle touches, like the way he'd grasp the back of her neck whenever he walked by.

Scott had never been a toucher, and neither had her parents, and Abby had never realized until now how much that casual kind of contact meant to her. She reveled in it. But there was more to it than that. He also made her feel so wanted, so special. Every morning, before he left for the day, he'd find a way to get her alone. And every morning, Abby would stand at the door and watch him disappear, already missing him, feeling as if some of the joy had drained out of her day.

But even without Conner, her summer was fantastic. She loved working in the garden, and she loved spending time with Mary, and she thrived on her visits with Kate McCall. She loved her long meanders along the creek, and her rides with Conner when they got the chance. It had been years since she felt so rested and content, or as energized as she did at Cripple Creek. This summer had given her a whole new perspective on life.

Thinking about her personal rejuvenation, Abby knelt in the corner of the courtyard garden, swatting away a mosquito, then used the trowel to dig out a clump of couch grass. She wondered how many hours she'd spent out here, puttering and weeding, or out in the vegetable garden. She'd never had time to really garden before, and she found it suited her, suited her nature—suited her need for both beauty and order. But mostly she loved the feeling of accomplishment and satisfaction she got out of it.

The portable phone, which she'd left on the veranda, rang. Pulling up another clump of couch grass as she rose, Abby got up, brushed the dirt off her knees, then picked her way through the garden until she got to the flag walk.

The caller was on the third ring when Abby reached the veranda. Pulling off one garden glove, she hit the connect button with her thumb, then lifted the instrument to her ear.

A familiar voice greeted her. "Hi, Abby. It's Joanne." Abby's expression brightened. Joanne had been a client of hers for years, and a solid friendship had developed, a friendship that Abby had heavily relied on at times. They chatted for a few moments; then Joanne explained the reason for her call.

"I've just landed a six-month contract in Chicago, and I'll be leaving the first week in September. The contract isn't really long enough for a lease agreement and, to be honest, I'd really rather not have a bunch of strangers knocking holes in my walls. But I don't want it standing empty either. So I wondered if you and the kids would like to house-sit while I'm gone. The only expense would be the utilities."

A chill radiated through Abby, and she sat down abruptly, her insides balling up into a hard, cold knot. Joanne's house. Close to the kids' school, handy to downtown. The kids loved Joanne's big old house— with its indoor pool, huge yard and a fantastic park just across the street. It was a phenomenal offer. And it was an offer she would have jumped at eight weeks ago. Now it made her feel sick.

"Are you there, Abby?"

Feeling as if her insides had just been excavated, Abby pulled off her other garden glove, then rested her forearm across her thighs. Her chest hurt and she was cold to the bone. Forcing aside the surge of panic, she rubbed a sudden tight spot in her temple. "Wow," she said, trying to dredge up some enthusiasm. "You've kind of knocked the wind out of me. That's a pretty generous offer."

She could hear the smile in her friend's voice. "Hey. Your solid advice really helped me over the years. I figure I owe you."

Abby tried to put a return smile in her voice when she rebuked her friend. "As I recall, you paid rather handsomely for my advice, Joanne."

There was a short pause, then Joanne spoke again. "The truth is, you're about the only person I'd want in there, Abby. You'd be doing me a favor."

Abby closed her eyes and massaged her head, the knot in her stomach getting worse. It was more than a generous offer. And she knew Joanne well enough to realize she never would have made the offer unless it suited her. The last thing Joanne would want was this to be seen as a gesture of charity. And for Abby, it was a golden opportunity. Six months would give her a chance to get settled in a job and find a place to live. She should have been thrilled. She felt like throwing up. Taking a deep breath to quell the sick feeling, she managed to fake enthusiasm—although her gratitude was genuine. Drawing another deep breath, she stepped off into thin air. "I would love to house-sit for you. When would you want us there?"

From that point on, it was all Abby could do to hold up her end of the conversation. But she did. After she got off the phone, she braced her elbows on her knees and covered her eyes. Two weeks. If she was to get back to Toronto before Joanne headed off, all she had left here was two weeks. God, where had the summer gone?

Dropping her hands, she stared numbly into space, another rush of panic stirring in her middle. This had come too soon—and she wasn't ready for it. She needed more time.

Her insides churning, Abby clenched her jaw, the panic climbing higher. All her life she had been the ultimate realist. Even before she'd left Toronto in the spring, she'd known what the reality was. And the reality was that she would come for the summer, go back in the fall. There had never been any question about her going back. The best paying jobs for a management consultant were in Toronto, she had contacts there, the kids' friends and school were there, her life was there. That was her reality. Cripple Creek was a respite, that was all. And now the new reality was that her days here at Cripple Creek were rapidly running out. Swallowing hard, she closed her eyes. God, she felt as if someone had just yanked the rug out from under her.

Suddenly unable to sit, she got up and headed for the gate, then stopped and paced the narrow flag walk, the agitation splintering into a dozen different reactions. Grateful. She was grateful that Joanne would make such a generous offer. And she was terrified— the thought of going back scared her to death. And she was angry. So angry. Angry at Conner, angry over his inaction, over his refusal to talk.

But that made no sense. How could she be angry at him for that? She had done the same damned thing—avoided any kind of confrontation. It wasn't as though she had even one single doubt about how he felt about her—she never doubted that—but it was an impossible situation. She knew that. It was too damned complicated, too entangled with too many people. Even without the kids it was bad enough, but with them in the equation—the truth of their conception—it was beyond anything she'd ever even considered. But she wished—God, she didn't even know what she wished. If wishes were horses...

Dragging her hair back from her face, Abby stopped, forcing herself to stand still, dread beating in her chest. Okay. Her time as a happy ostrich was over. And she had to face some cold, hard facts. Summer was nearly over. Her time had run out. And that shouldn't come as a big surprise. She had planned all along to go back.

And now she had to take the first step down that road.

Cold to the core, she turned toward the house. The longer she put it off, the worse it would be. With dread climbing up her throat, she climbed the steps and entered the house. She was grateful that Conner was gone for the day. Facing the kids was going to be bad enough. Facing him was going to be ten times worse. And she needed time to get her head on straight before she told him the news. It made her insides curl up just thinking about it.

She found the kids playing in the dirt behind the garage. Cody was building roads and Sarah was diligently making mud pies, decorating them with caragana pods.

Expelling the air out of her lungs to try and clear away the sick flutter, Abby folded her arms and rested her shoulder against the corner of the building, trying to manufacture an offhand demeanor. She watched them for a moment, then tightened her arms. Willing down the queasy feeling, she spoke, trying to make her tone upbeat. "Guess what, guys. We just got some good news."

Sarah looked up at her, mud smeared down one side of her face, a bright, scheming look in her eyes. "Guess what. I know how baby calves get made."

Cody gave his sister a disgusted look. "No, you don't."

Sarah puffed up, giving him an indignant look back. "Yes, I do so."

Feeling as if she'd just been flung off a Ferris wheel, Abby stared at her two children, totally discombobulated. Where in heck had all this come from?

As if reading the stunned look on her mother's face, Miss Sarah enlightened her. "Jake told me. When that eye man came. He told me how some of the momma cows need help making babies, so the eye guy comes and sema—semalates them." She gave her brother a superior look. "Jake told me. So I know."

Cody rolled his eyes. "You don't know anything. It's not the eye guy, it's the *AI* guy, and it's not se-malate, it's *inseminate*." He gave his mom an embarrassed look. "She just thinks she knows, Mom. Jake just told her a little bit about that artificial insemination stuff." Clearly pleased with himself for mastering more ranch lingo with the "artificial insemination" line, he gave her a sheepish little shrug. "He didn't tell her *everything* because she's a girl." His eyes brightened. "But the AI guy explained it all to me."

Totally distracted from her mission, Abby bent her head and pinched the bridge of her nose. God help her, she wanted to laugh. The things her kids were going to have for show and tell.

Finally able to keep her expression straight, she raised her head. "I see."

As if needing to distract his mother from the racier side of life, Cody redirected her. "You said guess what."

The dread came back with a vicious rush, knocking that bubble of humor right out of her, and Abby's stomach dropped away to nothing. Her hands suddenly clammy, she braced herself with a deep breath. "I just got a call from Joanne," she said, trying to inject some enthusiasm into her voice. "And she's going to be working in Chicago this winter, so she wants us to come live in her house."

Both kids stopped what they were doing and looked at her as if she had live snakes crawling out of her mouth.

Her stomach in knots, she hung on to her happy face. "Won't that be great? You'll be able to have a swim whenever you want, and we can go to the park every day."

Clearly upset, Sarah threw her mud pie on the ground and got up, giving her mother a hateful look. "You can go live at Joanne's house by your own self," she stormed, starting to cry. "But I'm staying here with Uncle Conner." Her chin in the air, she ran past her mother, jerked her arm back so Abby couldn't catch her. "I hate Joanne, and I hate her house. And I hate the park."

Giving his mother a look of contempt, Cody got up and followed his sister, his face white and rigid. He wouldn't even speak to her.

Abby leaned back against the garage and closed her eyes, a renewed sick feeling churning up in her. She had expected as much. They were going to hate her for this. And she couldn't really blame them. She'd let them get too settled in. She should have kept reminding them that this was not forever, that it was only a summer vacation.

Forcing herself to straighten, she stared across the open space, a terrible ache enveloping her chest. She wasn't sure how she was going to dig herself out of this one.

Gathering her resources, she heaved a sigh and pushed away from the garage. She was going to have to try and explain it to them, to get them to see reason. It would just get worse if she left it.

She found them both in Cody's room, sitting side by side on the edge of the bed. Sarah was sobbing and Cody had his arm around his sister, a belligerent look on his face. He looked so much like Conner— so much—and Abby's throat closed up even more.

Needing a couple of seconds to get herself together, she picked up a pair of dirty socks off the floor and tossed them on the chair. Trying to keep her expression even, she went over to the bed and crouched down in front of her kids. She fingered the rolled corner of the bandage on Sarah's knee, then she looked up at them, her face somber. "I know you don't want to go back to Toronto," she said, her voice quiet. "But we only came for the summer, guys. You knew that." She touched the bandage again, trying to figure out what the best way was to say it. Feeling pretty darned miserable herself, she looked back up at them. "I've got to get a job. We can't live off of Uncle Conner forever, and you have to start school pretty soon. And all your friends are there."

Cody gave her a disgusted look. "Not all our

friends. We've got friends here. The McCalls are our friends.''

Abby managed a wan smile. "I know you do, Cody. But you have to understand my position. I've got to get a job so I can support you guys. That isn't Uncle Conner's responsibility. That's my responsibility.''

Cody held her gaze a moment, then looked down and started picking at a scab on his knee. Her heart aching for her child, Abby caught him under the chin and forced him to look at her, her touch gentle. "I'm not trying to be mean here, Cody. You knew it was just for the summer, didn't you?"

Pulling his arm away from his sister, he trapped his hands between his legs, his expression downcast. He gave a halfhearted shrug, refusing to look at her. "Yeah," he whispered.

Her face wet with tears, Sarah snuggled closer to her brother. "But what about the ponies? And the kittens?" she sobbed, her expression stricken. "And Uncle Conner? He will be all by hisself.''

Her throat closing up on her, Abby reached over and gently smoothed down her daughter's hair, a fierce pain in her chest. Easing in a breath to try to release the painful cramp, she tried to smile. "I promise you can come back for other visits, sweetheart. And maybe Uncle Conner will come and spend Christmas with us." Abby wiped her daughter's face with the heel of her hand, holding on to her smile. "You'd like that, wouldn't you?"

Looking absolutely heartbroken, Sarah nodded, more tears spilling over. "But he's still going to be all by hisself, Mommy," she whispered through her tears. "And that makes me really sad.''

Hit with a terrible surge of unhappiness, Abby abruptly stood up and left the room, her vision blurring. Oh, Lord. This was going to be so hard. So very hard.

She went into her room and closed the door, clamping her hand over her mouth. She didn't know what she was going to do. She really didn't.

It took Abby a couple of hours to get it together. She was so emotionally exhausted, she couldn't have squeezed out another tear if she wanted to. She had a long, cold shower that got rid of most of the puffiness around her eyes and almost cleared her head. Feeling almost numb, she put on clean clothes and slapped on some makeup to cover the remaining ravages. Halfway fortified, she went down the hall to Cody's room. Sarah had obviously cried herself to sleep, and now Cody's quilt was pulled up over her. Cody was lying on the floor, a comic book spread before him. Twisting her hair up on top of her head, Abby secured it with a clip, then spoke, her voice very soft. "Are you okay, Chucker?"

He looked up at her and gave a discomfited little shrug. "I guess."

Abby stuck her hands in her back pockets. "I know how you feel, Cody," she said, her voice still very quiet. "I'm not ready to go home either."

He responded with a lift of his shoulder. "I know."

Knowing that sometimes a little was enough with Cody, she indicated Sarah. "Thanks for taking care of her for me."

Avoiding looking at her, he turned the page of his comic. "You're welcome."

Her expression somber, Abby studied her son a

moment, then turned and left the room. Times like this he was so much his father's child.

Feeling as if there wasn't a shred of lightness left in her, Abby went downstairs, the house oddly muted in the summer heat. She had pulled down all the shades early that morning to keep the cool air in and the heat out, and the still, false dusk suited her mood.

She entered the kitchen and went to the fridge, taking out a flat of eggs and a container of boiled potatoes. Unhooking one of the pots hanging over the huge range, she set the eggs in it, then filled it with water, placed it on the stove and turned on the burner. Taking a stainless steel bowl from the baker's rack, she picked up a paring knife and began slicing potatoes for potato salad.

She should be happy, grateful, relieved. Instead she felt miserable, depressed, totally emptied out. She had needed a reality check, and Joanne's phone call had certainly been that. And now she was trapped by someone else's agenda. She couldn't avoid reality any longer. She'd taken the easy way out, and now she was cornered. And it scared her to death.

Then there was Conner. She knew exactly how it would play out when she told him—his expression would close down and he would pull back into himself. And that would be that.

She experienced a rush of hurt, and she closed her eyes, making herself take a deep, even breath. What in hell did she expect him to do? That was who he was, and it was how he lived his life. And she had gone along with it. Mostly because she was a coward. She wasn't even sure what she did expect him to do— ride to the rescue this time as well? Even after they got involved, she'd known it would never go beyond the summer.

Feeling completely drained, she tucked a loose wisp of hair behind her ear, then went back to slicing potatoes. Maybe it wasn't as bad as she thought. Just because it was the end of the summer, it didn't necessarily mean her relationship with him was over. There was Christmas and next summer. Her stomach balled up when she thought about telling him. And as much as she dreaded it, she knew she was going to have to do it before the kids got to him.

A rap on the screen door made her jump, and Abby expelled a long breath, then called out. "Come on in."

She heard the sound of someone wiping their feet on the hemp mat, then Henny appeared in the doorway, her gardening hat resting on her back, a pail in her hand. The wrinkles on her face creased as she gave Abby a wide smile. "That leaf lettuce in the south corner needed a thinning, so I figured you could use some." She set the pail in one of the sinks. "And there's some radishes and green onions in there, and a few baby carrots—enough for a meal."

Abby wiped her hands on a towel and went over to check out the produce. "Thank you, Henny. I was going to go myself after I got the potato salad made."

Henny took her gardening gloves out of the pail and laid them on the counter. "Fixed a bucketful of salad myself this morning. Figured the boys might like a cold supper. It's such a scorcher out there, I'm calling it quits. I've had enough for today."

Almost glad for the distraction, Abby took the bunch of carrots out of the pail and set them in the other sink. "What's everybody up to?"

"Well, the AI fellow was here this morning—he and Jake took care of those cows Conner wanted done. Some of the lads are moving bulls, and some are baling hay, and I think Conner is off fixing fence over by the river—Jake said they found some fence down there yesterday." Henny got a sly gleam in her eye. "Expect he'd appreciate a thermos of cold lemonade right about now."

In spite of how rotten she was feeling, Abby almost smiled at Henny's conniving. The older woman had handed her an opportunity to talk to Conner alone, and she knew Henny would keep an eye on the kids. But just the thought of telling Conner they would be leaving made her feel sick again. She also knew the longer she put it off, the harder it would be.

Keeping her expression neutral, she lifted out the bunch of fat red radishes. "He probably would." Her insides suddenly doing flip-flops, she avoided looking at the other woman as she began cutting off the tops. "I'll get this salad out of the way, then I'll run him down some lunch."

Henny took the paring knife out of her hand and wedged her way in front of the sink. "Well, now. Why don't you just scoot and let me do this? And I'll keep an eye on the tadpoles—it's too hot out there for them to go crashing around outside. Don't want them getting heatstroke."

Relinquishing her spot at the sink, Abby dried her hands, the flutter rising higher. She did not want to do this. She definitely did not.

The road to the river was unused and overgrown, years of neglect turning it into a narrow trail. Grass grew between the tracks and saskatoon and chokecherry bushes crowded in on either side, with barbed wire fences marking the boundaries. Abby skirted one very large pothole, the SUV rocking on the rough track, the branches of the wild berry bushes scraping against the side of the vehicle. In spite of the heat, she drove with the window down, her elbow resting on the frame, her sunglasses breaking the glare.

She loved this part of the ranch—loved the vastness, the spectacular vistas, the untouched beauty of it. With the exception of fence lines, this area was just as it had been a hundred years before, and she was always overwhelmed by it.

There was a gap along the west fence at the top of the hill, and Abby stopped, shielding her eyes as she stared out at the view. It was breathtaking, this country. The mountains, the forested eastern slope, the spiny backs of the foothills, the distinctive green of the aspens. There was no place like it in the entire world. And there was a sense of unfettered freedom here that she'd never experienced anywhere else. Shifting her gaze, she followed the lazy descending circles of a hawk, the wind whipping loose hair across her face. It was as if all this space allowed her to take a full breath, to expand her lungs to their total capacity, to shed all her constraints.

Conner had never talked about it, at least not to her, but she understood his commitment to the legacy of Cripple Creek. She understood how deep his roots went. And she wondered if he hoped that his son and daughter would carry on that legacy.

That thought gave her a funny start in her middle, and she gripped the wheel. How *did* Conner feel about that? She didn't have a clue. And what did he foresee for his kids? And for the two of them? What if she had it all wrong? What if he wasn't concerned about all the complications? What if he was prepared to say to hell with convention? What would she do if he asked her to stay? Was she prepared to jump in?

Abby got such a buzz from the last question that it made her insides go perfectly still. A funny lightness started to unfold in her, and she straightened right up. She had been wrong about him before. Maybe she was wrong about him again.

Feeling as if a hundred pounds had been lifted from her shoulders, she put the vehicle in gear and started down the final slope to the river. Maybe she was in for a big surprise.

She turned onto the narrow approach to the gate and found it standing open. Even though she didn't know exactly where he was working, he wouldn't be that hard to find. All she had to do was follow the truck tracks in the flattened grass.

The tracks led her right to him. The truck was backed into a clearing, the tailgate down, giving easy access to the tools and fencing supplies in the back. Conner was working on a stretch of fence that ran through a stand of aspen and skirted a rocky outcropping. He had his Stetson on, his shirt off, his hands covered in heavy leather gloves, and the sweat glistened on his deeply tanned back. He turned as she pulled into the small clearing, and he straightened when he saw who it was. He finished the splice, then stuffed the vise grips in his back pocket and started walking toward her. Abby watched him, a familiar warmth starting in her middle. He was a marvel to watch. Big, bronzed—and nearly naked. It made her mouth go dry just looking at him. Realizing where her thoughts were taking her, Abby turned and lifted a small cooler out of the back of the vehicle and set it on the running board. Then shading her eyes, she watched him approach. He looked hot and tired and just a little cranky. But he managed a warped smile as he pulled off his gloves and tossed them on the hood of her vehicle. "Your life isn't worth a plug nickel if there isn't a cold beer in that cooler."

She considered tormenting him, but decided it was not smart to bait a hot, tired, cranky man who'd been working in this heat all day. "I'm not completely stupid, Calhoun," she responded. "Of course there's a cold beer in there. Although," she added, letting him know he'd gotten off easy, "Henny suggested I bring lemonade."

He flipped open the cooler lid, pulled out a can of beer and popped the top, then tipped his head back and downed the entire can. Wiping his mouth with the back of his hand, he looked at her, a glint of humor in his eyes. "If you'd brought lemonade, I would have drowned you in it."

Abby gave him a cheeky smile. "Then aren't I lucky I'm such a clever girl?"

He grinned for real, grabbed her by the back of the neck and gave her a hard kiss. She felt the heat radiating from his body, and she could taste sweat and beer on his mouth. He released her, and gave her another rueful grin. "What else you got in that cooler?"

She made a face at him and dug out a plastic bag with a wet, chilled towel in it, then handed it to him. "This is the airline thing in reverse." Conner shot her a startled look, his eyes lighting up with appreciation when he felt how cold it was. He began wiping his face, arms and chest with it. Abby dropped the empty bag back in the cooler and closed the lid.

"And I brought you some fresh buns and cold chicken."

Draping the wet towel around his neck, Conner picked up the cooler and started back the way he'd come. "I've had enough heat for a while. There's some shade over here." He headed over to the rocky outcropping, found a flat ledge heavily shaded by a stand of spruce. He sat down, leaving room for Abby beside him. Then he opened the lid and reached for the containers inside.

Abby sat down next to him, hooking her heels on a ledge. They were on the side of a hill, and she could see right down to the river. She loved this high country—there were spectacular views everywhere, and she liked the feeling of being able to survey it all. Shortening her sight line, she noticed the bluebells—well, actually harebells—bobbing in the natural grasses. The color fascinated her; they were the exact same shade of blue as Conner's eyes. She tucked some loose hair behind her ear, then folded her arms across her knees, soaking up the sense of space that surrounded her. "This is so beautiful, Conner," she said, her voice soft. "It's just phenomenal." Remembering why she was there, she almost flinched, a burst of dread spiraling up inside her. She did not want to do this.

They sat in silence as Conner ate the lunch she'd brought him, the breeze ruffling through the aspen leaves and sighing through the spruce boughs. It would have been perfect if Abby hadn't been so tied up in knots. But maybe she was making mountains out of mole hills. Maybe he would surprise her and be willing to talk about Joanne's offer. Another shot of dread flooded her system. And maybe not.

She heard him crumple another beer can; then he closed the lid on the cooler. He leaned forward and rested his arms on his knees, staring off across the valley. Finally he spoke, his tone quiet. "You got something on your mind?"

Her insides rolling, Abby picked up a small pebble from the ledge and tossed it into the grass. Her stomach balled up when she forced herself to speak. "I got a phone call from Joanne today." She paused, then took a fortifying breath and forged on. "She's got a six-month contract in Chicago, and she's offering us her house for the duration."

There was a very tense stillness; then he spoke, an edge in his voice. "When?"

Abby couldn't look at him. "She's leaving after the Labor Day weekend. And she'd like us there before she goes."

He didn't move a muscle, and Abby held her breath. It was almost as if he hadn't heard her. Then he abruptly got up, snatched the cooler and headed toward the SUV, his long strides leaving a trail in the grass. Any hope she might have had that his reaction would be different evaporated like smoke. Her heart climbing up her throat, Abby scrambled off the rock slab and went after him, a lump of dread settling in her belly.

He had the towel and cooler in her vehicle by the time she caught up to him. His expression completely shut down, he turned away from her and yanked on his heavy gloves, deliberately avoiding her gaze. "You'd better head back. I've got another stretch of fence to fix."

The muscles in his jaw flexed, and he stalked off in the direction of his truck. At a loss how to deal with this, Abby stared after him, the dread spreading through her whole body. Knowing she couldn't leave matters like that, she started toward the truck. But Conner tossed the posthole auger that had been lying on the ground into the back, slammed the tailgate shut, then climbed in the cab. And without so much as a glance in her direction, he started the vehicle and headed down the hill. With the wind dragging her hair across her face, Abby watched him go, stunned by his anger. On one level, she had been prepared, but she had never expected that kind of rebuff. Never. Not from him. She had never felt so abandoned, so cold and alone in her entire life.

Conner never came home that night. Abby waited up for him until well after midnight. She kept hoping against hope that he would show up, but deep down she knew he wouldn't. But she waited anyway, her insides in knots. The only place she could hold the panic at bay was in his room, a pillow from his bed clutched against her, the scent of him providing a kind of barrier. She tried to dredge up some anger of her own, but she couldn't even manage that. She understood Conner Calhoun better than anyone might have guessed, and it nearly killed her, knowing he had simply gone to ground. But there wasn't a whole lot she could do about it—not when he kept so many things off-limits. Those non-topics were such a formidable barrier. And she couldn't see a route through that minefield. So she sat on the edge of his bed, hugging his pillow, emptiness upon emptiness piling in on her.

It was just before five in the morning when she heard the back door open, and she dropped the pillow and got up, her heart leaping in her chest. Trying to still the nervous clamor inside her, she went into the kitchen, uncertainty gripping her. He was in the mud-room, one foot wedged in a bootjack to pull off his boot. He looked awful—haggard, unshaven, his eyes red-rimmed. His hand braced against the wall, he glanced up when he heard her, his face set in grim lines. Not quite knowing what to say or do, Abby folded her arms, her uncertainty doubling. She spoke, her voice unsteady. "I was worried about you."

He pulled off the other boot, then bent over and set the pair on the boot rack, the muscles in his jaw hard. Finally he straightened and looked at her, his eyes flat and his expression completely closed down. "You had no need to worry."

He hung his jean jacket on the hook, then stuffed his gloves in the pocket, his profile like stone.

Realizing he wasn't going to say anything else, she took a step onto shaky ground. There was a catch in her voice when she spoke. "Please talk to me, Con-ner."

He cast her an inscrutable glance, then tossed some fencing staples on the shelf. "There's nothing to talk about," he answered, his tone as flat as his eyes. "We both knew this day was coming. And we knew all along where we were headed."

Avoiding even the slightest contact with her, he slipped past her into the kitchen, and Abby leaned against the door frame and closed her eyes, a terrible ache swelling up inside her. It was as if he'd just slammed a door in her face. And it was the first time since he'd come into her life that Abby felt as if he'd totally shut her out. And it was a devastating feeling.

She heard his bedroom door close, then a few sec-onds later, the shower, and she clenched her jaw, the ache intensifying.

Unable to bring herself to go upstairs to her empty bed, Abby went into the living room and wrapped herself up in the afghan, then curled up on one of the sofas, a hollowness around her heart. She watched the sky lighten and the shadows fade, and she faced another reality she had been skirting for a long, long time. She had always cared about Conner. Always. But somewhere along the line she had fallen in love with him.

Only what she felt for Conner was so very different from what she'd felt for Scotty—so very different. She had fallen in love with the bright, talented boy in Scotty. With Conner, she had fallen in love with the man. Admitting that to herself made her tremble with an odd kind of alarm. And the reason for that alarm was that she didn't know when it had happened. She couldn't look back at one definitive moment. It was as if it had been there all along—like some great dormant creature, suppressed by her commitment to his brother—and all it had taken was something as insignificant as his placing his hand in the small of her back to bring it to life.

The chill of morning crawled inside her, and Abby drew the afghan tighter. She was so accustomed to having him in her life, she wasn't sure how she would manage if his withdrawal was permanent. And she was terrified that it was. Feeling completely depleted, she closed her eyes and huddled deeper into the blanket. An entire night without sleep—she wasn't sure how she was going to make it through the rest of the day.

She didn't even want to think about the rest of her life.

Chapter 9

It was a crash in the kitchen that woke Abby up, but it was the sound of her son's loud admonishment to his sister that had her up and moving before she was totally awake. She just knew from his tone there had been another disaster.

A male voice gave a quiet command to her son, and Abby's stomach took a nosedive. Conner was in the kitchen. The thought of facing him made her insides drop, and for an instant, she considered walking out the front door. But she couldn't walk out on her parental responsibilities. She rounded the corner and hauled up short. Conner had a barefoot, pajama-clad Sarah hooked up in one arm. Sarah had her hands clamped across her mouth, her eyes alight with glee, obviously delighted to be suspended in midair. Conner was scraping together pieces of a broken cereal bowl with the side of his boot. And there was splattered milk and cereal everywhere.

Slightly dizzy from getting up so fast, Abby steadied herself on the door frame. Cody appeared from the mudroom with a dustpan and broom, his expression going wide-eyed when he saw his mother. He was quick off the mark to declare his innocence. "It wasn't me, Mom. It was Sarah. She was swinging that stupid rabbit around and she knocked my bowl of cereal off the table."

Conner glanced up, his expression going very still when he saw her. Abby avoided his gaze. Instead she fixed her daughter with an exasperated glare. "Sarah?"

Sarah, who was still hanging like a rag doll in the hook of Conner's arm, flashed her mother a pleased grin. "Uncle Conner swooped me up so fast, my jammies just about came off."

Abby's head was still so filled with thick, gray fog, she just couldn't quite get her brain around that, and she raked her hair back with her hand. The corner of Conner's mouth lifted and there was a tiny glimmer of amusement in his eyes. He pulled up the back of Sarah's sagging "jammies" as he set her on the table. "I swooped you up so you wouldn't cut your feet." He tapped the end of her nose in unspoken reprimand. "You weren't watching where you were going, little one."

She climbed into his arms. "I liked it."

The glint intensifying, he lifted her up and turned her toward Abby. He avoided Abby's gaze, and his tone had an odd, rough quality to it when he spoke again. "Yeah. But you woke your mom up, and I thought we agreed we wouldn't do that."

There was something in his tone that made Abby's chest fill up, and she swallowed hard as he passed her daughter to her. The awful lump was still lodged in her throat when she spoke. "Just leave it, Cody. I'll clean it up."

Conner was so close that the heat from his body engulfed her, and it was all she could do not to grab onto him. She expected him to move away, but he didn't. Instead she felt a light touch against her shoulder, and she swallowed again, that one single touch nearly undoing her. Not knowing what to expect, she looked up at him, her stomach lurching when she saw the dark, somber expression in his eyes. He held her gaze for a long, electric moment, then he drew a deep breath and stepped away. His voice was very gruff when he spoke. "We'll take care of this," he said, crouching down to pick up the pieces of broken crockery. "You'd better check her feet just in case."

Hit with such a heavy rush of emotion, Abby tightened her hold on her daughter and headed for the door, her vision blurring. The fact that he'd touched her filled her with such relief, but it also broke her heart. And she wasn't sure how either one of them was going to get through this. Because she knew he was hurting just as much as she was.

That incident in the kitchen seemed to alter things. Granted, he never got that close again, but he stuck around—and she had the sensation he was watching to make sure she was okay. That should have made her feel better, but in some ways it made her feel worse. Because it became even more evident that there was this huge stretch of no-man's-land between them, a space he refused to cross. And Abby had no idea she could feel so awful, so empty, so damned sad. She hadn't known this degree of unhappiness even existed—the kind that knotted her up inside and made her heart ache. And there were moments of such unmitigated sorrow that she had to go upstairs and shut herself in her room, unable to hold those feelings at bay.

By midafternoon, Abby was so wrung out she was totally numb. Knowing she had to keep busy or all those feelings would ambush her again, she stripped the kids' beds and hauled everything down to the laundry room. She stuffed the sheets in the washer and altered the setting, recognizing the fact that she had to snap out of this. If they were leaving in two weeks, she had to get their stuff organized. She shut the lid and started the machine, a shout from outside drawing her attention.

She went to the window, her chest getting tight when she saw that Conner was with the kids, and Sarah was hanging off him. Folding her arms, she stood staring out, her throat closing up and an awful ache climbing up her chest. She wondered what it was going to be like for him when they were gone—when the children he'd sired were no longer there. It was going to leave a huge hole in his life. And she knew that he would miss them as much as they would miss him.

Recalling her first encounter with all the things he had kept hidden, Abby abruptly turned from the window, a funny feeling rising up in her chest. She didn't understand why, but she suddenly had to know.

Her whole body on edge, she headed for Conner's room, her heart pounding, her hands cold. She was crossing a line—she knew she was crossing a line—and what she was doing was wrong, wrong, wrong, but she just had to know.

The blinds were pulled and the room was dark, and

Abby's nerves clenched up as she entered. It had only been two days since she'd last been in his room, but it seemed longer—much longer—and for some reason, the familiarity seemed almost foreign. Knowing she had no business being in there, Abby swallowed hard, the flutter in her chest getting worse. She hesitated. Then bracing herself, she crossed the room and opened the third drawer of his highboy. Her stomach dropped. The pictures were no longer there.

Overcome with another wave of sorrow, she slipped out the door onto the veranda, fleeing to the solace of the courtyard. Folding in on herself, Abby huddled on the top step of the veranda, the pain so intense it tore her apart inside. She didn't know why the absence of the pictures hurt her so much, but it did. It was as if by removing the pictures, he had put her out of his life. And she didn't know what she would do if he pulled away completely—she just didn't know how she could handle that. Leaving him was bad enough. Losing him altogether would be unbearable.

So wrapped up in her own misery, Abby was oblivious to everything around her, and it wasn't until Conner sat down beside her that she was even aware that he was there. Grasping the side of her face, he pulled her head against him. "Don't, Abby," he whispered, his voice rough and uneven. "Don't."

Turning into his embrace, Abby pressed her face against his neck, unable to check the overwhelming unhappiness gripping her. It was as if a dam had broken and she no longer had any control over the awful feelings pouring out of her. She couldn't stand it if he withdrew permanently from her—she just couldn't.

Stroking her arm, he pressed her head tighter against him, his arm around her back. He never said anything, and there was a remoteness to him, but he continued to hold her.

It was a long time before Abby was emptied out enough to regain some control, and it was even longer before she was finally able to let the last of it go in a rough, shuddering sigh. She felt so raw inside, it was as if she had been stripped. Wiping her face with the back of her hand, she drew a deep, unsteady breath, then let her head rest on his shoulder. Closing her eyes, she huddled in the warmth of his body, the terrible hollow feeling persisting in her chest. He might be close physically, but he had never been so far away emotionally. And she was sure if she made one wrong move, he would be gone. Conner Calhoun knew a whole lot about erecting barriers.

Feeling totally wrung out, Abby tried to absorb some of his physical warmth, wishing she could just climb inside him and stay there for the rest of her life. But other than his hand on her arm, she got no response from him. Twisted around in an uncomfortable position, Abby reluctantly straightened. Without saying anything, Conner withdrew his arm and pulled a paper napkin out of his shirt pocket, then handed it to her.

Abby wiped her nose, then wadded up the napkin and looked at him. His profile was like stone and there were white lines around his mouth she had never seen before. Even without those tight lines, he would have been formidable. Not stopping to consider the whys and wherefores, she spoke, her voice unsteady. "Come to Toronto with us."

There was an instant—a split second—where time

seemed frozen. Then he abruptly turned and got up. His body rigid, he crossed the veranda and entered the house, flipping the screen shut behind him. Too depleted to react, Abby folded her arms on her knees and rested her forehead on them, a numbness spreading through her. So that was it. Without saying a word he had given her his answer. It was over. And there was no going back.

Abby went out of her way to avoid him after that. It was just too damned hard otherwise. But she found out that hope was an impossible feeling to extinguish, and every time she heard him or was around him, she would experience that frantic flutter of hope—that he would retract that awful wall of silence. But then it would happen all over again, that awful sick rush, when she had to realize he was never going to give. It got so she couldn't eat and what little sleep she got was fractured with senseless ''what might have beens'' and ''what ifs.'' And she got so she dreaded going to bed. God, she had never felt so alone in her entire life.

It was four days after the incident on the veranda that she got a second call. This one was from the head-hunting firm in Toronto. A clothing manufacturer was recruiting a manager for their human resources department. They were very impressed with Abby's CV and wanted to set up an interview with her. The employment agent told her it looked like a perfect match, and the pay scale was outstanding.

A heavy sensation sitting on her chest, Abby stood in the kitchen, the phone pressed to her ear, listening to the agent rattle on. The company was so anxious to interview her that they were prepared to fly her and the kids back to Toronto. And they would even make the flight arrangements. Abby listened, her insides shriveling up. Somehow a potential job offer made her departure more definite, more real, and she leaned back against the cupboard, her throat growing tighter by the second.

Without even a glimmer of enthusiasm and close to tears, she made the move that would end it all. She agreed to an interview date, a date that meant they would have to leave for Toronto in four days.

Abby hung up the phone, then went to stand before the kitchen window. Folding her arms against the awful cold feeling, she stared out, her expression stark. Four days. It would all be over in four days. She should be relieved. Because she knew she couldn't go on like this—living with the unbearable tension. But she wasn't sure she could go on living without him, either. That would be worse than anything she had ever endured.

Knowing she was going to sink into a painful space if she stayed locked in her thoughts, Abby swallowed hard and turned toward the door. As much as she dreaded it, she had to tell the kids, and she had to tell Conner.

She found Conner in the barn. He had one of the Cripple Creek three-year-old colts cross-tied in the shed row, and he was grooming him out. Abby knew this was the horse he was sending to Chase McCall for training, and she guessed that Conner was getting him ready to go. A radio was playing, the sound overlaid by the twitter of sparrows in the rafters.

Realizing he hadn't heard her approach, Abby paused, the heat of the sunshine doing little to dispel the chill in her. Wishing there was an easier way to do this, she rubbed her arm, trying to warm her skin, her chest tight with dread. Finally scraping together a modicum of courage, she entered the barn, her heart suddenly far too big for her chest.

Clearing her throat, she spoke, her voice uneven. "Conner?"

He turned and looked at her. He had on a blue plaid shirt and faded blue jeans, his dusty straw Stetson pulled low over his eyes. His face gave nothing away. Resting the brush on the horse's rump, he stared at her.

Feeling as if she was unable to get a full breath, she stuffed her hands in the pockets of her jeans. It took every ounce of strength she had to hold his gaze. "I just got a call from the head-hunting firm in Toronto. They have a position they want me to interview for."

Conner stared at her an instant longer, then tossed the brush in the tool caddy. He picked up a curry comb, then pulled up the colt's tail and started combing it. His voice was clipped when he finally responded. "Is it what you want?"

She had to swallow before she could speak. "It sounds very good."

Finally he looked at her, his expression fixed, the set of his jaw inflexible. He never made any comment, and Abby compelled herself to speak. "They've set up an interview for this Friday."

The muscles in his jaw bunched as Conner stared at her; then he turned back to his task.

Abby watched him for a moment longer, wishing that she could say something that would make him respond, something that would get him talking. But she knew that was never going to happen. Feeling more distanced from him than she ever had, she

turned and headed back to the house, shivering as the
sun went behind a cloud. She wasn't sure how she
was going to get through the next four days. They
were going to be the longest four days of her life.

The rest of that day was a total loss. The kids went
into another major sulk when she told them the news,
and Abby was just too tired to even try to reason with
them. Needing to get off on her own, she got a hoe
out of the shed and went down to the garden. The
sun beating down on her, she set about hilling potatoes as if the survival of the universe depended on it.
Today she wasn't going to think about anything. Today she was simply going to be. Tomorrow she would
start packing up for their impending move. She simply didn't have the energy to start dealing with it
today.

Which was not a good plan. By the following day,
the kids had formed a united front and were in full
opposition. One being ornery was bad enough, but the
two of them together were impossible. She wanted
them to cooperate. They were in full revolt. She
wanted them to help gather up their stuff. She caught
them trucking off the things she'd stacked on her bed.
They got into another war in the kitchen, when Abby
wanted them to take their rubber boots and spare jackets to their rooms so she could pack them. Cody got
silent and stubborn, but Sarah was openly defiant, and
Abby ended up yelling and sending them to their
rooms. Feeling as if she were being undermined at
every turn, Abby headed toward the laundry room,
her stomach dropping when she saw Henny standing
in the open doorway, a horrified look on her weathered face.

Feeling as if her nerves were in total shreds, Abby

tipped her head back, too emotionally battered to make any kind of explanation.

The older woman crossed the room and put her arm around Abby's shoulder and gave her a comforting hug. "Now there. Don't let 'em get to you, honey. Kids can be little monsters when they sense they've got you on the boards." She patted Abby's back, her tone kind. "And I know those two. They know you're feeling bad, so they're going to play it for all it's worth. Those little tads are hoping if they act up enough, they can get you to change your mind. They don't see your side of it at all. Kids at that age tend to be self-centered as sin—so don't you worry." She patted Abby again, then piloted her into a chair. Her tone changed to one of amusement. "Just so you know, I yelled at mine plenty, and it don't seem to have warped 'em too bad. And I can't say that they hold it against me. At least they keep coming home for my apple pie."

Giving up a shaky laugh, Abby wiped her face with the side of her hand, then looked up at the foreman's wife. She let out a long breath and shook her head, giving the woman a wan smile. "It's been a bad, bad day."

Henny sat down across from her and grasped Abby's hand, giving it a firm squeeze. "It's understandable, honey. They don't want to go back. And neither do you. But you gotta, and that makes it hard." She smiled and patted Abby's hand. "Tell you what. Why don't I ride herd on them two, and why don't you take off on your own for a bit."

Abby wearily tucked some hair back, then met the older woman's gaze. She really should go into town. She hadn't told Mary that they were leaving before the week was out, and she was darned sure Conner hadn't said anything to her. And it didn't make her heart leap with joy, knowing she was going to have to be the one to tell her.

Feeling as if all her energy had just been sucked out of her, Abby balled up a piece of lint, then looked at Henny. She managed a wry smile. "Are you sure you really want to step into that minefield? They aren't exactly happy campers right now."

Henny grinned. "Don't you worry about me and the little ones. We'll sort things out quick enough." She reached across the table and gave Abby another pat. "Now you get along. And if you're going for a drive, take the coulee road—it's right pretty this time of year. All kinds of wild flowers in bloom."

The drive was exactly what Abby needed. And the coulee road was definitely one of her favorites.

She smiled again for Henny's benefit. "Maybe I will. And I could pop in and see Mary as well."

Henny patted her hand again. "That sounds like a fine idea. And you just take your time. The tads and I will manage just fine."

The coulee road probably added five miles onto the trip to town, but it was worth it. And Henny was right; the wild flowers were spectacular. She stopped along the way and picked Mary a big bouquet of bluebells, wild yarrow and something that looked like yellow tansy. And by the time she reached the nursing home, Abby felt almost restored. Almost.

Mary wasn't in her room. Abby located an empty vase and put the flowers in it, then took the arrangement with her when she went looking for her mother-in-law. She found her outside on the terrace, sitting

in the shade of an apple tree, a book open on her lap.
She wore a silver dressing gown Abby had sent for
Christmas, a pink shawl around her shoulders, and she
was watching sparrows take dust baths in the earth
under a spruce tree. Her eyes lit up when she saw
Abby, and she turned her wheelchair to face her.
"Oh, my. What a beautiful bouquet. There is nothing
like wild flowers, is there?"

Abby set the flowers down on the patio table by
Mary's wheelchair, then bent over and kissed her
mother-in-law on the cheek. "I thought of you as
soon as I saw them."

Her mother-in-law's voice was full of appreciation.
"Thank you so much, my dear. They're lovely."

Sticking an upbeat look on her face, Abby sat down
on the wrought-iron park bench facing the other
woman. "So what have you been up to today?"

Mary studied her daughter-in-law, the smile leaving her eyes, a thoughtful, perceptive look appearing.
She didn't say anything for a moment, then she spoke,
her voice soft with concern. "Whatever is the matter?"

It was the kindness that did it—that genuine com-
passion and understanding that came from deep
within this woman, the woman who had borne one
brother and become a mother to the other. And without warning, Abby's unhappiness blindsided her, and
she had to look away. Lord, she did not want to leave
here. She did not. There was the sound of tires on
flagstone, then the touch of Mary's crippled hand
against hers. As if realizing Abby couldn't handle any
show of sympathy, the older woman spoke again, her
tone more businesslike. "I think you'd better tell me
what's going on, Abigail."

Feeling like a big baby, Abby swallowed hard and straightened her back. God, she was getting so fed up with herself. She hated women who cried over everything, and she hated the fact that she had become one of them. She'd been reduced to tears more times in the past week than she had in her entire life. Lord help her, it was time to get a grip.

While her marriage had been falling apart and Scotty had been on drugs, she'd still been able to hold it together. Not so now. Straightening, she swallowed hard and stared off across the immaculately kept lawns, trying to inject some enthusiasm into her voice. "Actually, it's good news. I've heard from the employment agency I signed on with in the spring, and I've got a job interview on Friday. And it sounds as if it's a peach of a job—exactly what I was looking for."

There was a brief silence, then Conner's stepmother spoke. "Well," she said, her tone carefully controlled, "I see." There was a long pause, then Mary spoke again, her tone quiet. "I suppose that means you'll be leaving soon." Abby heard her reposition her wheelchair and lay the book on the table. Then her mother-in-law spoke again. "I expect it was exactly what you were looking for in June. It's probably not at all what you want right now."

Startled by Mary's observation, Abby swiveled her head and fixed her gaze on the older woman. As if oblivious to Abby's reaction, Mary Calhoun gave her daughter-in-law a guileless look. She maintained eye contact for several seconds, spoke, her voice perfectly calm. "I know about the children," she said, as if casually commenting on the weather. "Scotty told his father and me before Cody was born. He thought it was the right thing to do."

Abby was so flabbergasted, she felt as if she were suddenly hanging in thin air. She stared at her mother-in-law, not sure she'd actually heard right. As if reading her daughter-in-law's mind, Mary answered with a confirming smile.

Abby finally got her wits collected. "You knew?"

"Absolutely."

"But you never said a word."

Mary smiled and again shook her head. "It wasn't our place, dear. That was for the three of you. We felt it was better if we just kept our noses out of it."

Feeling as if her insides were still airborne, Abby abruptly got up and paced to the edge of the terrace, her thoughts in a whirl. Scotty had told his parents. She couldn't believe that they had known all along. She turned and faced her mother-in-law, the strange sensation floating through her. "Does Conner know that you know?"

Mary gave up a truly amused smile. "That sounds like a line from one of those dreadful soap operas, Abigail. Does he know that I know that he knows."

Not sure what to do with her hands, Abby stuck them in her pockets, trying to keep the rising tone out of her voice. "Well does he?"

Tugging the light shawl around her shoulders, Mary shook her head. "No. We all realized he would not be comfortable with that." She tipped her head, sunlight catching in her snow-white hair. "Above all, my eldest son is a very private, honorable man, Abigail. In fact, my son measures his life by what is right and honorable, just like his father." Her expression altered, and there was something almost feral in her eyes as she stared off, as if looking into the past. "And he is my son. He was mine the moment I laid eyes on him—he was such a solemn, serious, dear little boy. So I made him mine. And he's mine as much as Scotty was your children's father." She turned her head and looked at Abby, an apologetic smile appearing. "I'm sorry, my dear. I get a bit defensive about Conner. He deserves much more than he's ever gotten out of life."

Hit with a surge of guilt, Abby turned and faced the lawns, shaken by Mary's comment. Her mother-in-law was right. He had deserved more. So much more.

Mary continued. "It always amazed me how different the two boys were. Scotty always stood up and took what he wanted out of life. Conner was never like that. He's more like his father—he stood back and simply watched." There was a touch of amusement in the other woman's voice as she continued. "I knew that right from the beginning with John. I knew if I wanted him, I'd have to go after him."

Sensing there was more, Abby turned, sudden interest sharpening her attention. Mary met her gaze and chuckled. "I was actually quite brazen, my dear. I surprised even myself."

Abby laughed and tipped her head to one side. "Well, it doesn't surprise me. I always knew there was more to you than meets the eye."

Mary gazed up at her daughter-in-law, a twinkle in her eyes. Then she looked down and began carefully straightening the folds of her dressing gown with her twisted, crippled hand. After a brief silence, she spoke again, her voice quiet. "I don't believe in destiny. It's a concept that is far too convenient—absolves us of free will or assuming any responsibility. And I learned a long time ago that happiness doesn't always get served up on a silver platter. Sometimes we have to go after it. And sometimes we have to stand and fight for it.'' She set the final pleat in place, then looked up, her expression unsmiling. ''Don't let life pass you by, Abigail,'' she said, her tone very soft. ''In the end, what other people think is of no importance.''

Upended for the second time by her mother-in-law, and shaken to the core, Abby abruptly turned, folding her arms tightly in front of her. She could not believe it. Mary Calhoun knew. This sweet, white-haired lady who looked like an aged angel had it all figured out. Somehow or another, she'd guessed what had been going on all summer between her and Conner. Then another thought cut through the daze. Abby wondered how long Mary knew what she knew. Closing her eyes, she rubbed the bridge of her nose. Lord, it did sound like a bad line from a soap opera.

As if once again oblivious to the effect her comments had on her daughter-in-law, Mary spoke, her voice perfectly natural. ''Now, how about you wheel me and this beautiful bouquet back to my room. It's almost tea time, and they're serving strawberry shortcake. We wouldn't want to miss that, would we?''

Abby let her breath go in a rush and forced her body to relax. She was not going to think about anything for the next couple of hours. She was putting everything out of her mind. Except her insides didn't get the message. They were still all tied up in knots.

Sticking a smile on her face, she braced herself and turned to face her mother-in-law. ''Tea time it is.'' Grasping the handles of the chair, she turned toward the ramp that accessed the back of the lodge, the crazy flutter still banging away in her chest. She was willing to bet that tea time was not the only thing that Mary Calhoun never missed.

The fluttery feeling persisted throughout the entire afternoon, and Abby wasn't entirely sure how she managed to act halfway normal. The truth was that she felt a little like a kite caught in the wind, being jerked from one place to another, disassociated from any kind of anchor.

But in spite of the willy-nilly feeling, she stayed until it was time for Mary to go to the dining room for dinner. And for some reason, it was especially hard to leave Conner's mother—maybe it was knowing that there wouldn't be that many more visits, or maybe it was more complex than that. It was almost as if Mary had burrowed past Abby's own facade and touched something Abby didn't even know existed. And Abby had never felt closer to her. She faced another fact; it wasn't just Conner she'd be leaving behind.

Needing time to think, Abby took the coulee road back to Cripple Creek, pondering Mary's perceptiveness, wondering how the woman had put it all together. It wasn't as if she and Conner had been blatant about their relationship—in fact, they had, by an unspoken agreement, been very discreet.

Feeling suddenly very shaky and claustrophobic, Abby abruptly pulled over onto the verge of the narrow, gravel road, then got out of the vehicle, stuffing the keys in her pocket. Still shaky, as if she'd had too much caffeine, she climbed through the barbed wire fence and waded through the wild grass to a rocky outcropping overlooking the shallow valley. Huddling

on the slab of granite, she stared out across the pan-
orama, the jagged gray mountains nearly free from
snow, a purple haze settling around them.

She had only three days left here. Just three. And
she had never been so afraid in her entire life. And
Mary's shrewd comments only made it worse—it was
as if she saw something that Abby couldn't. Clasping
her hands under her thighs, Abby rested her chin on
her upraised knees, trying to compress the rush of
panic in her chest. She had to put that out of her
mind—how little time she had left. She had to stop
thinking about it, or she'd never get through it.

Deliberately she focused on Mary's comments,
wondering again how her mother-in-law had ever put
it all together. A strange sensation unfolded in Abby's
belly, and she took a deep, careful breath. What if
Mary had put it together a long time ago? What if
she had been aware of how Conner felt about his
brother's wife all along? What then?

Feeling as if her brain was about to explode from
overload, Abby closed her eyes and tried to shut everything down. She couldn't think about that anymore. She just couldn't. She couldn't let herself think
about anything.

Concentrating on her breathing, she inhaled all the
fragrances that surrounded her—the perfume of the
wild sage she'd crushed walking to the rock, the smell
of dust and balsam poplar, the scent of damp earth.

Keeping her mind empty, she continued to focus
until she found a kernel of calm. Then, careful not to
disturb the surface of that calm, she got up and went
back to the vehicle. Now if she could just extend that
feeling over the next three days.

The house was empty when Abby got back to the

ranch, but there was a note on the kitchen table in Henny's handwriting, saying that the "tads" were eating in the bunkhouse kitchen with the men. Dragging the strap off her shoulder, Abby set her handbag on the counter by the phone, then pulled her hair back, securing it with an elastic band.

Glad to have the house to herself, she went upstairs to change, her stomach contracting when she found four boxes neatly stacked on the top landing. They were all expertly taped shut, notes in Cody's handwriting stuck to each one, listing the contents.

The sight of those boxes hit Abby hard, and she very nearly lost it. But she clamped her teeth together and went into her room, pulling her cotton top over her head. Obviously Henny had a hand in getting the kids to collect their stuff. She wondered what the foreman's wife had said to get them to cooperate. Recalling that she had made a promise to herself that she wasn't going to think about anything for the next three days, Abby peeled off her good shorts and pulled on the sweat suit lying at the end of the bed. She had three more days to get through—and she had to do whatever it took to get there.

Pulling her ponytail free from the collar of her top, she went down the hallway to Cody's room, where she got another shock. His suitcase was lying on the window seat, half packed, and there was a neat pile of his stuff beside it. Her chest tight, Abby checked the drawers and found all but one empty, as was the closet. Experiencing the now-familiar sick feeling, she went to stand in front of the window, her arms tightly folded. Her expression fixed, she stared through the space in the trees, her gaze fixed on the revolving windmill. She could remember when Conner had installed the high-tech windmill as an auxiliary for the ranch's power supply. It had been how many years ago? How many? She couldn't remember.

Having managed to distract herself from the nearly full suitcase, Abby abruptly turned and left the room. She didn't even bother checking Sarah's room—she wasn't equipped to check it, at least not yet.

Feeling as if the walls were closing in on her, Abby went downstairs and out the back door. She just could not face the rest of her own packing right now. She needed to take her mind off what those boxes signified. And she had never known Henny to be without a pot of coffee on.

She found the older woman in the huge kitchen attached to the bunkhouse, rolling out pastry, a dozen pie plates stacked up by her elbow. She smiled when Abby entered. "Well, howdy. Did you enjoy your visit with Miz Mary?"

Abby leaned her hip against the big work island, watching Henny's expert hands in motion. "We had a great visit. She seemed better today."

"That's good." Henny turned the pastry, then continued rolling. "Just so you know, the tads have gone with their Uncle Conner. He's taking that colt over to Chase's place for training."

For some reason, that bit of news hit her hard, and it was all Abby could do to keep breathing. Avoiding the other woman's gaze, she folded her arms. Her voice wasn't quite steady when she spoke. "I owe you big time, Henny. I saw the boxes the kids packed at the top of the stairs. I really appreciate that."

The older woman dusted the pastry with some flour, then started rolling it out again. "Oh, that wasn't me, honey. It was the boss. When he came in and I told him what a merry chase those two had been giving you, he gave 'em a little talking to. Told 'em they were making things darned hard for you." Picking up a knife, the other woman quartered the huge expanse of pie pastry, sliding each piece into a pie plate. "He took 'em upstairs and got things started up there. Spent most of the afternoon up there with them. Then took 'em to Four Corners store for an ice cream."

Hugging herself to keep everything in, Abby clenched her jaw, her lips feeling stiff and unresponsive. It took her a moment before she could pull it off. When she spoke, her voice was almost normal. "Well then I'll have to thank him."

Under normal conditions, she would have stayed to help Henny, but she made an excuse that she had to get back to work; then she left, her insides a mess. She hadn't thought it possible, but preparing to leave was getting harder and harder. Too hard. She almost wished they were leaving tomorrow. Each day was worse than the one before.

Chapter 10

She didn't see Conner at all that night. He dropped the kids off, but didn't even come into the house. Which didn't surprise Abby. And it certainly didn't make her feel any better. But then, she couldn't have felt any worse. By eleven o'clock, she had such a vicious headache, it obliterated everything else. Almost grateful for the distraction, she took something for it and went to bed, but she couldn't go to sleep either. So she lay there in the dark, her mind drifting. It was well after midnight that she recalled Conner telling the kids when they were still in Toronto that they could sleep on the veranda.

The pain in her head giving way to a whole different pain, Abby dragged her arm over her eyes and locked her jaw, determined not to let that kind of emotion take her under. It was so stupid, but it nearly killed her, knowing they wouldn't get that chance, at least not this time.

Finally dredging up some self-directed disgust for how she was behaving, Abby got out of bed, yanked her sleep shirt down, then gathered up the quilt and a pillow. Okay. Her kids might not have slept on the veranda, but she could. For some reason she had to do this for herself.

Not wanting to wake the kids, she tiptoed down the stairs in the dark, clutching her pillow and blanket. She crept through the house and out onto the east veranda, closing the screen door quietly behind her. Dragging the pad off one of the chaise longues, Abby tossed it on the floor. Then she folded the quilt in half and placed it on the mattress, tossing her pillow on top of it. Feeling almost defiant, she climbed into her makeshift bed and stretched out on her back, her hands tucked under her head. She couldn't remember the last time she'd done something like this. Actually, when she thought about it, she wasn't sure she had ever done anything like this.

The smell of evening scented stocks filled the warm air, and Abby turned her head, studying the night sky. The stars were so dense and bright and beautiful, and seemed so close, she would have sworn she could reach out and touch them. She had never seen night skies like that in the city. Never. Filling her mind with the awesome spectacle, she watched the sky until her eyes grew so heavy, she couldn't keep them open.

It was the squeak of a floorboard that dragged her out of sleep, but before she was fully alert, she felt a hand rest against her jaw.

She opened her eyes, her heart contracting when she realized Conner was on one knee beside her, his hand on her cheek. He was naked except for a pair of jeans, and his hair was damp, as if he'd just had a shower. Not sure if it was a dream, Abby wet her lips and spoke, her voice husky with sleep. "Conner?"

He made no response, his face obscured by shadows, but even in the faint starlight, she could see the rigid angle of his jaw. But what she couldn't see, she could feel in him—and it was a terrible tension, as if he was clamping down on some awful emotion.

She heard him try to clear his throat as he dragged his thumb across her cheek. His voice was rough and very uneven. "You shouldn't be out here."

He shifted his position, sliding his arms around her, gathering her up as if to lift her. Overwhelmed by a mixture of sharp relief and unbearable sadness, Abby wrenched her arms free of the blanket and wrapped them around his neck, hanging on to him for dear life. Locking her jaw to keep her own emotions contained, she pressed her face against his neck, a sob trapped in her chest. He clutched her head against him, his rib cage rising sharply; then he made a ragged sound and put her down, pulling her underneath him as a violent shudder coursed through him.

A feeling of deliverance pouring through her, Abby dragged one leg free, holding on to him with every ounce of strength she had as she twisted under him, clutching him even tighter as his full weight settled between her thighs. It was as if every feeling she'd ever had for him had been magnified a hundredfold, and she turned her face against him, tears slipping down her temples. He was everything to her. Everything. And she was so grateful for this reprise. So grateful. She wanted to tell him what was in her heart, but she couldn't; it was just too full.

Abby caught the back of his head, her fingers tangling in his damp hair, emotion upon emotion piling up in her. It was as if they were fused together by desperation, by their individual sorrow, by all the things they couldn't say, and it was too much. Far too much. And it got even worse when she realized his face was wet against hers.

Not Conner. Not her rock, her anchor. Not that kind of anguish. Clenching her jaw to contain the awful pressure in her chest, Abby shifted her hold, trying to completely enfold him, trying to tell him without words that she would do anything to keep him safe.

Expelling his breath in a violent shudder, Conner roughly turned his head and tightened his hold, nearly crushing her. With tears still relentlessly sliding down her temples, Abby cradled his head, absolutely unable to swallow. She knew in her heart that he had never intended this to happen. But she also knew this was his final goodbye. And it nearly killed her.

Tightly closing her eyes to try to dam the tears, she continued to hold him with all her strength, afraid if she loosened her hold just a little, he would disappear like smoke.

She had no idea how long they lay like that, clinging to each other, afraid what would happen if they let go. But Abby's arms were quivering when Conner finally stirred. His chest rose sharply, pressing against her as he took in a deep, uneven breath, then she heard him swallow. "I think I hear Sarah," he whispered, his voice rough with strain.

Her insides sinking, Abby opened her eyes and listened, and she too heard the soft, "Mommy? Where are you?"

Closing her eyes again, she clutched the back of his head, not wanting to let him go—but also knowing she couldn't let her daughter find them like this.

Shifting his hold, Conner caught her by the face, then softly—so very softly—kissed her, his mouth warm and moist and unbearably gentle. Abby was blindsided by that gentleness, and she tried to grasp him, but he pulled her arms from around his neck, deepening the kiss for just an instant. Then he tightened his hold on her wrists and rolled off her, his arm across his eyes, his jaw rigid.

Abby tried to think of something to say, something to hold him there, but she heard Sarah start down the stairs. Stripped of his warmth, Abby reluctantly rolled over and got to her knees, pausing to touch his mouth before she got up.

She did not want to leave him like that, she did not.

"Mommy?"

A wrenching regret made her blind, and she stumbled as she got to her feet. She had to try twice before she could get the screen to release.

Entering the dining room, she pulled the screen door closed behind her and started toward the stairs, her nightshirt skimming her knees.

She found Sarah standing two steps from the top, her bedraggled bunny clasped in one arm. Abby smiled at her daughter and picked her up, straddling her on one hip.

She pressed her daughter's head against her. "What's the matter, pumpkin?" she whispered, brushing back Sarah's hair from her face.

"I woked up and got cold. And I went to your room, but you weren't there. And I got scared."

Kissing her daughter on the forehead, Abby cuddled her closer. "You don't have to be scared, sweetie." Abby carried Sarah up the stairs and back into her own room. She tucked the six-year-old into her bed, then sat on the edge, rubbing her daughter's back until she drifted off to sleep. Assured that Sarah was sound asleep, Abby left the room, closed the door soundlessly behind her, then flew down the stairs.

Let him still be there, she beseeched mentally. *Please let him still be there.*

But the veranda was empty, the cushion replaced on the chaise. Abby stood there, her arms folded tightly to quell the awful sense of loss rising up inside her. Heartsick, she went back into the house, experiencing another jolt when she saw her quilt neatly folded on the sofa, her pillow lying on top of it. It was as if he'd removed all evidence of what had happened on the veranda.

For the first time, Abby experienced a spurt of genuine anger. How dare he? How dare he disappear after that? With her throat cramped and her jaw stuck out a mile, she headed for his bedroom, but just as she approached the door, she heard a vehicle leave the yard. She recognized the sound. The spurt of anger gave way to the terrible, terrible feeling of loss, and Abby turned and went back to the east veranda, staring out into the shadowed courtyard. And without a doubt, she knew the interlude on the veranda was his last goodbye.

Abby stood looking out over the courtyard until fingers of light seeped over the eastern horizon, wishing she could be angry, bitter, disgusted—any other feeling would do, as long as it obliterated the great, cumbersome sorrow eating away at her.

It was over. She knew it was over. Mary had been right about her elder son—Conner was an honorable man. And he lived his life by that creed. Using

Mary's observation as a distraction to keep from thinking about the sound of finality, the sound of that solitary vehicle leaving the yard, Abby considered that quality in Conner. She had always been aware of it, but she had never really thought about it. Now that she had, she realized it was one of the traits in him that she respected most. And she recognized that he measured everything by that.

Feeling as if she had just stumbled onto something very significant, Abby wondered how his sense of honor had affected them. As long as she had known him, he had been upright and honest in his dealings with everyone. She doubted if he had ever betrayed anyone—certainly not his father, or Mary. Not likely the Hendersons and certainly not her—

A funny feeling unfolded in her belly, and Abby straightened, the sensation buzzing through her. But what if he felt that he had betrayed his brother by getting involved with his wife? Abby was suddenly so wide-awake, she felt as if she had received a shot of pure caffeine. What if he did feel that, and what if that was one of the reasons he refused to talk?

Knowing she had indeed stumbled onto something significant, Abby dissembled it all in her mind. It would explain so much. And suddenly she was truly angry. Only it was at herself. She had been so damned self-absorbed about her relationship with Conner, she had never once taken the time to consider it from his side. Of course he wasn't going to say anything. How could he? Even if he had wanted to bring it up, he wouldn't, because it could have appeared that he was diminishing her. And he would never do that. Never. That would be dishonorable. He would simply shoulder the responsibility and say nothing.

Suddenly wired, Abby started pacing back and forth in front of the French doors, her expression fixed. The more she thought about it, the more she was sure Conner's behavior was about Scott. Which was fair. Maybe they had betrayed him.

Abby recalled the feeling she'd had that first day in the vegetable garden, after she had found the pictures of her, when she had Henny tell her about Conner's breakup with the bank teller. It had confused her, that feeling she'd had, as if she had missed out on something—had lost something rare and special, something that was not hers to lose. Now, in the light of dawn, she faced what she had kept deeply buried—and it was that she had missed out on being Conner Calhoun's wife.

Shaken by that realization, Abby closed her eyes and rubbed her forehead, her insides churning. But Scott had also betrayed them both. He couldn't face up to what he'd done with his life and had taken the easy way out. But now, given the circumstances, how would he react if he knew that Conner had stepped in to look after his family?

Abby's head came up and she stared at the garden, her chest full of an impossible lightness. She knew exactly how Scotty would feel. Because he had said so long ago. In fact, he had said it on more than one occasion—if anything ever happened to him, he didn't need to worry, because he knew he could depend on Conner to look out for them. Conner would never let him down.

Right from that first Christmas she had spent at Cripple Creek, it had been apparent that the only person Scotty truly looked up to was Conner. Another thought occurred—one that set her insides into hyper-drive. What if Scotty had known all along how Conner felt about her? And that was why he'd said he could depend on Conner to look out for them?

Feeling as if she had just discovered something so enormous and so significant, Abby was totally stunned. She stared out at the silhouettes on the horizon; she believed her husband. And she knew, as sure as she was standing there, that Scotty would be comforted by the fact that they were all here with his older brother. She knew it.

But that knowledge didn't alter things. Scotty was only part of the issue. And some of the others, like the parentage of her two children, weren't all that simple. Now Conner had gone to ground. Abby wasn't even sure what she would have done if he hadn't. Conner was formidable in his silences.

By the time the first rays of sunlight peeped over the horizon, Abby was so mentally battered that she couldn't hold one coherent thought for more than two seconds. Knowing she had to stop going around and around in her mind, she went into the kitchen and put on a pot of coffee, the room silent and still.

She poured herself a mug and went upstairs. With her chin set, she started clearing out her room. She didn't think. She didn't stop to ponder. She just did it.

She kept at it until the kids woke up just after ten, which did not bode well. When they slept in that late, they usually both got up with chips on their shoulders. And she was right. She heard Cody first, then Sarah whining and banging on the bathroom door, demanding to be let in. The whining grated like nails on a blackboard. Knowing after a night with no sleep, she was not going to be awash with patience, Abby went downstairs to fix them breakfast.

The whining accelerated into a yelling match. Normally she would have gone upstairs to straighten the situation out, but she closed her eyes and held her breath, counting to twenty. Ten just wasn't going to cut it today.

A few moments later, they appeared at the table, both of them trying to tell on the other one, and Abby smacked their bowls of grapefruit down on the table, glaring at both of them. "I'm in no mood for this, you guys. So can it." Hit by the fact that she would be giving them breakfast here only twice more—tomorrow and the morning they left—Abby turned and braced her hands on the counter, her eyes clenched shut, the shock of reality hitting her. Conner was gone—and there was nothing she could do about it. God, it was over. Really over. Their life here was down to a matter of hours.

Sarah's voice rose to a shrill whine. "Mommy! Tell Cody to stop making faces at me! Make him stop."

"You're just a big baby. I'm not making faces at you."

"You are so making faces at me. He's making his nose look like a pig's! He's making pig faces at me, Mom!"

At her absolute limit, Abby whirled, the muscles in her neck tensed, her teeth gritted. She went over to the table, braced her hands on the wooden surface, her face inches away from her children. Her voice was very, very quiet when she spoke. "You two *will* shape up, and you will do it right now. I am tired of arguing with you over every single thing, and I am tired of your bad behavior." She straightened and shoved the chair against the table, her voice shaking.

"I know you don't want to go back to Toronto, and I don't want to go back either. But we *are* going back. And that's final." She pointed to the door. "So you two get up those stairs, and you get the rest of your things together, and I don't want to hear another word out of you. Is that clear?"

Sarah flounced off her chair, her face crumpling into tears. "You're so mean. You're the meanest mommy in the whole world."

His face white and his jaw jutting forward in anger, Cody put his arm around his sister's shoulder and glared at his mother, then turned very solicitous toward his sobbing sister. "Come on, Sarah," he whispered, guiding her toward the door. "I'll read you a story, okay?"

Abby had had enough of them colluding against her, and she leveled her finger at him, her voice rising. "That's enough of that, Cody. Sarah, go to your room." She waited until her daughter disappeared, then she fixed her gaze on her small, defiant son. "There aren't going to be any stories. And there is not going to be anymore stalling. I want your room finished by noon."

His face pinched and white, he cast her another hateful look and shoved the chair out of his way, then stomped out of the room. "I wish Conner was my real dad," he yelled back at her. "Then I wouldn't have to go with you. I could stay here with him."

It was as if he gave her a shot of electricity. Experiencing such a sharp hot-and-cold rush that she had to grasp the back of the chair to steady herself, Abby stared into space, her expression frozen.

He wished Conner was his real dad. It was as if those words had thrown open a door to possibility—

a door she had never considered, a door that let in a whole new set of options. What if the kids were told the truth about their conception—that Conner had, in fact, sired them. Then what?

Would they be able to grasp it?

Remembering the two of them telling her about the conversation with the AI technician, Abby knew that they would. Would it affect how they felt about Scotty? No. They loved their father, what they remembered of him. But those memories would fade, unless she and Conner were to keep them alive....

A thousand sensations sizzled through her, making her so lightheaded she was almost dizzy.

Would it be wrong to tell the kids the truth?

As if Scotty were right there beside her, she heard his voice, from that Christmas long ago, when she'd told him Conner had agreed. *Maybe someday we can do something to make this up to him.*

And she knew. She knew what Scotty would want.

Hit with soaring, effervescent sensations, Abby paced across the kitchen, then paced back, her heart racing, her thoughts in a crazy tangle, everything spinning around in her head.

But one thought was delivered whole and intact. Maybe honor went both ways. Maybe it was time she did the right and honorable thing.

She stopped dead in her tracks, possibilities and options flashing through her mind like bright lights. Her heart rate going really berserk and a crazy kind of hope taking hold, she pressed the heels of her hands against her eyes, trying to grasp on to a thread of rationality. She needed to use some caution here— she needed to think this through. She needed to use her usual common sense.

But that little voice in her head popped up, making rude comments about her common sense.

A huge feeling burst in her chest, and Abby dropped her hands, that same unbearable lightness zipping through her. To hell with caution.

Spurred on by a crystal-clear surety, she headed for the stairs and sprinted up them, feeling more clear-headed than she had in her entire life.

She found both kids in Cody's room, putting things in the suitcase on the floor, looking like the most pathetic little orphans on the face of the earth.

Her heart doing crazy barrel rolls, she grasped the door frame, needing to anchor herself. Her tone was sharp—intense.

"Did you really mean what you said, Cody? About wishing Conner was your dad. Is that really the way you feel?"

He looked at her, obviously confused, then he exchanged a perplexed look with his sister.

Trying to force some calm, Abby took a deep, stabilizing breath. "I need to know," she said, a tremor in her voice.

The kids looked at each other again, then Sarah reached over and took her brother's hand. "Tell her," she whispered, crowding against him.

As if uncertain what was going on, Cody stared up at his mother, then answered, defiance in his eyes. "Yes." Drawing his sister even closer, he spoke again, his lips colorless. "Both me and Sarah." His chin came up as if he was challenging her. "Both me and Sarah want him for our dad."

Hit with a giddy weakness, Abby closed her eyes and held on to the door, forcing air into her lungs. And something hard and tight let go in her chest.

There was a chance for all of them. If she didn't blow it. There was a chance. Gathering her strength, she crossed to the bed and sat down, her knees quivering, her heart fluttering like crazy. Managing a not-quite-steady smile, she held her hands out to her kids. "Then come sit here on the bed. I have something to tell you."

With them on the bed watching her with big round eyes, she told them the truth. Grateful for their previous educational experience with the "eye guy," she told them how she and Scotty couldn't make babies by themselves, and how Conner had helped them. So he was also their dad, just like they wanted.

There were a couple of technical questions that were straightforward and far easier to answer than she'd expected. The only hard question came from Cody, when he wanted to know why they had kept it secret. It took Abby a minute to find the right words, then she explained that they hadn't wanted to confuse them, and the reason she was telling them now was because she knew their dad would want her to.

Cody sat there watching her for the longest time, and she held her breath and waited, her insides jittery, her nerves stretched to the limit.

Then Sarah folded her arms and stared at her mother. "So if Uncle Conner is kinda our dad, why do we hafta go back to Toronto?"

She wanted to hug her daughter in the worst way, but she felt obliged to play it out. "Well, if you kids are okay with this, I don't think we should go back. I think we should just stay here."

There was a split second of silence, then they both tackled her, knocking her off the bed and onto the floor. Both kids landed on top of her, and Sarah grabbed her mother's face between her hands, making Abby look at her. "You mean it, Mommy? You really mean it?"

Laughing at their response, Abby hugged her. "Yes, I really mean it."

Cody let out a whoop and piled off her, pulling his arm down in a scoring gesture. "Yes!" he crowed. "Yes!"

Sarah scrambled off her mother, grabbing her brother by the arm, her voice urgent. "Come on, Cody. Come *on*. We gotta put our stuff away 'fore she changes her mind!"

As if spurred by that urgency, Cody stopped, his eyes getting very big, then he ran for the door. He collided with his sister, who had turned to ask her mother something. "Can we tell?" Sarah demanded. "Can we tell Jake and Henny?"

Upended by the question, Abby froze; her first panicky thought was to say no. But then an odd stillness settled on her. Cody turned, his expression suspended, as if her answer was critical. Knowing the die would be forever cast by her answer, she sat up, those crazy little butterflies loose in her chest. Henny and Jake were as close to family as anyone could get. She swallowed hard, then answered, her voice perfectly steady. "Yes, you can tell them."

For a split second no one moved, then both kids shot out the door, and there was a thunder of racing feet on the stairs, and Cody's yelling at his sister to hurry up.

Hit with the enormity of what she'd just set in motion, Abby didn't move a muscle. She'd turned them loose, all right, and now there was no turning back. The die was definitely cast.

But the feeling was superseded by another—a kind of wild, crazy disregard. She got to her feet, that same feeling of unbearable lightness zinging through her. Well, since she had turned the kids loose with that kind of information, she might as well burn all her bridges.

Knowing she was throwing all caution to the wind—and just a little terrified by her wild abandon and total lack of common sense—Abby marched downstairs to the phone in the kitchen. Before she lost her nerve, she called Joanne, called the head hunter, then called the clothing manufacturer. And she told them all the same thing. She was not coming back to Toronto. She was staying at Cripple Creek.

When she hung up from the last call, she was feeling so shaky that she thought she just might get sick. She couldn't believe she was doing what she was doing—it was just so unlike her to jump in so over her head. It just wasn't her.

But still on a roll, she rummaged through her handbag and found the business card she needed, then she placed one last call. That one was to the moving company that was storing her household effects. With the same disregard, she made arrangements to have everything shipped, including her car, to Bolton, Alberta, and the Cripple Creek Ranch.

By the time she concluded that call, she was in much the same condition as after she'd given birth—drenched in perspiration, shivering like crazy, and higher than a kite. She thought maybe she'd totally lost her mind.

She was just replacing the receiver when Henny and Jake came rushing in, both of them all in a flutter, their eyes wide with astonishment.

Shaking so badly she could hardly stay on her feet, Abby looked at them, a little flutter of panic breaking loose. But there was Sarahlike defiance in her when she spoke, her voice shaking just as bad as she was. "I'm not going back. So help me, I'm not."

Henny didn't move for an instant, then she tipped her head back and lifted both fists toward the ceiling, her jubilation ringing out. "Thank you, Lord. Thank you!" Her face wreathed in joy, she came over to Abby, wrapping her up in a crushing hug. "We've been praying for this, Abby girl. We have. We can't tell you how glad we are."

Needing something to hang on to, Abby closed her eyes and hugged her back, the trembling getting worse.

Henny patted her back, simply mothering her. "Now there, there. What you done was the right thing, honey. Sure as I'm standing here."

Needing to sit down, Abby grasped Henny's arm as she reached for a chair. Jake was watching her, concern stamped on his face. "Are you okay, missy?"

Henny flapped her hand at him, dismissing his worried tone. "Of course she is. She's just a little shook up, that's all."

She set a glass of cold water on the table in front of Abby, then patted her head. "Must admit, I'm a little shook up myself. Never thought all this would come out."

Abby went very still. She focused on wrapping her hands around the cold glass, then she fortified herself with a deep breath. "You knew?" she asked very carefully.

Henny patted her shoulder. "Well, we wondered. I

knew Conner's real momma, and there's something about Cody that reminds me of her.'' Henny patted her again, then bustled around, putting on a fresh pot of coffee. "We wasn't dead sure, but we speculated."

Abby tipped her head back, a bubble of hysterical laughter rising up. She kind of figured that Henny and Jake were aware of what had been going on over the summer—but the other secret? Maybe the whole darned county had it figured out.

Stripping off his hat, Jake grinned and hiked his thumb in the direction of the barn. "Them young 'uns are right outta their boots. They're out there standing on that old fuel platform, yelling at the top of their lungs that they're staying." Still grinning, he hooked his hat on one chair as he sat down at the table. Then he reached out and patted her hand. "We're truly glad you're staying, missy. You and the tads are exactly what the boss needs."

Abby felt her blood drain to her shoes. When she'd gone into orbit and rebelled against high-minded convention, she had not once considered how she would face Conner with her decision, and now it scared her to death. She didn't have any doubts about what she'd done—not one, single doubt—but telling Conner was not on her top ten list of fun things to do. And to make matters worse, she didn't even know where he was.

Sure she had lost all color, Abby let her breath go. She clasped her hands together, swallowed hard and braced herself to meet the foreman's gaze.

It was as if he read her question before she had time to really formulate it, because he gave her a surprisingly gentle, fatherly smile and spoke. "I expect he's holed up in that line shack over by Dead Horse

Canyon—you know the one, where we all went fishing a few years back.'' He glanced up as his wife set a cup of coffee in front of him, then he leaned one elbow on the table. ''His truck's parked behind the barn and Big Mac is gone. So I 'spect he rode over there.''

Abby did know the place. She also knew it was at least a four-hour ride by horse to get there. The camp was used mostly in the spring as a staging area for roundup, and normally, the horses were trailered over and back. The road wasn't great, but she had driven it a number of times over the years. The worst part was that it was going to take her almost an hour to get there.

Henny laid her hand on Abby's shoulder, her tone kind. ''We'll mind the tads, honey. You go on. I figure you two will need some time on your own anyhow.''

Abby wasn't really sure how she made it up the stairs. Needing normal activity to ground her, she flew into her room, her mind going a mile a minute. She couldn't really believe she'd done what she'd done. That kind of reckless behavior was just not a part of her character. One minute she was elated by having thrown caution to the wind, and the very next instant, she was in near panic. But one thing was for sure—she had to get out of there fast, or she'd lose her nerve.

She threw on some clothes and tossed some things in her shoulder bag. She was halfway down the stairs, the strap of her bag hitched over her shoulder, when she stopped and looked down at what she had on. Shorts, T-shirt, nothing out of the ordinary. But her mission was anything *but* ordinary.

Abruptly she turned and raced back up the stairs, dropping her bag at the top landing, peeling her T-shirt off over her head. This called for something special.

Dumping her suitcase on the bed, she rummaged through the pile of clothes until she found what she wanted. It was a dress that was very similar to the one she'd been wearing in the photograph that Conner had taken years before. A simple, sleeveless dress that buttoned up the front, with the long full skirt gathered under the bust. The kind of dress that was ultra feminine, the cream-colored gauzy fabric scattered with dainty, old-fashioned bunches of bluebells, lilies of the valley and tiny rosebuds. The bluebells seemed significant somehow.

And for the first time all summer, Abby took real pains dressing. She pulled her hair up in a deliberately tousled sexy style, which seemed to take forever to get just right. She was such a mental wreck after she finished that she had to do some very deep breathing exercises to calm her nerves—honest to God, she felt as if she were right back in the middle of a long delivery. Taking another breath to steady her hands, she applied her makeup. When she was finished, she stood back and assessed her handiwork. She grinned at herself, that light feeling coming back in a rush. Lord, she was definitely going to mess with his mind. Realizing she had wasted a horrific amount of time, she practically had to tear the room apart to find her blue sandals, and she was back to being close to panic when she put them on.

Totally disregarding the disaster she was leaving behind, she grabbed her bag as she flew down the stairs. An hour. It was going to take her at least an hour to get there. And it was going to be the longest hour in her life.

The sky was scudded with white clouds by the time she turned onto the narrow road that led to the line shack, the sandy track beaten smooth by previous rains. The line shack, which was situated on a rise of land and surrounded by alpine meadow, wasn't really a shack at all. It was an old log cabin covered in Virginia creeper and tucked up against a stand of aspen.

The natural meadow was lush and high with brome grass, the heavy heads mixed with a riot of colorful alpine flowers—the bright coral Indian paintbrush, the purple wild aster, the yellow daisies. With the mountains as a backdrop, the scene was absolutely breathtaking, and on any other day, she would have dug her camera out of her shoulder bag—but not today. Her hands weren't steady enough to take pictures today.

She parked by the pole corral constructed in the shelter of spruce trees, then gripped the wheel and closed her eyes, the unbelievable scents wafting in through the open window. A new hatching of butterflies broke loose in her chest. All the way here, she had practiced dozens of soliloquies in her mind—very eloquent soliloquies—of what she was going to say to him. And now that she was here, she couldn't hold on to an entire thought, let alone utter a complete sentence.

Tossing her sunglasses on the dash, she opened the door, leaving her shoulder bag on the seat and the keys in the ignition. She got out, her knees nearly giving way under her. She slammed the door, then crossed to the pole fence, her heart going a mile a minute as she crawled through.

Inspiration. She needed a shot of inspiration right now.

Feeling as if her heart was climbing up her throat, she started across the meadow, the grass and flowers swaying in the breeze and brushing against her long skirt. Her mind racing, she broke the blooms off random bunches of flowers, frantically trying to come up with the right words. Lord, she needed the right words.

The sound of galloping hooves set off a flurry of panic, and Abby stopped, the butterflies multiplying. She gripped the ragged bouquet of flowers, her gaze fixed in the direction of the sound. There was a hill on that side, one that dropped away to the creek.

Horse and rider came into view like an apparition rising from the ground, and Abby watched them, her throat so paralyzed she couldn't swallow. This was it. This was the rest of her life.

Conner reined the gelding in when he saw who it was, and it was all Abby could do not to press her hand against her chest. Fortifying herself with Mary's words about having to go after happiness sometimes, she started toward him, the panic giving way to a strange soaring calm. This was right. Without a doubt, she knew this was right.

Her gaze fixed on him, she approached horse and rider, her throat closing up for entirely different reasons when she got a good look at his face. *Ah, God, Conner,* she thought, *you are so hard on yourself.*

Her heart full to bursting for the torment she saw stamped on his face, she considered telling him that she had explained the truth to the kids, then changed her mind. There were other things she needed to say first. Taking a deep breath, she spoke, her voice uneven. "Did I ever tell you that Scotty told me once that if anything ever happened to him, he knew he could depend on you to look after us? Did I ever tell you that, Conner?"

Conner didn't move so much as a muscle, and he sat staring at her, his hat pulled low over his eyes. His jaw was unshaven and grimly set, and even from thirty feet away, Abby could feel the rigid tension in him. Big Mac tossed his head against the reins, then lowered his head and began cropping the grass. Abby paused, the flutter suddenly back. Unable to hold that unwavering stare of his, she began plucking bits of grass out of the bunch of flowers in her hand. She tried to make her tone offhand. "Just so you know, the kids and I don't want to go back to Toronto. We've decided to stay here. So I told Joanne I couldn't look after her house, and I fired the head-hunter—and I also cancelled the job interview." Badly flustered by his stoniness, Abby wet her lips and turned toward the cabin, scrambling for some excuse, any excuse to break the tension. "I think I'll just go in and put these flowers in some water."

She had maybe taken five steps when she heard the saddle squeak, and her heart nearly jumped right out of her chest. Not sure what to expect or what to brace herself for, she kept on walking.

His voice cracked like a whip. "Stop right there." She stopped, erected a smile to dazzle, then turned. He was standing beside Big Mac, one hand on the saddle and one on his hip, and there was a coiled energy in him—as if he was stretched to the limit. His expression was downright formidable. She had a hard time hanging on to that smile.

His features looked as if they'd been hacked out of

granite, but there was something dark and intense in his eyes, something so tormented that made her throat ache and her chest fill up.

His gaze locked on her, he spoke, his voice low and ragged. "What in hell are you doing?"

Trapped by the intensity of that gaze, Abby stared at him, all her feelings for him swelling up inside her. How could she have ever considered leaving him? Her rock, her anchor, her knight in shining armor. She loved him. He was everything to her—and everything she wanted. She had to swallow before she could speak. "I'm doing what's right for us," she said, her voice catching. "I know this is what Scotty would have wanted, us all here together. And it's what I want. And it's what the kids want. I love you, Conner. You have no idea how much I love you." She tried to smile, but there was so much emotion jammed up in her chest, her vision blurred. "Don't you know that you're my rock, my anchor, my knight in shining armor?"

Certain she was going to lose it, she turned toward the cabin. She knew he needed time. Time to wrestle with his honor. He would come to her when he was ready. He would—

She was nearly yanked off her feet. One minute she was headed toward the cabin; the next she was whirled around and hauled into his arms, his unchecked strength nearly crushing her. Relief ripping through her, she got her arms free and then locked them around his neck, a sob breaking loose. And that unbearable lightness burst inside her, and she knew, knew they had found their way.

Tossing his hat aside, he tightened his hold and roughly turned his face against her neck, his chest heaving, his voice cracking and nearly inaudible. "Abby. God, Abby."

Locking her jaw to stop the debilitating ache in her throat, Abby grasped the back of his head, molding herself against him. Her throat was so tight she could barely get the words out. "You are going to keep me, aren't you, Conner?"

Hauling in a deep, ragged breath, he tightened his embrace, his face still buried against her neck. "God, I thought I'd lost you," he whispered roughly, holding her as if he couldn't let her go.

Tears burning her eyes, Abby clasped his head even tighter. "You can't lose me," she whispered unevenly, holding him with every ounce of love she had in her. "This is where I belong."

She could feel him struggling, and it broke her heart—but it also lifted her up with a pure, effervescing joy. Because he was also holding her as if his life depended on it. And with such love—with such binding, unrelenting love.

Conner hauled in another deep, uneven breath, then flattened his hand on her back, his voice raw with emotion. "Marry me, Abby. Stay and marry me."

Tears slid free, and Abby twisted her head and pressed her mouth against his jaw, her love for him overflowing. He had finally said all she needed to hear. It was as it should be.

Early morning light filtered in the narrow windows of the cabin, a kind of stillness settling in that could only be found in the high country.

Abby lay on her stomach in the narrow cot, a heavy flannel sheet twisted around her, her head resting on her folded arms. Just barely awake and still fuzzy from sleep and a night of very good loving, she watched Conner shaving at the old-fashioned wash-stand stuck in the corner. He had slipped out earlier for a swim and to turn Big Mac loose in the horse pasture and load the tack in the SUV.

His hair was still damp and his torso was bare, and he looked absolutely magnificent. Watching him scrape away shaving foam, she smiled sleepily. She had whisker burns where no respectable woman should have whisker burns.

It had been quite the night, and she was certain she hadn't had more than an hour's sleep. She had no idea how many times they made love, but every time was like an affirmation of the beginning of a whole new life. And Conner had held nothing back.

But just as importantly, they had talked. They had talked about Scotty, and they had talked about them. It wasn't until the middle of the night, when he had made love to her yet again, that Conner had finally told her in words that he loved her. It was then that she told him about finding the pictures. And it was hard for him—really hard for him—to admit how he'd felt about her all those years. They had talked until the sky got light. And she told him in very specific terms how he made her feel. She told him everything.

Well, everything except that she had told the kids the truth. Her smile fading, she watched him rinse off his razor in a washbasin, her mood suddenly sober. She couldn't put it off any longer. She was going to have to tell him now.

Finished shaving, Conner rinsed the remaining foam from his face, then pulled the towel free to dry his face.

He turned and saw her watching him, and a slow smile appeared, lighting up his eyes. Tossing the towel on his saddle bags, he came over to the cot, his boots thudding on the plank flooring. Placing one hand beside her head, he bent over and gave her a long, soft kiss. Rolling over on her back, Abby wound her arms around his neck. She would tell him later.

It wasn't until they were almost home that Abby faced the rather significant lapse on her part. Somehow it just hadn't seemed right to tell him in the cabin. Then Conner had found her camera in her shoulder bag, and he insisted on a picture of her in the field of flowers. Abby had understood about the picture and why it was so important to him, and it made her heart fill up, knowing why he wanted it. That hadn't seemed the right place to tell him either.

They were halfway home when she finally screwed up her nerve. Conner was sitting in the passenger seat, his head tipped back against the headrest, his eyes closed, his hand warm against her thigh. Nerves climbing up her throat, she tightened her grip on the wheel and wet her lips. "I hope you realize that the kids got quite an education from the eye guy."

He turned his head and looked at her, clearly not having a clue what she was talking about. "What eye guy?"

It wasn't what she saw in his eyes that neutralized the nerves. It was how he was absently caressing the inside of her leg—the kind of intimate touching that assured her more than anything else possibly could. She shot him a smile and focused on the road. "Well actually, it was the AI technician. Between him and Jake, they pretty much explained how it works."

She glanced at him again, and he was watching her, his eyes narrowed. ''Are you okay with that?''

Abby smiled again. ''I'm fine with it.'' She tightened her grip even more, then took a deep breath. ''Since they had such a solid foundation, I thought it would be the perfect opportunity to tell them how you helped their dad and me make them.''

Conner's expression froze, and he looked as if she'd poleaxed him. ''You what?''

She gave him another easy smile. ''I know Scotty would have wanted them to know the truth, so I told them.''

Conner continued to stare at her; then he abruptly tipped his head back and closed his eyes, and she could see the muscles in his throat work. Not wanting to think of what he was experiencing, especially when she was driving down a winding gravel road, Abby stared straight ahead. She negotiated a tight S-curve, then pressed the programmed number on the mobile phone. It was Cody who answered. ''Hi, Hon. How are you doing?''

There was a funny quiver in his voice. ''Are you coming home?''

''We'll be there in about twenty minutes.'' She was going to say more, but he abruptly cut her off.

''Okay, bye.''

Bemused by her son's abruptness, Abby disconnected, then glanced at Conner. She could tell by the way muscles in his jaw were bunching that he was having a hell of a time, and she swallowed hard and covered his hand with her own. Her anchor, her rock. Her own throat got unbearably tight. Finally she had been able to give his gift back to him.

Conner never said anything, but he turned his palm

up, gripping her hand with a viselike hold. Abby could only guess what kind of emotions he was wrestling with. Her gaze fixed on the road, she caressed his hand, trying to tell him by touch alone that she understood.

It wasn't until they turned onto Cripple Creek land that Conner finally moved, and Abby glanced over at him, her heart contracting with a wealth of emotion when she saw the look on his face. And her throat got even tighter. It was about time that Conner got back just a little of all he'd given. He had never expected this to happen. She could see it on his face.

Her jaw locked against the ache in her throat, Abby turned and fixed her gaze on the tree-lined lane, her heart giving a painful little lurch when she saw a dark head, then shoulders, then an entire body appear over a hill. It was Cody, and he was running flat-out. Abby had to clench her teeth to keep her own emotions in check. She knew what he was doing. He was running to Conner.

She knew the instant Conner spotted him; he nearly crushed her hand in two. Abby kept going until she was nearly to Cody, then she braked, and Conner was out of the truck before the vehicle stopped moving. Her vision blurring, Abby watched as her son threw himself into his biological father's arms, winding his arms and legs around him like a human octopus. Her chest so full she couldn't see, Abby put the vehicle in Park and got out, folding her arms tightly in front of her. This too was as it should be.

Wiping away her tears, Abby managed to take a breath without the pressure in her chest getting away on her. She had just closed the car door when another form appeared over the hill, little legs going like windmills. With Cody still clutched in his arms, Conner started toward Sarah, and Abby watched, a sudden gust of wind catching at her dress and hair. Her vision blurred again as Conner swept up their daughter, their son still clinging to him.

Filled with joy and happiness so pure that it made her feel weightless, Abby managed to swallow, her heart full to bursting. Everything she ever wanted was right here on this road. Her kids. Her rock. Her anchor. Her knight in shining armor. Smiling through her tears, she started walking toward them. Walking toward the rest of her life.

Epilogue

Huge snowflakes drifted by the window in the tack room, sliding through the halos of lights in the yard, draping everything in a coat of white. Conner paused at his task, watching the snow build up in the pines. From this angle, he could clearly see the outline of the house. It was hard to miss, draped with string upon string of Christmas lights, the tiny icicle lights hanging from every gable and eave. Even the trees in the front yard were decked out in colored lights, the falling snow sending up colorful auras. His wife had taken over from Mary, spreading color and light all over the place. A twist of humor surfaced. It was a good thing they had their own source to supplement their power supply, and plenty of wind to drive it; he didn't want to think what their utility bill would be without the windmill.

He turned back to the workbench where he was adding reins to a brand-new, hand-tooled headstall he had picked up that morning. Abby didn't know it yet, but the kids were getting their very own horses for Christmas—beautiful, registered paints that Chase McCall had found for him. When he'd suggested the kids have their own horses, Abby had put her foot down. No horses. She said they already had plenty at Cripple Creek, and they didn't need their own. They were overindulged as it was. Conner grinned. He figured since she kicked up such a fuss and got her way over the lights, it was only fair that his kids get their horses. His kids.

A sudden cramp formed in his throat, and he bent his head and gouged his eyes. It still caught him unaware at times—how damned lucky he was. He'd never expected to get it all. Never. But he had. And he figured he was the richest, luckiest S.O.B. in the whole damned country. He couldn't want for anything that he didn't already have.

He lifted his head, his gaze catching on a grouping of pictures over the workbench. Where there was once only one, now there were three. There was the one of Mary and his father, of course. And now there was one of Abby, walking toward him in that field of flowers up by the line shack—the one he'd taken the day after she'd shown up there. The day she'd altered the course of his life. But he didn't need a picture to remember that. If he lived to be a hundred, he would recall that moment in living detail—that image of her coming through the flowers toward him. He had never expected to see her there—a vision in that filmy dress, a little bouquet of flowers in her hand. A soft smile hovering around his mouth, he reached out and touched the frame. No, he didn't need a picture to remember that. But he'd hung it there, beside the one of Mary and his father. Because that picture of Abby was his new beginning.

The other one was of all of them—he, Abby, Cody and Sarah. It had been taken in the courtyard on their wedding day. The trees were festooned in ribbons, the garden was vivid with flowers, and Abby, who wore his grandmother's wedding dress, had a bouquet of roses in her arm she'd gathered from that very garden. And that picture was there because it was their first day as a real family. Conner reached out and brushed some dust off the glass, his throat getting tighter. She was so damned beautiful that day—that old-fashioned dress, with flowers in her hair—and there had been so much love and joy on her face, it still made his chest seize up when he looked at it. His wife. His kids. He was damned lucky, all right.

Conner heard the outside door being dragged open and closed again, then a muttered curse and footsteps. He recognized the footsteps. He chuckled to himself and shook his head. It had taken him and Jake two days to string all the bloody lights, and he had put up the last string just that afternoon. It had been a cold, rotten job, and Jake had finally got fed up and stomped off, muttering under his breath. And by the time Conner finished, he was so irritated by her pickiness, he could have strangled her with the last extension cord. But he had the nasty feeling that his wife wasn't finished yet—she was probably on her way to petition for yet more lights, probably figured they needed to do the trees along the lane. Hell, they might as well; they were already lighting up the whole damned country. They had only turned them on that evening, and already they'd had two neighbors stop by to see the display.

Abby entered the tack room, snow in her hair, the smell of cold clinging to her, the shearling coat he'd bought for her pulled snugly around her. Leaning back against the workbench, Conner folded his arms and stared at her.

She angled her head, giving him that disarming look of hers, a definite twinkle in her eyes. "Hi. Are you talking to me yet? Or are you still steamed?"

Conner gave her a dry look. "Hell, the whole country is experiencing an outage because of our drain on the power grid. Why should I be steamed?"

Laughter dancing in her eyes, she came over and slid her arms under his fleece-lined mackinaw, looping them around his waist. "Poor, poor Conner. You are *so* hard done by."

Looking into her eyes, he straightened, then rested his arms on her shoulders, a smile trying to break loose. "I know you're up to something. I should save myself a whole lot of grief and just dump you in a snowbank."

She grinned and kissed him, giving him a hard hug. "Thank you for indulging me, love. It really does look beautiful."

He pointedly held her gaze, one corner of his mouth lifting. "I am not putting up one more string of lights, Abigail. So don't even think it."

She chuckled and hugged him again, the warmth of her body infusing his. "I don't want anymore lights. I just want to know when you're coming in."

There was a wisp of hair clinging to her cheek, and he carefully brushed it back, a sudden rush of emotion impacting his chest. God, but he did love this woman. His voice was gruff when he spoke. "What did you have in mind?"

Her gaze softened and she ran her hand up his back, a twinkle in her eyes. "Not stringing lights, that's for sure."

Conner tipped his head back and laughed, then returned her hug. "This might be worth checking out."

Once outside, Conner took a deep breath, enjoying the smell of snow and cold air. It was a truly gorgeous night, the distinctive stillness of falling snow muffling the yard. As soon as he closed the door, Abby slid her arm around his waist as he draped his over her shoulder, matching his stride to hers. And Conner looked up, recalling the night when Cody had first called, when he had avoided going into the dark, empty house. Now the windows were bright and welcoming, and lights twinkled everywhere. And he had the woman he loved more than life at his side. His kids asleep in the house.

He really did have it all.

*   *   *   *   *

Silhouette®

INTIMATE MOMENTS™

presents a riveting 12-book continuity series:

a Year of loving dangerously

Where passion rules and nothing is what it seems...

When dishonor threatens a top-secret agency, the brave
men and women of SPEAR are prepared to risk it all as they
put their lives—and their hearts—on the line.

Available May 2001:

CINDERELLA'S SECRET AGENT
by Ingrid Weaver

As a sharpshooter for the SPEAR agency, Del Rogers was determined to
capture an arch villain named Simon. Love and family did not factor into
his mission. *Until* he found the Cinderella of his dreams in the form of a
pretty, pregnant waitress. Helping to deliver Maggie Rice's baby girl was
all in a day's work. But keeping his heart neutral was an entirely different
matter. Did this chivalrous secret agent dare indulge in fantasies of
happily ever after?

*Available only from Silhouette Intimate Moments
at your favorite retail outlet.*

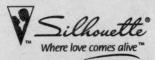
Silhouette®

Where love comes alive™

Visit Silhouette at www.eHarlequin.com   SIMAYOLD12

Beginning in May from

INTIMATE MOMENTS™

**The will has been read.
Destinies have been decided.
And the Delaney siblings are about
to discover what family really means.**

a brand-new series by
CARLA CASSIDY

Mark Delaney has set in motion a most daring plan.
He's taken on a new personality to fool those who
tried to kill him. But how long can he hide the
truth from a woman determined to love him...
no matter who he has become?

MAN ON A MISSION
MAY 2001 (IM #1077)

And watch for more powerful stories as
The Delaney Heirs continues, only from
Silhouette Intimate Moments.

Available at your favorite retail outlet.

Where love comes alive™

Visit Silhouette at www.eHarlequin.com   SIMDEL

SILHOUETTE® MAKES YOU A STAR!

Look in the back pages of all June Silhouette series books to find an exciting new contest with fabulous prizes! Available exclusively through Silhouette.

Don't miss it!

Silhouette®

Where love comes alive™

P.S. Watch for details on how you can meet your favorite Silhouette author.

Visit Silhouette at www.eHarlequin.com   **STEASER**

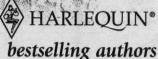

HARLEQUIN®

bestselling authors

Merline Lovelace
Deborah Simmons
Julia Justiss

cordially invite you to enjoy three
brand-new stories of unexpected love

The Officer's Bride

Available April 2001

HARLEQUIN®

Makes any time special®

Visit us at www.eHarlequin.com   PHOFFICER

Silhouette® —

where love comes alive—online...

eHARLEQUIN.com

your romantic life

—Romance 101——
♥ Guides to romance, dating and flirting.

—Dr. Romance ——
♥ Get romance advice and tips from our expert, Dr. Romance.

—Recipes for Romance——
♥ How to plan romantic meals for you and your sweetie.

—Daily Love Dose——
♥ Tips on how to keep the romance alive every day.

—Tales from the Heart——
♥ Discuss romantic dilemmas with other members in our Tales from the Heart message board.

All this and more available at
www.eHarlequin.com
on Women.com Networks

SINTL1R